UNGUARDED

MARYANNA ROSE

For my dad, Tim Rose.

You have believed in me, smiled at me, and loved me my entire live.

No girl was ever luckier.

Let's stay in touch!
Sign up at www.maryannarose.com to get occasional updates, and to hear when the next book in The Ties of Blood series is out!

No, life had never been easy, and I didn't expect that to change. But I thought I'd found a place to at least exist in the shadows.

But the people I thought I could trust couldn't save me. And the ones I feared were monsters worse than I'd imagined.

And help, oh yes, because help must eventually come to the stubborn who refuse to give up. . .when help came it seemed far too late and almost more frightening than the nightmare I was trying to escape.

If only I could wake and find it was all a dream. Or a nightmare rather, for there wasn't a soul who would call this reality a dream. . . at least, not at the beginning.

ONE

*K*arlsruhe, Deutschland -
22. Oct. 1940

Sweat rolled down my back and into my eyes. I shoved the last three loaves in the oven and the door snapped shut.

"Lena Weismann?"

I spun and lost my breath when I saw who asked.

He was tall and wore the distinct air of being above the law, any law. He was. "Are you Lena Weismann?" The man asked.

"Yes." I dug my nails into the palms of my hands. Don't faint.

"Get clothes and food together, enough for three days. Someone will come for you in an hour."

I held my breath and waited. For something else. Something to respond to.

He walked out and the door slammed behind him.

I shuddered with the walls of the bakery.

The room was spinning when I opened my eyes, I grabbed the counter, pulling myself up. I sat down? I held onto the slight glimmer of light. He'd only come for me.

The clock chimed and I jumped. The bread? No, I just put it in. Only minutes had passed.

I hurried out the back door, the air icy after the sweltering oven. I was halfway across the alley before I stopped, shivering, and stared at the door.

I had to go in, but I couldn't force my feet forward.

The door opened.

"What's wrong?" This time Aunt Gerta had reason to panic, but I needed her help. More than ever, I needed her. She pulled me inside. "Is it Tobias?"

I shook my head. "A man came. I have to pack some things."

Her eyes widened. "A man, Lena? Who?"

"I have less than an hour."

"Why did your uncle have to be gone today. He'd know what to do." She tightened her arms around me. "I'll go to. . ."

"It won't do any good."

"I have to try."

I shook my head. "Think of Tobias. It's not worth the risk."

Her eyes filled with tears.

"Take care of him. Promise." My chest twisted and I pulled away.

"But, Lena. What will I tell him?"

"I have a minute to get my clothes. I'll have the dark rye out unless..." I was helpless at comforting people, but today I didn't just lack the words. If I tried to say anything, I'd start crying and never stop.

How could I leave Tobias?

In two minutes I was done. I closed my eyes, hugged Aunt Gerta, then pulled away and hurried out the door. The cold welcomed me and I sucked in an icy breath to keep from thinking. An eerie stillness in the streets hurried me into the bakery.

Ten steps from the house to the bakery but I could feel eyes on me, waiting to see what would become of me. Maybe caring, maybe not, but waiting till it'd be too late to do something even if they wanted to.

The door opened. It hadn't been an hour.

"When will you be back? What do I tell Tobias?" Aunt Gerta whispered.

I shuddered, the pain in my gut doubled. "I don't know anything. But promise you'll keep him safe." I didn't turn around. I couldn't.

She grabbed me in a hug.

"You should go. If someone sees us together, it could raise questions," I pulled away when she didn't. "Please?"

Aunt Gerta let go and left, the door sucking the air out with her.

I wiped my eyes and looked around. The bread racks were still being filled. It was rare that I left before they were empty. Uncle trusted me to take care of his bakery while he picked up the flour. I was failing him.

Food. The man said to bring food. Bread would last and I couldn't face aunt Gerta again.

I pulled a loaf from the cooling rack and wrapped it in a towel, pushing it into my bag.

The clock's ticking hammered in my head while I stacked the raising baskets, scraped the counter, swept the floor and carried the crock of dough down to the cellar. I wouldn't be mixing dough tomorrow. I climbed back up the steps and let the trap door slam with a cloud of flour.

I grabbed the broom and swept again, focusing on the corners, getting the cracks I never had time for. There had to be something I needed to do, but what?

The bread.

The wisps of steam had quit curling out the cracks around the oven door and the smell of ripe wheat was close to burnt.

I grabbed the peel, pulled the oven open and shoved it in, pulling out the first three loaves and shaking them onto the

3

rack. Now I was warm, and the rhythm was familiar and soothing. Almost numbing.

The last one, always so far back. I stretched and stood on tiptoe and shoved the peel as far as I could then pulled it out. Dark but not burnt.

"Finished?" The deep voice was close.

I jumped. Blinding heat seared into my arm and I pulled away from the oven door. Taking a deep breath, I turned around.

A soldier stared down from across the counter and anger seeped into his eyes.

I turned away, my heart in my throat. I couldn't breathe. I picked up my bag and came around the counter, forcing myself to face him.

Something worse than fear tightened my stomach.

He reached towards me, his hand big and callused.

I closed my eyes.

"This way."

I looked up.

His jaw tightened and he backed up, dropping his hands to his sides. "I'm not going to hurt you."

I walked to the door, then it swung open and hit me. The world tilted and I hit the floor.

"What's taking so long?" A new voice boomed through the room. "What is it Karl? What's going on with you?"

I gripped the floor. My head rang and the cold wind from the open door shot into my arm.

"Leave it Max. Attend to your own assignment and stop interfering with mine." This voice, the soldier's voice, was close and mad. Was he mad at me?

The door slammed shut and the bakery was silent.

"We have to go."

I kept my eyes closed and used the door to stand.

"Can you walk?"

What would he say if I said no? I opened my eyes and walked, carefully.

"I'm sorry you got knocked down." He stayed close at my side, but he needn't have worried. There was no way I could run right now, even if I had somewhere to go.

The Rosenbaums came up Gossman strasse with three soldiers. Frau Rosenbaum's mother was with them. Were we being taken to the same place?

I shuddered at the possibilities.

"Are you alright?" The soldier asked.

I looked up; the darkest eyes were peering down into mine.

His eyes drew together, and his forehead creased with lines.

"I'm fine." Why was he asking?

He stopped and stared at me. His face hardened, the stiff angry look filled it again. He didn't need a gun like the rest were pointing. He scared me without a word.

Several other groups were ahead.

I walked again when he did, keeping my eyes ahead, away from the scar on his neck, the eyes boring into mine. My foot caught on a rock and I fell to my hands on the jagged edge of the street. I pushed against the rocks and tried to get a breath. I didn't want to see his anger right now. My head settled and I opened my eyes.

His held out his hand.

Did I have a choice?

"I'm sorry." I could feel my face going red. But I got up, took a deep breath and started walking again, keeping my eyes on the ground. I jumped when I felt his hand on my elbow.

"I'm trying to keep you off your face," he said.

Noise ahead brought me back to the nightmare that was reality. The train station was crowded, there were so many people I sucked in a breath and looked up at the soldier by my side.

What was going on?

People were sitting on the ground. Old people and children with their mothers. I felt my stomach churn, the crying of a little boy made it hard to see.

The soldier led me to the edge of the crowd and let go of my arm.

I wiped my eyes and looked up.

He turned away.

"Thank you for catching me," I said.

"Don't thank me," he said, his face full of fury. Then he turned and strode away without looking back.

The sun was overhead, but it wasn't hot, simply less cold than earlier. The clock in the square chimed, it had already been two hours.

"How long are we going to be waiting here?" Someone asked.

The constant murmuring stilled, all wondering what else they would tell us, if anything.

"We don't know yet." The brusque answer was repeated by several of the guards. Some were police, some were soldiers.

A woman's skirts swished when she walked by in the street, her basket banging against her leg. She kept her eyes on the ground and hurried. I couldn't blame her; I'd probably do the same thing.

What could make this any worse?

My heart stopped when I realized what would.

"Why?"

The voice asking the question tore at my heart. I scooted towards a stout woman a few steps away and hunched down behind her.

"But why, mama? Where's Poppy?" Tobias's little voice carried across the street, one of many children on their way from school. I peeked up and saw my aunt trying to hurry

Tobias down the street. She looked over and shock covered her face when she met mine.

I shook my head, "Don't," I mouthed. "Don't let him see me."

I shuddered and wrapped my arms around my head. What would she answer, what would he believe about me from now on?

The pain of losing him reached up and took my breath.

"Poppy."

My stomach knotted. No. But I looked up, my aunt stood frozen, her face desperate but she couldn't stop him. I couldn't have stopped him either.

He'd seen me and was flying across the street. His face lit up, he didn't know anything was wrong.

I gulped and stood, stumbling around a few people to get to the edge of the group. Then a tower stood in front of me. Between me and Tobias.

"Can I tell him goodbye?"

"Who is he?" The answer was gruff. The guard grabbed him and held him back. "Is he related to you?"

"No. I worked for his parents. I was-"

Tobias was struggling with the guard. "Poppy," he said again. He wasn't being hurt but he didn't understand. Why wasn't I rushing towards him?

"Let it be, Fritz. We had no orders against it," the voice from a few steps away was familiar and deep, the response immediate. The soldier who'd picked me up was there again.

But I couldn't care less who gave the order.

The guard let go and Tobias plunged into me.

Tears clouded my eyes and I dropped to the ground, hugging him to me. Holding him up and grasping him closer, I only had a moment.

I looked up and saw my aunt a few yards away, waiting. Trembling. Be strong, I mouthed to her.

She probably didn't get what I said but she nodded anyway.

7

"Why didn't you come get me? Why-"

"You have to go home with your mother now," I interrupted, so glad he called her that. "I have to go, but you be a good boy."

"Why?"

I stroked his head and felt the little bump behind his ear. He'd had it even when he was a baby. "I love you."

The guard shifted his feet.

I gulped down the tears brimming and forced my mouth into a smile. "I love you," I whispered again, pulled his arms from around my neck and set him down.

"Go with mama now," I touched his cheek one last time then gave him a little push. I smiled when he looked back.

Aunt Gerta took his hand and pulled him away.

He looked again right before they rounded the corner and I smiled and waved.

Aunt Gerta didn't look back once.

I sat and put my head in my hands. My heart was pounding, the pain circled and circled gaining strength every time. He was gone, I'd just said goodbye.

But if I showed what I was feeling, if they suspected at all. I shuddered and my lungs burned for air. I took a breath and tried to stop the tears from coming.

It wasn't a nightmare.

Nightmares always featured my father in some ghastly way and they always ended before I lost Tobias.

TWO

$\mathcal{I}$ sat still, keeping my arms tight around me. My heart was tearing in pieces, but I had to be still. Still and quiet.

Tobias would be home soon, eating his dinner and getting soup on his sleeves.

Despair crept up and pulled at the strings tied from him to me.

Tobias.

A laugh from nearby brought me back to reality.

My arm prickled. Later the pain would drive me distracted but now I couldn't feel it. I was shivering from deep inside, but I wasn't cold. I was too numb to feel anything. Like I was trapped inside someone else who was shivering and burning.

Shouting woke me. The street beneath me was cold.

Shadows had crept up; dusk had brought a train, and everyone was swarming to get on.

Why were they rushing? I rolled forward and sat up. A shooting pain shot up from my hand. I cried out before I could stop myself. The weight moved off my hand, I pulled it in and hunched in a ball.

Someone else banged into me and said something foul.

Then a tall figure stood beside me and I wasn't being pushed from every side. A hand reached down to me.

I gulped and stood alone, but my legs were stiff, my side pulled a stitch and I swayed. Two strong hands stopped my fall and suddenly I couldn't breathe. His hands were around my waist and I fought the panic that stole the air from my lungs. The darkness hid his face, was it hiding mine as well? What was he doing here again?

"*Stop it.*" I said to myself. He's doing his job. Getting rid of us. Whatever that means. I straightened my back and relaxed my shoulders as best I could. He let go, getting the hint I was trying to give. I shivered and backed up. I had to get away from whatever his devious plans were.

He stood watching, but I turned away and made my way to the train. It was clear now why they'd been hurrying. Everyone getting on now, like me, would be sitting on the floor.

The train pulled out and the town was gone in seconds. Soon it was dark and mostly silent. Guards paced back and forth. Fortunately, the one from before wasn't in this car.

"What's your name?" Someone whispered. It was a man nearby, bent with age. "Are you alone?"

I shivered and looked away; he might not recognize me but that wasn't mutual.

"You can be with my wife and me. You shouldn't be alone."

I shuddered at what he was implying. Had he seen the soldier outside, taking too much interest?

"What's your name? Are you from nearby?"

"She's scared Horst," someone else leaned down from the seat when the guard had turned away. "Are you all alone dear?" The woman meant to be kind; I could hear that.

But my skin prickled remembering their words a few years ago.

"Don't worry, dear, you're not alone," her hand on my

shoulder like a claw, her words stung. For I knew what they were. Empty.

"Lena Weismann," I said, louder than a whisper. The hand on my shoulder froze. "My father's name is Alfred Weismann." I couldn't hold it in. I couldn't take the fake kindness. They didn't want to help me, they wanted to help a random, innocent - and most of all - Jewish girl.

She pulled away from me, cursing my blood.

I sighed; it was nothing new.

The night was endless with constant stops. Where were we now? Still in Germany but why were we here? We stopped again and two women at the front of the train car stood.

"Sit down," the soldiers said standing at the doors. "No one's getting out."

Indignant replies swirled around. I crouched close to the side of the aisle.

We didn't move for more than an hour, by then the guards were more than unhappy. At least I could try to sleep. They had to stand.

Another stop a few hours later jolted everyone awake. The two babies in the car cried and worse was the old people who wanted to. It was dawn when we started again, but only a few kilometers down the road everyone groaned when we slowed again. The guards and the guarded.

I curled to the side and rested my head against a bench. Closing my eyes, I tried to think of grass and trees, something calm.

A shove from above sent me sprawling into the walkway, *"Mischlinge."*

Then a sharp boot sent pain racing up my ribs and someone fell on me, the sharp butt of a gun digging into my leg. I rolled out of the walkway, away from the side I'd been on.

The soldier stood, cursing me. "Six months in constant skir-

11

mishes with not a scratch. One little Jewess and my face is sliced open."

I held my breath, hoping the pain would leave my side. Hoping he wouldn't act on the anger in his voice. The door opened and I kept my head down.

'Forget me. Please, forget me.' I begged the silence.

"Stand up." The words were right above me.

I pushed my hands off the muddy floorboards and stood, holding onto the back of the seat nearest.

"If anyone gets in my way again, you'll..." he paused. His breath sent prickles down my neck. "Suffer the consequences." He didn't sound as angry, but I was more scared than before. Then he grabbed my arm and pulled me down the steps to the platform.

Only soldiers milled around.

I ventured a look at his face and my stomach knotted.

He dragged me towards the station building nearby. It was small, dark, empty.

"Fritz."

We stopped, his hand around my arm shook.

"Yes sir?" He sounded nervous and he turned, taking my other arm.

The pain as he grasped the open burn dragged a cry from my lips.

He spun me around, adding to the haze the fog had already created.

"Where are you going?" The deep voice growled. "Answer me."

I shivered though it wasn't growling at me. I knew that voice, and once my eyes could focus, I saw the soldier who once again could scare me without even talking. He was staring straight at me. I tried to back up but the fingers biting into my arm kept me close, and he kept coming closer, getting taller and taller till I was staring up at him.

The guard beside me shook me, rattling my teeth, but it broke whatever it was that held my eyes to the soldier, huge and terrible above me. Terror, exhaustion, whatever the hold was, I was glad to be free of it.

"Get back to your post."

His grip got tighter and tighter the longer we stood, digging into my burn.

I groaned and closed my eyes.

He saluted and pulled me away.

"Leave her."

We stopped. "Lieutenant?"

My arm was on fire, but I could hear the confusion in his word.

"Leave her." The voice was deep, the dead certainty rang through."Any other questions?"

He released my arm instantly and I stumbled. He turned and marched quickly away.

I straightened and looked up. He must know what he just saved me from, or was he saving me? My stomach churned, the intensity of his stare unnerving. Lieutenant, he wasn't just a random foot soldier.

My heart thudded; I took a step back.

The tall soldier came closer again. I froze when his hand came up to strike me. I closed my eyes. Then a hand was on my arm pulling me forward.

He strode down the line of rail cars, there were so many. So many and all full of people.

A stitch in my side pulled, I gasped for breath and stumbled.

He slowed but didn't release me. "You get in a lot of trouble, don't you?" He slowed even more. "Don't you have anything to say?"

What was he going to do to me?" "Thank you."

"That's not—" his face hardened. "I didn't mean that." So he did know what the guards intention had been. "Were you going to run?" He slowed even more. "You think you can make it alone?"

Was he taunting me?

His eyes pulled in and lines spiked up his forehead. No, he was serious, just like he'd sounded.

"If I say no you could say I'm lying, if I say yes you could—" I pulled in a deep breath. "What would you have me say?" I hugged my free arm to my side pushing against pain. Why had I been so sharp with him? He could shoot me if he wanted. I bit my lower lip. Why did he ask?

The fog of the night rose up around us and mixed with the steam swirling from the train, it was almost like we were all alone.

I shivered, my jacket wasn't doing much. Especially since I didn't even have both arms in. My burn wasn't hurting much right now though. Thank goodness he hadn't grabbed that arm.

I waited for something to happen. And it did. We stopped at the last car on the tracks.

He led me up the steps.

"They sent her back, too crowded," he said. This car had the same faded benches and closed windows and it looked just as crowded. Maybe even more.

"Sit." He ordered.

Shivering against the animosity around me, both from the guards and those sitting, I huddled where I was thrust.

Wind hit my face when the door opened and mud splattered my hand when two soldiers stamped past. "Another day or two and we should be done."

They were anxious to be through. But what of us? Where were we headed? We'd probably wish ourselves back here again within minutes. Or hours, I added taking a breath and gagging again. The bit of air from outside only made it harder to breathe when the door was closed again.

"Can we open some windows?" The woman was braver than I.

"Please?" I found my mouth opening unbidden. "Just a small ways?" I stood and looked at the soldier.

The woman's mouth twitched towards a smile, but she didn't and I wouldn't have wanted her to. She held her baby closer and slumped into the corner of her seat.

The soldier came down the aisle towards me, the other woman forgotten. Only a bit taller than me, he came close, too close. The smell of meat and ale and tobacco mixed in his hot mouth and smacked my face making me gasp for the stale air of the rail car. I almost lost the little bread I ate all those hours ago.

"What are you doing?" he asked.

I stared at my feet.

Heavy brisk footsteps came from behind. "Answer me." The soldier said roughly.

"What?" Someone asked. "What is it?"

There were eyes on me from every side, soldiers before and behind, all the benches full of people watching with nothing to do but worry.

"I was asking for. . ." I swallowed. The silence was unnerving. I looked back and my stomach dropped.

He was here again, the tall soldier with his eyes on me and only me.

The short tobacco smelling soldier whirled me around. "You're in the way," he said and thrust me aside. "Sit and shut up." Easier said than done in the crowded car.

It was darker now. There wasn't much moon so I couldn't see the trees. "Where are we going?" A little girl asked. She'd been good all day, but she wanted to get off. Wanted to be done.

Her mother's murmurs were indistinct, quiet. But it was what we all wondered.

Should I have run weeks ago?

The torture of knowing I could have dug into me. But Tobias. My finger knotted in my hair before I noticed I'd started twisting.

I looked around, was anyone else was wondering the same thing? Was anyone thinking of running now? Was anyone thinking at all? Everyone I could see was tired, afraid, and resigned.

Was I resigned? Did my face look hopeless? There were only three guards on this car. Only two on the last one. Was I the only person thinking this?

We were sure to stop soon. We couldn't seem to go far before some important train needed the tracks, and we got sidelined again. Once it was dark, if I was quick, could I slip away?

I was already on the floor. If I could get closer to the door, it was less crowded at the end. Of course it was colder too - that's why.

With each passing of the guard I scooted another foot, they didn't seem to notice.

Then one tripped on me.

"Why are you here?" He asked.

"There's nowhere to sit," I pointed to the corner by the door. "I was trying to get out of the way."

He shrugged. "Stay out of the way."

I hurried on and slunk down. The guard didn't give me another thought. That tall one would have, thank goodness he wasn't on this car. A shiver went down my spine.

Sitting this close to the door was colder. I dug in my bag and pulled out some socks. It took tugging to get my shoes off, but I did and added the extra layer.

Bread sounded dry, perfect. I ate a little. The night was so long in coming I almost fell asleep. Maybe I did. Then I realized with a jolt that we weren't moving. The train had stopped. A blanket of silence covered the whole car and the guards were on the other end.

Squinting, the sign through the window was almost visible. We were in France, we traveled west? That was something. All the bad rumors had been from the east.

But I had to try something. The creeping sense of doom grew stronger the further we went.

The doors opened and all the guards got off.

Right in front of me the door stood open. No one was looking. I slipped my bag over my shoulder and eased forward. The floor creaked under me, I felt my heart jump into my throat.

But no one moved. No one even looked my way, though some whispered now the guards were gone.

The beating of my heart was so loud, I put my foot on the first step. I crept down another. And another. I peeked around the corner.

Most of the guards were in the station.

Walking along the rail car I headed towards the closest building, that wasn't full of guards.

If I could get there, I could hide till the train left. And if anyone who found me later didn't notice my French was from the south. There were so many if's...

Now I had to cross several yards, away from the train, and I couldn't stop and blend into the shadows if someone looked over. My feet felt like rubber.

"Who are you?" Someone shouted. I froze and looked up. I hadn't thought of this. It was the tall soldier. The Lieutenant.

Run, Lena, run.

I turned and ran.

THREE

*T*he town was close.

Dark shapes loomed up and missing fence posts and water pumps was hard as I ran. I stopped to catch my breath in an alley. Once I could hear past my breathing everything was quiet, too quiet. I crept back and looked around the corner.

Several soldiers were running, one of them towards me.

I spun and took off running. I was in someone's garden now. I tripped over a pumpkin; the vines tangled around my legs. I lost my breath, but I pushed up and stood again, running before I could get any air to my lungs.

Footsteps clattered on the street nearby.

Pain ran up my legs, pain dug into my side, but I kept running.

A thud ahead brought me to a stop. I turned and ran towards the woods.

"Henrik. This way." They were close, the woods too far off.

I looked around the small street, leading from one big road to another.

Houses stood quietly, shutting me out. Nowhere to hide. The footsteps were getting closer. On two different sides.

I spun in a circle, both directions were blocked. My head swam and I sank to the ground, leaning against the low fence beside me. I held onto it to still the spinning in my head. I gripped the slats of wood and splinters dug into the palms of my hands.

They were right behind me. "She must know someone here."

"We can't go door to door. Some wouldn't tell us if they had seen her and most wouldn't understand us anyway. We crossed the border a few hours ago." They were so close.

My hands were slick with sweat, my back ached from the bent position, but I refused to breathe. I refused to make a sound.

It wasn't working.

"What was that?" They stopped, listening. Listening for me.

Seconds ticked by. Eighty-four I counted. What was I going to do? I couldn't hold on much longer. My hands slipped a little and I held tighter, biting my lip.

"Let's go," the soldiers walked away, looking down every street that turned off.

I watched them go, keeping hold of the fence. Don't look back, I begged.

At the corner they stopped and looked back.

I held my breath, but they didn't seem to see me. I loosened my hold and sank back on the ground. Boots a few streets over echoed in my head but they continued without stopping or coming down this street.

The town was so quiet. I looked around, someone must have heard the train. Someone had to have seen me get off.

The sound of the train. It was pulling out. I didn't want to be on it, not even a little. But it was my link to home. To Tobias.

I stifled a choking in my throat and straightened myself out. Standing, I looked around. Which way it was to…where?

I didn't even know where to go.

Aloneness filled me. Then terror.

Then a sound I couldn't believe, couldn't reason out.

Boots.

But the train had left, I could hear the echo of it fading, but it had certainly left. It was gone. And someone was not on it. Of course they wouldn't let me escape.

Quietly I started walking towards the woods. Where the soldier was, I couldn't tell exactly but I had to do something. My luck wouldn't let someone walk past me twice.

The guard from the first rail car. If it was him, a jolt of pain covered every bit of me. At least it made me hurry.

Now I saw why I hadn't been able to see the sign from the train. Clouds parted above and the whole road was clear. I could see now.

He'd be able to see me too.

My legs went faster. I couldn't hear anything now. Whoever was still here, looking for me, must have gone the other way.

The tall trees beckoned to me, they were so close.

I should be safe enough if I didn't go too far in. I took a deep breath and looked both ways across the street. Should I cross or go around? My finger got caught in my hair before I realized I was standing still, in plain view. I had to get across.

I hurried but my fingers were getting stiff now from the cold, and my legs were sore.

In the middle of the street I froze. A prickle on the back of my neck made my stomach drop. I turned slowly, the shadow I'd seen, had I seen a shadow?

There was nothing anywhere. I hurried on. The woods were so close. It was almost light with all the moonlight, but tonight the light didn't make me smile. The light was like a flashlight out to find me, expose me.

But I was close. I breathed a sigh of relief.

Furious barking from across the courtyard brought a scream

from somewhere close. I clapped my hand over my mouth. I was the one who screamed.

A scuffling in the house, a light came on.

The dog lunged against a rope.

I backed away and tripped on a branch but somehow didn't fall. I ran for the woods.

The dog barked like he knew I was meant to be caught. Somehow he knew I was running. Branches pulled at my hair, vines and huge ferns grabbed at my feet, but I didn't stop. I kept running past the ache in my lungs, when would I have enough to breathe again? Past the tearing in my legs, I couldn't stop.

That soldier was coming after me. He was sent to bring me back.

It was almost morning. I dreaded and yet longed for it. Only walking now but I was so tired it was torture.

When I'd had Tobias, I found a way to keep going. But for me, I wanted to stop and sleep.

A branch slapped my face. I backed away and hit the tree. I sank where I was, gripping the bark of the tree. Something that was real and staying in place.

My head ached, but it wasn't dripping. I felt over the part that hurt the most, at least I hadn't gashed it open.

Blood on your face doesn't help you blend in.

I fought with sleep, but it swept over me. Curling up against the tree I gave in.

I was cold, even with the sun in my face. Rain was drizzling down and I was soaking wet. I sat up against the tree and shivered when a gust of wind blew past.

A branch snapped nearby. The soldier couldn't have found me. Could he?

Getting on all fours I backed up then stood up, stumbling to move but forcing my legs to take me away. Every part of me begging to quit.

When I hit a road I stopped.

A road.

Quickly I got to the other side of it and staying in the trees I followed the road.

I looked up, the sun was setting already. I'd slept the day away. What had the soldier been doing? Was he long gone or right behind me? I looked back seeing nothing but trees, ferns, and more of the same. It was just another wood.

Soon my stomach was making so much noise if I had to hide it wouldn't do any good. I sat down and dug into my bag. I should still have some bread.

My bag was still on my shoulder, but it was empty. Had I dropped everything?

I sank against a log and closed my eyes. I just wanted to sleep.

The moss on the log was soaking wet, and after a minute so was the back of my dress. I stood and kept walking along the road. Surely someone would help me here. Surely I'd find something to eat.

A wagon was coming up the road.

I could ask for help.

I froze behind a big tree, waiting for it to get closer. Waiting to see if the driver looked like he would help someone or not. I watched each step of the horses but what was I looking for?

The driver looked like. . .a person. Who was to say if he'd help me or turn me in? What was I looking for?

I could ask for a ride to town. I could ask, something. What should I ask? What should I say?

The wagon rolled by and disappeared around a bend in the road.

I couldn't decide if he looked safe or not. I couldn't risk it.

Walking again, I fought with myself. What was I going to do? Walk for now, that was enough to think about.

Someone else was in the road behind me. I knew it, but I couldn't ever see them. They always hid when I turned around. Walking forward was hard, I wanted to see what was behind me. And I didn't know if I should be going forward, or the other way entirely. I might be going right back to the town I ran from.

Once it was too dark to avoid tripping, and I'd tripped and fallen three times I let go and collapsed on the ground. A fern tickled my face, dousing my face with water.

The rain wasn't falling now. It was the mist of evening, covering everything.

After I woke, I found the stream of water I heard during the night. I couldn't believe how thirsty I was after being soaked for so long. I stuck my face in the water, it was icy and quenched my dry throat, but the water made me shiver. I washed the dirt off my face, or tried to. My hands were dirty themselves, it was hard to know if I made my face better or worse.

Then I followed the road again.

If I were brave, walking into the town wouldn't be hard.

At least the town wasn't the one I'd come from. I didn't know where I was, only some small town, somewhere in France.

I walked down the one little street and everyone was staring. Or was that my imagination? Was there dirt on my face?

"Do you need any work done?" I asked at the store.

"No," the woman said.

"Never," the man almost shouted.

I hurried out and saw the soldiers in the square. They were here because we'd won. They'd won. The Germans were the invaders here and if I were these people, I wouldn't want me either.

But I was hungry. Very hungry. So I kept asking.

I finally got a yes after asking three more times, and I set to work. I didn't want to add anything negative to the image of what Germans were seen as here.

Hard calluses lined the hands of the man who'd said yes. I swept quickly, then took up the rag and cleaned the counter.

"Thank you," I said when he looked at me.

He grunted and motioned.

I hurried to him.

"Here," he pressed some coins in my hand. "Go now. I can't do any more."

What? I only started.

"I want to help you," he looked around, his hands trembling and not from old age. "But I can't do anything more. Please, take it and go."

"I've only just started," I said, holding out the money. "I can't take money I haven't earned."

"Take it," he said stepping away, leaving the money in my hands. "Please, it would ease my conscience. But go now. Before someone," he looked towards the door again.

I backed up. "Do you have a back door?"

He sighed and relaxed his shoulders."Of course." He led me back.

I hurried from it not looking back. The money clutched in my hand I hurried around buildings, hurried away, putting distance between the kind- hearted man and me before I could bring trouble on someone else.

FOUR

$\mathcal{H}$aving everything wouldn't make some people happy. Having only a little would make others extremely so. Was this whole thing happening because I wasn't happy? Because I wanted more?

"Who are you?" A man called out in German, shaking me from my thoughts.

I turned slowly. What should I say? What would he believe? "*Qui estu?*" I held my breath. Please don't speak French, please. I couldn't remember if I'd said the question right. Or what it was I'd said. I prayed digging my nails into my palms, but the pain was too slight to stop the shaking in my chest.

"Of course, French. Never mind," he said, waving me off and shaking his head.

I focused on walking away, not tripping, not starting to run. Was every town full of soldiers? How was I going to get anywhere, or food for that matter? Looking up at the trees, they all seemed to be bending towards me, pressing me further down than I was already. Small and at their mercy.

At the mercy of anyone who found me.

My hand still clenched the coins. A train would take me far

away, and quickly. Walking down the road I looked for signs. For towns and rail stations. Surely there would be some way to find a train and head in the opposite direction.

I stopped in my tracks, where had we been heading? I shuddered when I realized — I had no idea. I didn't even know which way to run.

But I had to keep going, if they found me, they might find Tobias.

They couldn't find Tobias, I had to keep going.

At the next town I was still trembling. I could do this, I told myself. I just had to wait a little while.

Before I knew it, it was night. I huddled where I'd sat to rest.

Huddled in a ball, I closed my eyes. It was darker, but there was less to see. The night came on, noises made me jump and hold my hand over my mouth. But close to a town, a town this big should be enough incentive to keep wild animals away. I hoped so. I prayed so.

The wind blew, loud and soft going back and forth. Keeping my eyes closed didn't help. I could imagine more than I could hear.

The night dragged on. Sleep stayed away, but so did wild animals.

I waited for the light to come. Someone would wonder why I was here alone but coming in early would be worse to explain.

The sun was shining in my face when I woke, I stared up at the sun and sighed. I was almost warm everywhere except my feet. They were still ice cold.

I stood up then fell back faster.

Ice cold and numb. My fingers were cold too, but I untied my shoes after a bit of trouble. I rubbed at my feet and looked around.

No one had found me, thank goodness. My feet were so cold, I kept rubbing and rubbing but they were numb. They didn't hurt, but that was worse, I knew that was worse. I pulled off my socks and looked around.

No water in sight, but I found a creek last night. I shivered before I got close. I closed my eyes and fighting everything in me, stuck my feet in the water. In winter people used ice to thaw their feet, this should work.

A few seconds was all I could take.

My feet were still pale when I lifted them up. I stuck them in again and held them in longer. Pin pricks and then needles on fire told me I'd done enough.

My feet bright red now I sat on the bank. I couldn't walk yet, but at least they were thawed.

I crawled back to find my shoes where I'd left them.

It took so long to get them back on I wanted to cry. First from the frustration, then from the pain. My feet were thawed but they were burning. From the inside out.

Finally I stood and holding on to a tree I started walking.

Ignoring my feet, I kept moving. Walking into town I shoved away the fear that'd kept me in the cold last night. I went through the town and didn't see the train station.

But I'd seen tracks. There had to be a station.

I could feel eyes watching me when I started through the town again.

Why was it hard to find, wouldn't it be in the middle of town?

I bought some bread, but nothing more, I didn't want to go from store to store. One person hating me was enough. Or was it indifference? I couldn't tell. These towns were mostly French but so many soldiers were around. I needed to go somewhere there wouldn't be soldiers.

A map. I needed to find a map.

"Train station?" I asked an old man. He pointed down the road and hobbled on, in the opposite direction.

My feet were thawed now, the pain more than distracting.

Perhaps I could sit for a few minutes. Maybe no one would notice.

Walking down the street of a small town, without getting noticed. A foolish idea. Especially in this town, swarming with soldiers.

That street didn't lead to the train station. The next didn't take me there either. Soon I stopped in an alley and leaned against the wall. It was chilly in the shade. I rubbed my hands together.

A curse came from across the street.

Across the street, in the ally opposite, a man cursed again. It was a soldier, it was two soldiers.

I shrank against the wall and kept still in the shadow.

They were fighting, one had his arm wrapped around the other's neck.

I edged along the wall, trying not to look in that dreadful alley.

Someone was getting hurt.

Should I do something? But what? Maybe it was just a fight, soldiers did that. Men did that. That was normal. Wasn't it?

I looked back. One lay on the ground now, the other stood and looked at me.

My throat went dry. The soldier was looking straight at me. I backed up along the wall.

But he just stood, watching. Watching me leave.

No, I breathed, don't follow me.

He stared up the alley but didn't move.

I turned and ran, not even looking to see if he followed. I ran into several people who muttered but didn't stop me. No one seemed to care why I fled, or were they too scared?

Someone grabbed my arm, pulling me to a stop. "*Was ist los?*"

That definitely wasn't French. It was a German soldier, speaking German.

My stomach dropped.

"What's wrong?" He repeated. "What's your name?" I looked up and searched the man's narrow eyes.

"Your papers," his grip tightened, though his face was composed.

"I lost them."

"I knew you were German. Why are you here?" He waited a moment. "Speak."

"I'm lost," I said and it was true enough - I didn't have a clue where I was.

"Why are you here, alone, in France?" He asked.

I gulped.

"Come."

I pulled away. "I'm not running."

But he held on, his fingers bit deep. He pulled me along the street, up the block, into the police quarters.

I clenched my teeth to keep from screaming.

"No papers. No explanation for being here," the soldier said, releasing me in front of a desk.

"None?" The man sitting behind it looked up, his lips pressed into a thin line. "Did you search her bag?"

"Her bag?" The soldier looked at me again, his eyes moving to my bag, hanging on my shoulder. He pulled it off, handing it across the desk.

The officer looked through it then back at me. "It makes no difference what she did with her papers. Put her in a cell. She'll go with the others in the morning."

The soldier grabbed me and marched me through the doorway to the back room, then into a cell.

I watched him leave, the keys in his pocket. I couldn't be here, in jail. Alone and leaving Tobias without anyone. It wasn't real.

A new soldier came in, his mustache too clean, too neatly trimmed. He leaned against the wall, staring at me like I was an animal on display.

The bench was covered by a single blanket, but at least it was dry. At least I could sit out of the rain.

"I'll be back later."

I looked up.

The new soldier was at the bars now, his eyes promising things I didn't want to see.

I turned away and dropped to the bench.

"You can't ignore me when the captain's gone," he whispered through the bars.

So repulsive I wanted to hit him, but no doubt he'd welcome attention.

He walked out, his words ringing. It was clear what he meant and he wasn't bluffing. He'd be back and the thought made me heave, but there wasn't enough food left in me to lose.

"It's another. Yes sir," a sharp clang when he hung up. "Werner."

Quick footsteps passed the doorway.

"Tomorrow you'll take her to the station."

"Yes, sir."

"Before it's light out. We don't want another scene."

I was pressed up against the bars listening. But that was all they said.

The outer room had gone silent.

I shuddered when the cell door clanged shut. The snicker of one guard and the other's comment. "We'll wait till the captain goes home."

Huddled on the pallet I pulled the blanket around me and I tried to block out their talk. Impossible.

"Kind of small, isn't she?" A laugh. "But feisty. Ran from the train, been on her own for days." The one talking now made me sicker than the first.

"She's a fighter."

The hours ticked by but not slow enough. I dreaded each centimeter the shadows crept forward.

Soon it was dark. Everything was worse in the dark.

The guard who brought in my supper set it down then stood, waiting.

I didn't move.

"Hungry?" He asked. His chuckle made me freeze. Then he ran his fingers along my arm.

The jolt was painful, zapping from my scalp to my toes.

"Fine, don't eat," he left and slammed the door behind.

My stomach cramped at the thought of food, I leaned over and looked at the tray. The greasy smell of the beef slapped me in the face. I lurched back and my head hit the wall.

The smell of kerosene drifted into the room. No, it was too early to light the lamps. And didn't they have any electric lights here?

I sat up and looked out the windows.

It was dusk.

The captain was leaving. "I'll be back to sign for her transfer."

Something burned in the pit of my stomach. I burrowed deeper into the flat mat on the hard pallet, under the thread-thin blanket.

My throat closed, choking a scream trying to get out. I couldn't breathe past the fear. It was so much worse knowing what was coming.

Heavy boots clicked, the front door slammed. The building was silent.

After a few minutes I gasped, I'd been holding my breath too long. Someone was talking, but I couldn't hear a word.

A chair scraped across the floor, it creaked when someone sat. I couldn't take this waiting much longer. It was killing me, this waiting.

"Will you be long?"

"Why? Anxious to sit up all night?"

"Finish your paperwork."

The cell I was in was one of two, the doorway leading to the front room centered between like a big gaping hole. There wasn't anything else in the whole room. I looked around, a filing cabinet stood in the corner.

It looked new. Too new, like it came with the replacement soldiers.

Maybe it had, we Germans were nothing if not thorough.

But what would the file say about me? Would there be a file on me?

Would anyone know what had happened? Where I was being sent?

Their laughter broke the quiet.

I leaned over the side of the bed and studied the tray of food. There was a bread roll beside the thin greasy broth. I could eat some bread. I reached for the roll and a sharp searing pain dug into my arm. Into my burn. Blood trickled down my arm and onto the tray, onto the bread in my hand. I dropped it, then jumped when it hit the spoon splashing the stew on the ground.

One of the guards looked in, his eyes went to my arm. Maybe he'd leave me alone, and the mistake of drawing their attention would be for good instead of bad.

"Poor thing, want me to make it feel better?" The offer was taunted, but he didn't come closer.

My stomach knotted at thoughts that came unbidden. I couldn't breathe.

He stood staring a long minute till finally he turned and left the doorway.

Alone I curled my knees under me. My hair was loose, strands sticking to the moisture on my face.

A lock on the front door was thrown.

All at once the room was full of noise. The ticking of the clock. The rain on the window hammering hard enough to break through the glass any second. The boots tramping from the front room to the back.

To this room, to the door of my cell. The key in the lock.

I covered my ears, my hands were shaking, I couldn't stop them.

Someone grabbed my hair, pulled my head back. I froze, I couldn't breathe.

"Don't be like that," the voice was smooth and grotesque at once.

I closed my eyes, clenched my hands.

His finger was sickening how it traced down my face and started down my neck.

My heart beat so hard I couldn't breathe, I pulled away, my hands punching whatever they found. Then I fell, my head hitting a corner of something that sent shooting pain in every direction. A cry escaped me.

"Broke my nose. You little witch. Serves you right to get knocked on the head," he stood over me and grabbing my arms pulled me up. "Think fighting back will help?" He shouted into my face.

I twisted away and tried not to puke.

"Dieter," he called, then he leaned close and whispered. "You should have behaved before."

I looked to the door. Maybe Dieter would stand up to what he was doing.

Someone filled the doorway. His grin settled into my mind and my last bit of hope faded.

I was falling, but there was nowhere to fall. I was firmly in the grasp of this miserable excuse of a man. And another was circling.

A scream came out of nowhere.

"Shut her up," Dieter came into the cell.

The first one shook me. "Quiet."

I couldn't stop. I couldn't.

His hand came at me.

Stinging needles covered my face, I gasped, choking on something.

"Don't get her all bloody," Dieter said. "And if you bruise her face the captain will see."

They were both so close, I couldn't get free of them. My back tingled with cold, and something else. They were shaking me. And I shook from the inside.

"Fight in this one, like I said."

The room swam, I closed my eyes.

"Maybe not," the other said. "Pathetic."

A finger traced my jaw and I pulled away. It was pointless but I couldn't ignore the horrible touch.

A laugh echoed, then a thud somewhere close by.

The painful claws in my arms were gone, the bed rose up and hit me square in the back. I gasped for breath, the air gone from my lungs and the pain in my head hammered.

"Who the hell?" Another thud, then silence.

I lay still, tried to open my eyes but something blocked them. My face was slick with something. Blood trickled into my mouth. Blood. I was covered with blood. I was gagging on blood.

"Are you alright?" The words were near and quiet in the silent room.

I pressed my hands to my face and rolled away.

"How bad are you hurt?"

I finally got my eyes open. A shudder ran through me.

Another soldier stood close to the bench, he looked familiar.

"I'm sorry, we have to go now," he leaned towards me. Slow. His hands coming close.

I pulled away, blackness covered my eyes.

FIVE

*T*hudding in my head pulled me awake. Light poured into my eyes blinding me. Sitting up I threw my hands out to grab something, to find something to stop the spinning. My head was on fire.

"Are you alright?"

I cringed away from the voice and hit something soft. I opened my eyes, the back seat of a car.

It wasn't the car I was seeing, though it was the nicest one I'd ever seen, let alone been in.

It was the soldier sitting in the front seat waiting for an answer. A soldier. In a car, with me.

My heart beat so loud it was all I could hear.

"Lena?"

He knew my name. How did he know my name?

"You don't remember me, do you?"

I turned towards him again, but some hair drifted into my face. A clump of hair matted with blood. I swallowed looking at it, then pushed it away. "How do you know my name?"

"I was the…" he looked away.

The soldier who'd picked me up. I knew who he was now.

Everything inside my head was spinning. Why was he here? Why did he stop those soldiers? "Why?"

"Why what?"

"I don't understand," I sucked in a breath. Every bone in my rib cage ached when I moved.

He reached over the back of the bench. His hands came towards me.

I froze.

He fisted his hand and pulled it back. "I stopped those—" the pause was ominous. "Those animals, then you blacked out. I drove till I had to sleep. And here we are."

But where had he come from? How did he find me? I left the train days ago and he was here? I looked at him. "But. . ." but what? What did I want to know?

"I'll explain later," he said. "Are you hungry?"

I looked at my hands. They were coated with something.

"I have water."

I looked up, my stomach coiled instantly. He was still watching, waiting. Why did he want me to wash?

"If you'd rather eat first that's fine," he waited. "I'm not going to hurt you."

Was my fear that obvious?

He pulled something out of his pocket and held it over the seat.

I looked from it to him.

"This is a picture of me with my sister," he reached it the slightest bit closer.

My heart sped but I took it.

It was a picture of him with a girl about ten.

"I promise," his voice shook. "I promise I won't do anything with you I wouldn't do with my sister."

My throat tightened, my fingers felt numb on the picture.

"I don't have a plan and I'm not going to tell you what to do. But I want to try and help."

After a minute I felt his hand touching the photo. My heart lurched and my hands trembled but I kept them where they were.

His hands trembled now.

I let go of the photo and leaned back "What now?"

He moved a few things around. "Want to get cleaned up a little? It's been a long day."

I shook inside but nodded. "Yes."

He got out of the car and came around with his canteen. He opened the door beside me and a rush of cold air brushed my face. And he was so close. He held out a cloth.

After a few minutes my face felt a little cleaner and my hands looked a little cleaner. Where did all the blood come from?

"Hungry?" He handed food over the seat. "The more distance between us the better."

"Where are we going?" I asked when I could speak.

"You were walking back to Germany ever since you left the train. I've headed south."

"You were sent after me when I ran?" This didn't make sense. He should have caught me sooner.

"Do you have any friends in Switzerland or Spain?" He looked back. "Or in France? Preferable southern France."

"Have you been following me this whole time?" I asked.

He turned back to the front.

"What's going on? Who are you anyway?" It was a trap and I'd fallen for it. He wanted to bring me in himself. I hurled myself out the door and ran for the woods.

I couldn't see through my hair. I reached up to brush it away as I ran and gasped, the pain in my ribs killing the motion. A stitch in my side pulled.

With my other hand I moved my hair, then I stopped.

The soldier stood before me.

I leaned over and held my side, panting, trying to catch my breath.

"Lena."

I shuddered and closed my eyes.

"My name is Karl. I understand you're afraid. You have every right to be," he paused.

I leaned against a tree and looked up at him.

He just stood there. "I promise."

I swallowed.

"Let me help you," he held out his hand.

Could he be telling the truth? Could he be trying to help me? I stared at his hand. He wasn't forcing me, it was an offer. A choice.

I took a breath and started back towards the car. Hair in my eyes again, I brushed it out of the way in time to see a tree branch coming at my face. Not in time to stop from hitting it.

Karl caught me, his big hand catching me before I hit the ground.

I shuddered, the shock of hitting the branch nothing too feeling his hands.

"I'm sorry," he let go and backed up.

I drew in a breath and looked up at him. He looked mad. "You didn't do anything wrong."

He looked around. "We should get out of here."

Did someone catch up already? I walked carefully. Tripping again wouldn't be good, my head hurt in too many places already. "I didn't have a chance of getting away, did I?"

His silence was answer enough. Then he opened the door for me.

I stopped, the seat was smeared with blood. My blood. I felt for the gash on my head and pressed my lips together when I found it. My stomach twisted, but I got in.

Karl was in his seat in an instant and starting the engine. "We've got to hurry," he looked back at me. "And find somewhere for you to get cleaned up. We won't be able to avoid notice like this."

Avoid notice. The trees rushed past and it was hard to think past the haze and the pain. Why was he here?

"Hungry?"

I looked up. He was so close. I fought the panic and took a deep breath. I shook my head. The shooting jabs made me draw in a breath.

"You should try to eat."

I sat still, trying not to heave at the idea of food.

"Oh, no," he said a minute later.

I froze when I saw the muscles on the back of his neck tense.

"Lie down."

"What's going—"

"Lie on the floor," he said slowing down. "And cover up with the blanket."

I lay down but there wasn't a blanket.

"Hurry."

"There isn't a blanket," the blood on the seat. "What about the blood on the seat?" I whispered. How close were we? What should I do? I rolled over and faced the ground. My head pounding, my heart pounding louder.

But what about the seat?

My fingers brushed against something. The blanket. If I could get it on the seat?

The car stopped. I banged into the back, a metal bar dug into my shoulder.

Karl rolled the window down.

"Your papers?" The command from outside stilled the blood running through my body. Was this his plan? Did he plan to get rid of me like this?

"Your reason for traveling here?" A shuffling of papers. The

39

papers I did have would be more trouble than none at all. How was I to get anywhere without papers?

"I've been sent to find someone," that was Karl.

"Very good," the commanding voice said at last after more questions. The car started to move forward.

"Halt!" this command was unexpected. And so much worse for it.

"What's with that blood on the seat?"

Karl laughed. What was wrong with him? "We were on leave, sir, and one of the fellows had too much brave and too little to back it up." He lowered his voice. "Someone had to take him back. Now I have to find a way to repair the damage. At least I haven't broken half my ribs."

They were looking at the back seat.

I stopped breathing, clamping my eyes shut.

The minute dragged by. And another minute.

"You're headed towards, let me see. Straight south? Yes, you'll find it's a large enough town. You should be able to get help there."

"Thank you, sir," Karl said, working the gears but the engine didn't start.

My stomach couldn't take much more.

Then the car moved, but at such a miserable pace it was hard to know for sure we were moving. Then we went faster, taking curves without slowing and picking up speed with every minute.

The tension in the car faded but I felt sicker and sicker with each moment. "Can I get up?" I whispered. Then louder. "Karl?"

"Wait," came his soft reply.

I slumped and stayed still.

Finally, he slowed and called back. "You can get up now."

I sat up.

"It's better to get farther away."

I got on the seat and sighed. My head was spinning, and my

body ached from lying cramped for so long. "You didn't sound scared."

"Should I have been?" He asked. "They could easily be me you know."

"Because I'm in your car. That means something to most people you know," I paused for a breath and waited for him to look back. "And what you're going to do. That's another thing."

"That's another thing we need to talk about."

I waited for something, anything to figure out what was going on.

"What do we need to talk about?" My heart sped up. Could he hear it?

Could he hear how scared I was?

"It'll wait," he said and then we drove for hours in silence.

The shadows of evening were coming on now. All at once the car felt small and I was so small in it. Powerless, again. I was in his power. "What's going on?"

"I thought you were asleep. I promise I'll explain," he said slowing the car. "But first we need a story."

"A story?" A rock jolted the car, banging me against the back of the seat. Holding my head in both hands, trying to hold the pain inside I looked up. "I don't understand."

"We need an explanation for why we're traveling, together," he hesitated over the last word. "Because we need to stop and I think it should be alright to stop at an inn tonight. It's too soon for anyone to know."

"Know what?" Was he trying to confuse me? "What are you talking about?" I leaned forward and everything spun. Cold air brushed my face, but just my face. Why wasn't I cold anymore, after all these days of being cold? The ground swayed under me.

Tight arms were around me. Someone carried me.

The blood pounded in my veins; my head swam.

"Hang on," Karl whispered.

I focused on not screaming, my hands clenched unbidden.

"Thank you, sir," Karl said.

What had he told them?

"The missus will see to Sophie," a man said.

I flinched. Did I really prefer Karl to an unknown woman? My mouth went dry.

"She's awake," said the man, a strangers voice so close.

"Sleep's what she needs. Sophie," Karl said. "I found an inn. Just a minute and you'll be fine."

He spoke to me. A fake name. That's what he meant when he talked about thinking of a story.

The room buzzed with muffled talking barely out of understanding.

The clanking of dishes made the ache in my throat impossible to ignore.

"I'm thirsty," I whispered.

His arms tightened and he leaned his head close to mine. "One moment," he whispered, then put distance between our heads.

The hoarseness in my throat turned to pain. Did he read my thoughts? Heat filled my face and my lips were dry, but I wouldn't wet them.

We went up a flight of stairs. Karl carried me the whole way, as if he'd done this before. As if he did it every day.

"Just a minute now," the man said from somewhere ahead. "A nice room here."

Something deep in the pit of my stomach clenched and I pressed my lips together. I gagged, but still I had nothing in my belly to lose.

His heartbeat sped under the thin shirt between us.

I froze. Could he feel mine?

"Thank you. I'll be down shortly," Karl said at the door.

This room wasn't as bright. I unclenched my eyes and saw the door closing behind a grey haired man.

The silence was overpowering. Every breath Karl took seemed to echo from one white-washed wall to the other.

Mine was even louder. I closed my eyes again.

He lowered me to the bed.

I was on the bed but still in his arms. My head hurt, the room was closing in. He was close. So very close. Hardly touching me now but there was little air between us.

He pulled away. "I'm sorry."

I kept my eyes closed. If he couldn't see mine maybe he couldn't guess my thoughts. "You didn't have much choice."

"The landlady will come up, she can see to your head," Karl said backing towards the door. "Is that alright?"

I sat up. "What's the story."

He gripped the door handle. "I didn't give one. I asked for a room. Say anything you like."

"Wait."

"Make it up," he looked back and shrugged. "Aren't girls supposed to be good at that?" A muscle in his jaw pulled.

"Karl."

He faced the door again.

"What if you don't like what I say?"

"I won't care one way or the other," he said and left.

I stood and the room swayed. I sat back down.

"I'll call you when we're through," a woman came through the door with no warning. "You go downstairs with the menfolk."

Karl met my eyes through the doorway.

The woman was closing the door. What was he trying to say?

It was closed in his face and I was left, alone, with the woman.

SIX

a jolt woke me, I opened my eyes.

Karl was backing up. "We have to go."

It was still dark out. It was hours to morning.

"Why?"

"It's too dangerous to stay. Can you get up?"

I sat up, my head spun, the blankets slipped away.

His face tightened and he looked away.

A chill covered me. All I had on was the loose shift the woman had brought me. Heat filled my face and then, "I don't know where my clothes are. She said she'd dry them out but I—"

"I found these by the door a few hours ago," he dropped them beside me, still not meeting my eyes. "Is that everything?"

My dress and stays, the white of at least one slip. "I think so," I swung my legs over the side.

"I'll wait outside," he whispered and disappeared.

I dressed in a hurry then went to the door. "Karl."

The door opened, he looked around the room then grabbed his pack off the floor. "Let's go."

I stepped out and he closed the door.

"Hurry," he slung on his pack and ran for the stairs, somehow without making a noise.

I hurried down the hall after him, the blood in my ears so loud I couldn't hear the boards under my feet.

At any moment a door could open on either side and we'd be caught.

Then the door to the right did open and a soldier stepped out into the hall. Karl was past, the man stood between Karl and I.

The running had ended before it hardly began.

"Who are you?" The soldier's look was calculating, while he dragged out the words.

I waited for an idea, but my mouth was so dry I couldn't make a sound.

"What are you doing here so early?" He came towards me.

Karl was behind him, his eyes calm. He hadn't left me.

I took a breath. "I work here. I have to start breakfast."

"You're not the—"

Karl slammed his hand on the soldier's neck and caught him when he collapsed. Then he dragged him into the room, closed and locked the door and took the key.

I stood, frozen in place.

"He's not dead," Karl said. "But we're running out of time." He grabbed my arm and pulled me down the stairs, through the kitchen and out the back door. We were moving so fast.

I held my breath, *don't get sick.*

He stopped at the car, wrenching the door open. "Lie down."

My legs were stiff but I got in.

"I wanted to leave the car behind," he wrenched the gear stick around with a savage shove. "But we missed the train."

"Why?"

"Every time we have to buy petrol someone sees us. It's not safe."

"No," I sat up. "Why are you helping me?"

"Does it matter?" He hit the gas pedal.

The mist of the morning surrounded the car, making the road ahead almost invisible.

Run away. A voice rang in my head. *Run away.* I wanted to shout at the voice. How could I run when we were speeding down the road?

An hour went by in silence. Then another. He'd saved me again. No one would go to this much trouble to trick someone. Would they?

He pulled off the road, shutting off the car. Then he turned in the seat and faced me. His eyes made me gulp, though he had plenty to be mad about. "We need to get food in the town coming up," he sounded focused, not especially mad. "We need a story. Can we pretend to be together?"

"I don't know."

"We look too different to pass as siblings."

"I'm not good at pretending," I looked away. "And no one would believe we're together."

His hands on the back of the seat in front of me made my stomach clench, a perfect reminder of the other reason it wouldn't work. If he put his hands on me again, I might not be able to keep from screaming. Last night was lucky. And this morning I'd been more scared of the other soldier.

"Why wouldn't they?" He pulled me from my thoughts. "Do I look too old for you?"

My toes curled and my neck broke out in a sweat despite the chilly day. "No one would believe it."

"Why not?" He spread his hand in question.

My stomach knotted.

"You're not giving me a reason."

"I'm too plain."

"That's the last thing we have to worry about," he turned around and started the engine. "I can't believe that's what you were worried about."

46

I gulped. My hands were clammy and the sign for a town in two kilometers didn't help. "I've never done this before."

We passed the first house of the town, close enough to see a rag stuffed in the small corner of window that had a crack. "I mean I've never had someone before."

His knuckles whitened on the steering wheel. "That makes us even," his tone so different from a few minutes before.

"What?" My hand clapped over my mouth.

"We'll pretend together. We need food and I can't think of any other reason we'd be out together," he stopped in front of a little bakery. He opened the door and held out his hand.

I pressed my lips together.

He leaned closer. "It's more noticeable if I don't." He pulled me out and put his hand on my side, closing the door with the other.

My face burned while the panic started to bubble. I bit my lip.

"This won't take long," his arm around me helped me stay on my feet and play the part. Karl asked for bread and rolls in French but it was stilted and stiff. His accent so rough.

The baker looked at me. "What's going on here?" He said in French. "Do you need help?"

Karl looked at me. The smile on his face didn't reach his eyes. "Can you smile or say something?" He whispered.

"No, I don't need help," I said a little breathless. "I'm fine."

Karl stiffened at my side.

"Very well," the man said, wrapping the loaves in paper. He leaned closer when he brought the loaves around. "Are you sure?"

"Yes. Thank you," I said, trying to keep my voice steady.

The flour coated his arms up to his elbows, like Uncle's when he scooped flour to mix the next day's bake.

I swallowed and focused on the bread, on not tripping, on

the door we were about to go through. Not on his hand almost touching my side. I pressed my lips together.

We got outside and Karl opened the front door, stepping back.

I looked up.

His face was impossible to read. "Later," he said, but his eyes weren't on me.

I got in, beside him this time, instead of the seat behind.

He got in and we were down the road a second later. "We'll have to make do with bread."

"Bread is fine."

He ground his teeth and shoved his foot into the pedal again. "Does he suspect?"

"I don't know."

Silence followed till my stomach growled so loud I couldn't be sure it was mine.

"You should have said something," he pushed the loaf towards me. "Eat."

I tore off a hunk and held it out. "You're hungry too."

He took it.

I tore into the loaf again. The crackle of the fresh loaf made me hesitate but I couldn't afford to think about home.

"Your French was, unexpected. Do you have friends here? Anyone you trust?"

"No." And I didn't. I didn't have friends anywhere.

"I hoped, when I heard you—"

"I don't. I'm sorry." What was his plan? Now that he'd wrested me from whatever lay at the end of that train, what did he plan to do with me?

"What did you do, before you were picked up?" He asked after a few minutes of quiet.

I looked up. "Nothing. I swear."

"That's not what I meant," he held up his hands. "Did your parents have a store you helped in?"

"I worked in a bakery," I looked out the window. "I've also cared for children. But I'm happy to do anything. Any kind of work."

"Don't say that."

I spun on the seat. "What?"

"Don't say you'll do any kind of work."

Blood filled my face. "I wasn't thinking."

"I know," He stared straight ahead.

I focused on the bread. "Thank you," I said once I could speak at all.

"The car is too easy to track," Karl said.

I didn't answer. I couldn't.

Karl shut off the car and got out. He walked away, pacing for a minute then leaned against the car. Any second he'd wrench the door open, furious, finished with me. His hands were inches away, on the other side of the glass. They were massive, powerful. He knocked out the soldier at the inn in a split second.

I stared at my own hands, then pulled my feet on the seat and dropped my head to my knees. A flood of cool air flowed around me a moment later, the door was open. I held my breath.

"We have to get away from here," he spoke quiet and close. Too close.

I shivered away from the cold before I could stop.

"I know it won't be easy, but it will get us far away and fast."

I dug my nails into my dress, clenching my fists along with my eyes. "I can't get on another train," I whispered. "I can't."

"Why? Do you think I'm going to take you back?"

The seat beside me dipped away, he was sitting now.

"No."

"We have to get as far away as possible."

I couldn't breathe.

"Can we talk about this?" He asked.

Why wasn't he yelling at me to look at him this instant? I sucked in extra air and looked up.

He didn't look mad. "Why can't we go on the train?" He dropped his hand to the seat, still several feet between us.

"I," I swallowed down a lump. "I'm scared of trains."

He straightened. "Is it trains or the people on them?"

I looked away. "The people."

"I promised, like a brother. I'll keep that promise and I'll keep you safe."

Who could promise such a thing? It wasn't possible.

I closed my eyes and pushed down the panic rising in my chest. There was nothing else he could do. He was trying to help, for whatever reason, and we had to get away.

"Lena."

I opened my eyes.

He was staring at me. "Is there anything I do that scares you?"

I clenched my hands to keep from shaking.

"I'll keep you safe."

I flinched when he reached out, then turned and slid my feet to the floor of the car. "When is the train due?"

"Soon," he got out and came around to my side.

I got out and pulled my bag after me.

He looked under the seats, sliding his hand along the edges. "We can't leave anything behind."

Anything that would help whoever was following us. I shivered and pulled my coat closer. When was he going to tell me why he was doing this?

He closed the last door and straightened, then he looked back at me.

"Ready?"

"Yes." Another lie. I wasn't ready to do anything but hide. I stayed beside him as we neared the town, though I couldn't copy his confidence.

He was so sure and calm.

"What's our story?" I asked when the quiet was too much.

He looked sideways at me. "I haven't much imagination."

I counted fence posts and forced myself to take a breath.

"We've already agreed we don't look like siblings," his thoughts were obvious, but there wasn't anything else to be done. "So we're together then."

"Married?" He asked.

My face was so hot, again. "Whatever you think."

"We don't have to say," he slowed his walk when we got to the main street. "If something must be said I'll take care of it."

My shoe caught on a rock, throwing me sideways. Karl's hand was tight on my arm.

"Careful."

The jolt singed every inch of my skin, but I forced my feet to keep moving. "I'm sorry."

"I'm sorry we can't stop. But we need to get food and the train will be in soon."

My stomach clenched at the mention of eating.

People noticed us, but didn't stop us. Karl wasn't the sort people stopped. He wasn't the sort a person would question.

The question was, why was he with me?

A whistle sounded in the distance.

"We need to hurry," Karl looked up and down the street than hurried.

I followed. Staying out of sight was impossible. Staying out of the way, that I could try to do.

We pushed into a small café.

A man got up from a table in the corner, he came towards us. His face red and his fists clenched, his feelings were clear.

Karl pulled me half behind him and faced the man. "Something on your mind?"

The man stopped. "I didn't know you were..."

Karl stepped towards him. "We're here to buy food. Is there a problem with that?"

I held my breath and tried to ignore the people watching, the size of the man's fists, the grip of Karl's hand on my arm.

"No," he went back to his seat, keeping his head down.

Karl strode to the front, his hand never loosening a bit.

I kept my head down and watched where I stepped. He didn't need me tripping right now.

"Let's go."

I looked up.

A paper sack was disappearing into his pack.

He led me outside and we kept walking. "I'm sorry about that."

"You defended me," only a hundred meters from the platform now. "You shouldn't apologize."

"Are you alright?"

The train bellowed smoke.

Karl moved into the smoke, towards the train.

Even as my courage sank, I couldn't help thinking about what everyone else was thinking. Karl was the very image of the fatherland's best. And he had his arm around me. It made me smile.

Then we went up the stairs of the last train car.

SEVEN

*K*arl didn't let go the whole time.

My pulse was pounding, from his touch or the train or people staring I couldn't say, but the need to scream and run grew with every second that passed. With every shiver of the train beneath my feet.

"Here," he stopped at the second to last row in the car and let go.

I sat down, careful to stare at my boots, then at the side boards. I counted the beads of rain on the edge of the window. It was raining? I hadn't even noticed.

"We're lucky. It's…" Karl's confidence was lost along with his words.

I looked around.

Only a few people getting on. But Karl had seen something, they must be dangerous.

"Tell me what to do," I whispered.

His hand on the seat tightened around mine.

It looked normal if anyone was watching but I felt the tension. I felt his fear.

He leaned towards me. What was he going to say? "Breathe. They'll notice if you pass out."

I took a deep breath and looked back outside.

The car wasn't half filled but the doors closed and the train lurched forward.

My hand itched under his, I fought the urge to pull away.

He let go, stretching out and shifting on the seat. Then he leaned closer, his head close to mine. "Are you alright?" He whispered.

"Yes," I let out a breath. "Are you?"

He sighed and coughed. "Yes."

I looked into his face, so dreadfully close. Did he enjoy danger?

"We're alright for now," he said then straightened and pulled his pack towards him. Opening it and pulling out something wrapped in paper. "Hungry?"

I reached for it and brushed the side of his hand. A jolt hit me, the pastry hit the ground. "I'm sorry."

He picked it up. "My mistake," his tone made me swallow.

I straightened and looked him in the eye. I bit my tongue and reached for it again.

The paper wrapped package was in my hand and I looked down. "I'm sorry."

"Let's eat and get some sleep," it wasn't for me he was talking.

I took a bite. I wasn't good at pretending. The pastry was good and I found I was starving once I got started. I wrapped up the half I couldn't finish and held it out to Karl.

"What?" He asked.

"I'm full."

"You have to eat," he didn't take it from my hand.

"I did," I said, starting to pull up my feet onto the seat, then I felt the mud and stopped. My shoes were soaked. Only saying his name in my head, my face got hot. He must know how he made girls feel.

He was leaning back against the bench.

I edged against the window but a bump pulled me closer too fast, my head banged hard and I gasped.

"Your head?" Karl whispered, his breath so warm against my neck I shivered.

"Yes, but I'm alright," I whispered back.

"You can lean against my arm if you want," he said. "It's softer than the window."

Was he joking? I sank lower in the seat and took a breath. "I'm alright."

He cleared his throat and I looked over. He was looking forward and when I saw the door open, I held my breath.

"Breathe," Karl said. "And let me do the talking."

I breathed and gripped a wad of my dress as the conductor came down the aisle with a walk so slow it was nothing short of torturous, I fixed my eyes on the trees passing outside.

The rain hit the window but the drops were slow.

"Tickets."

I looked up. My heart hurt, it wouldn't move. I was frozen, waiting for the next thing which must of course be bad.

Karl's big hand squeezed mine.

I looked up to his face.

"Breathe," he mouthed.

I looked away, inhaling and seeing nothing out the window but the reflection of the man in the aisle.

"Tickets," he said again. "And identification."

"Of course," Karl said rummaging through his bag. "They're newly issued."

I pulled out my bag and started looking. But Karl had the tickets and I didn't have any papers to go with it. What did Karl want me to do?

"We did leave in a rush," he pulled the tickets out and handed them over. "Did you find yours?" Karl turned to me.

"I'm looking," I said still poking around in the bag.

"What's the problem?" The conductor asked.

"I can't find my new papers," I said, finally looking up from my bag. "What will your father say? He went to such trouble."

"You don't have your papers?" The conductor asked. "Your tickets are in order." He looked from Karl's papers to me.

"We're just married sir," Karl put his arm around my shoulders. "And I have the week to get her to my aunt and uncle before I head back to the front."

"I see," he said. "And your name is?"

I couldn't answer. I felt my eyes tear up. Why was I crying now? I was scared to death.

"Sophie, talk to the man," Karl said his hand on mine. "There's no need to cry." His arm was tense around my shoulder. "Sophie."

I broke into tears. "Your father is going to be so upset," I couldn't answer, I didn't even know his last name. "I'm sorry."

"Your name."

Karl stood up. "It's Sophie Von Liedersdorf," he whispered. "I apologize. I can get a wire from my father at the next station. My father is Count Von Liedersdorf, advisor to field Marshall Von Milch."

He looked at me and Karl then nodded. "Very well. I'll see you at the station."

"Thank you, sir," Karl said, then sat down and put his arm around me.

The conductor left the car a minute later.

"It's ok, Sophie," Karl whispered, rubbing my arm. The name made it clear he was talking to the man watching us. "We'll get it straightened out. Try and sleep now." Then he pulled me closer. His heart was pounding so close I couldn't breathe. His face only a hand from mine.

Then his hands were on my back, both his big hands all but covering it. "It's okay," he said so close to my ear. "Lena, it's alright now."

My skin prickled, I choked and gasped for air. The whole time I fought everything in me not to resist him. My body rigid against him, I couldn't do anything but bite my cheeks to keep from screaming.

"Shh," Karl said, pushing me off him as he sat up.

I opened my eyes and straightened my back, it hurt after all the tension.

"Let's try to get some rest," he said, again for the others.

Was he mad I'd reacted so badly when he'd been so careful?

I risked a look at his face then leaned closer and put my mouth as close to his ear as I could. "I did try."

He turned his head and smiled at me. "You'll feel better after you get some sleep."

I stared up at his face, what was he thinking? I wanted to know. I needed to know. But my eyes were so heavy. "You're right," I said, though something was nagging. There was something that wasn't right.

The noise and motion of the train was dragging me under, but I couldn't seem to fall asleep. I wanted to, I tried to. Karl kept his hands away from me and I curled in the corner on my bag, but no matter how painful my eyes and worn my body, my mind wouldn't shut off.

The rocking of the train kept hitting the same spot on my head. I took a breath and another. Then the quietness hammered into my thoughts. Why was it so quiet? Was everyone asleep? Was I alone?

"Sophie?"

It was Karl, careful and using my fake name.

I opened my eyes.

Karl was close, he looked worried. What was going on?

"Are you ok?"

My back was sore, my arms felt odd. "What's wrong?" I tried to sit up and my headache spiked. I dropped back down, my hands gripping my head.

"Are you awake?"

I thought through answers, my head was killing me, three different points bent on being crowned strongest. "I'm awake."

His forehead was dripping with sweat, his coat was gone and his shirt was a mess. "Are you hurt?" His hand was hovering nearby, hovering but never quite touching me. His eyes on mine, he came closer, but so slowly I wasn't sure that he really was.

"You fainted," he whispered. "Are you okay now?"

"Yes. Are you?"

"You scared me," he looked sick. "I couldn't do anything to help you."

I put my free hand on the seat and sat up. A jolt of pain from my neck was enough to make me nauseous but he was so worried. "I'm sorry." I reached towards him, then stopped just before his face.

He stared at me. "Don't worry about it."

I closed my eyes to block out the look in his.

"Sorry," he whispered, sitting down beside me.

"Feeling better?" A smooth voice asked, an edge of something more to it.

I looked up and my spine tingled. My heart pounded in an instant. "Yes." It sounded loud to my own ears.

"Your husband was quite distraught," the man said, a sneer in every syllable.

"Do you have business with us?" Karl asked, putting his arm around my shoulders.

"Something bothering you?" He asked, his black coat flipping back as he shifted, something shiny at his side. "Or perhaps that's more your dear little wife."

"As you saw, she's not well and I'd like her to rest. If you have no business with us, be good enough to let her." Karl was tense. So tense.

"Of course. Forgive my intrusion." What did he know about us? What did I say? He turned and went back to his seat.

He made me want to puke.

Karl was stiffer than a board with his arm around me. He waited till the man sat down then shifted towards me. "We're getting off at the next stop. Be ready."

I squeezed my hand in his. I wasn't good at whispering.

Sitting with Karl's arm around me and the rain coming down in the dusk, I leaned back and tried to make sense of it. My head was hurting, but against Karl's side it didn't hurt as much. I felt safe somehow. It didn't make sense. How could I be safe here? I took a deep breath.

Karl relaxed around me.

"Sorry," I straightened.

The man in black turned around and looked straight at me. At us.

I froze.

Karl froze.

His arm was pinning me to his side and I couldn't move. I wanted to, but I couldn't. He was keeping me safe, so I relaxed back into him and closed my eyes.

A moment later he moved his arm away. "I didn't mean to do that."

"It's alright," I said. His instincts were to keep me safe. Then the train started to slow. I was almost sad.

"Don't freak out," he said turning his face towards me, his mouth so close.

My heart started to beat out a heavy rhythm again.

"Breathe and listen," he leaned towards my ear. "We're going to slip out the back." His arm came around in front of me. He was playing with the others in the car. It looked like something else entirely was going on.

It almost felt like it too. I closed my eyes and leaned into him though my throat closed, my heart fluttered in panic. I leaned even closer and whispered in his ear. "Why are you scared of that man? Is he-?"

His finger was on my lips. "Yes, Sophie," he said a little louder this time, though it was still a whisper. Then he leaned so close his lips brushed my ear. "He is."

I shivered.

The train was crawling to a stop now.

His hand on mine tightened.

I reached behind me for my bag. It wasn't there. "My bag," I whispered.

His hand, behind me already, reached further then threw the strap over my shoulder. "Don't forget to breathe," he said before standing and pulling me after him, his pack on his shoulder.

We were down the stairs before I could blink. Karl's hand on my arm kept me from falling on my face.

His arm circled my waist and we hurried through the empty station, into the darkness.

EIGHT

*S*houting came loud behind us.

My back hurt, but compared to my head it was nothing. How many different places had I hurt? In the train I must have hit something.

When the trees were close on every side Karl slowed. "Are you alright?" It seemed like that was the only thing he asked me.

"Yes. Where are we?" I asked.

"The middle of the woods," he said. "Are you up to walking awhile?"

"Of course. Are they following?"

"I don't think so," Karl said. "I waited till he was talking with someone. The conductor didn't have a chance to get back to the car so he couldn't have known."

Lucky for me the moon was out or I'd be in trouble. As it was I tripped every other minute.

"How are you feeling?" Karl asked again.

I stopped, turning to him. "You don't have to worry so much."

He looked at me, his eyes impossible to read, then kept walking. The words under his breath too low to hear.

I kept walking, I didn't want to know.

"You scared me. Like never before."

I kept going a few steps beyond him.

"You hit the ground so fast. I couldn't catch you. It was so fast," he stopped talking, his words strangled by something I couldn't see. By something only he could see.

"It isn't your fault."

"What happened?"

"Lots of people faint."

"Not like that. You blacked out from hitting your head," he stepped around me, blocking the path. "Have I done something wrong?"

I closed my eyes. "No."

"You were all but asleep. It was instinctive. Why do you fear me so much?"

"Do I have to answer?

"No. But tell me what I can do so it doesn't happen again. Tell me what I did wrong."

The echo of the wind in the trees was all that broke the silence.

"Men frighten me," I stared at his boots. "Even in my sleep."

He took a step towards me.

I sucked in a breath and clenched my teeth. I'd been so careful, but all at once it was painful and obvious and impossible to hide.

"I'm sorry I scared you. And I'm not trying to," he backed up. "Do you believe me?"

I couldn't even nod.

He took a deep breath and continued forward.

The quiet of the woods settled around us as we walked. Minutes ticked by with the moon shining down. Then the reality of what we were doing sank in.

"We're sleeping in the woods?" It was hard to believe. And

yet the world was tipped upside down and nothing was believable. I was sleeping in the woods with a soldier.

"I'm sorry about in the train. When I was whispering," his voice from ahead sagged a little. "I needed to warn you. I couldn't think of any other way."

"I understood, you had to do that." I gulped, the feel of his breath on my neck, his hand on my back almost the same as if it was only a second ago.

"No, I should've found another way," he almost yelled. His fists were balled up, the veins stood out on his neck.

"You got me away safe," I said stepping towards the fists so close to my face. "You kept that promise. You got me out safe."

He turned and kept plowing ahead.

My legs ached and my head throbbed at three different places. I wanted to ask if we could stop. It was on the tip of my tongue, but I bit it again. My tongue was raw from biting.

"We'll stop there," he said and stopped.

I sank to the ground.

"You should have told me you were this tired," he was next to me in a second. "Can you come a few steps more? I found a rocky ledge that'll keep us warmer."

A rock would keep us warmer? It didn't matter. I couldn't make my legs move now, it wasn't going to happen.

"Can I carry you? It's dryer over there." He waited for an answer.

Dryer sounded better, I tried to sit up. But I couldn't. I couldn't move. "Yes." I clenched my jaws together.

He slipped his arm around my back, his other under my legs. He lifted me and walked a few paces further then he set me down against a rocky wall. "Don't fall asleep." He pulled off his pack and pulled a blanket out.

"You're giving me your blanket?" He was doing so much already, he couldn't give me his blanket too.

"It's only a blanket, I have more than one," he wrapped it around me and backed up.

I sat there. Too tired to say anything more.

Something bright pricked at my eyes. Was it morning already? I was too tired. I couldn't face walking again. It was too much.

The brightness grew far too fast and it was warm.

I opened my eyes to a fire, but Karl was nowhere to be seen. I was alone in the woods with a fire to beckon anyone close enough.

The minutes passed and still he didn't appear.

I sat up and a blanket rolled away. Wait, there was a blanket under me and on top? "Hungry?"

I started and jerked away from the voice.

"Watch out."

Arms closed around my arms and a scream escaped and carried into the woods. Then I was flat on my back. A rock dug into my hip, a hand was over my mouth. I couldn't stop from slamming my fists into his chest. I couldn't get a breath, but I had to get free.

"Don't scream," he released my arms, loosened his hand on my mouth.

I sucked in a breath. I was free, not held down now. I took another breath and opened my eyes.

Karl crouched so close above me. "I'm sorry," he pulled his hand away and backed up.

I stared at the fire and waited for my heart to slow down. Waited for the air in my throat not to hurt so much. I looked at him.

His eyes were on me. "I'm sorry I scared you. And I'm sorry I slammed you on the ground."

I sat up. "You kept me from getting burned."

He crouched on the far side of the fire, but he was anything but relaxed.

"You were right. It is warmer with a rock behind."

His eyes were on me, boring in, trying to make something out, as if to read words plastered on my forehead.

I looked away. "I can't remember what you asked," I pulled my knees up and pulled the blanket around my legs.

"Are you hungry?" He asked, his voice low. Tense. Why was he always tense with me?

My stomach gnawed at my chest. "I am." It was painful seeing how he was now, so cautious. "It's not you, really." Though it was. A man, a soldier. It was shocking I hadn't taken to beating at him sooner.

He pointed behind me. "The food's in my pack."

I nodded. "I won't scream now."

He reached for it then sat a few steps away, dug in his pack and held something out.

I took it, not meeting his eyes. I didn't want to meet his eyes. "Aren't you hungry?"

"I ate."

The trees were blowing but there wasn't rain. We were lucky.

I scooted towards the fire. My hands were cold but not bad. I ate, holding one hand then the other to the fire.

Karl was staring at my hands.

Or was he? Why had he brought me out here anyway? What made him do this? I looked up and the look in his eyes made me shiver.

"What?" Then I bit my lip. I sounded upset. "If you want to ask something, ask."

"Why do I scare you so badly?"

I looked away.

"You're scared to death of me. Did I talk in my sleep?"

"No," I took another bite. If my mouth was full he couldn't expect an answer. But I couldn't swallow it. I chewed but the lump of bread only grew bigger. I stared at the fire, the flames drew me in. I forced the bite down, the lump hurt my throat.

"Done?" His voice was so close.

I jumped inside. "Sorry. I'm too tired to eat more," I held the bread out to him, letting my eyes trail down my arm and follow his to his face.

"You didn't do anything," a shiver ran through me.

He took hold of the bread and pulled my hand closer to him. "But?"

"You're still a stranger," I whispered meeting his eyes. "Strangers scare me."

He looked away.

"I'm safe with you, you've proved that," I had to make him believe me. "But it's instinctive."

His hand dropped from the food, cutting our link.

"I'll try not to scream next time."

He winced, then looked at me again, a contorted look on his face. "I'll try not to slam you on the ground and half smother you."

I set the bread down and held out my hand. It shook but I kept it there.

He slowly reached out with his, hovering so close. His eyes met mine, his hand found mine.

I caught my breath. It was no longer cold in the middle of the blowing wind.

His hand tightened around mine.

"You kept us from getting caught," I pulled my hand away and hugged my knees again. "Thank you."

"We should get some sleep."

"Yes," I agreed though I wasn't likely to sleep a bit.

He went to the other side of the fire and lay down and soon he was breathing heavy.

I pulled the blanket close though I didn't need to. Despite the wind I was warm. I curled in a ball and squeezed my eyes shut but my mind wouldn't stop. The memory of Karl's hand over my mouth and his eyes boring into mine. Then when he carried me, careful, he was so careful.

Like he didn't want to touch me.

Was there a girl back home he was comparing me to every time he looked at me? A girl with blond hair, not the indescribable shade between blond and brown that mine was? A girl that was beautiful and didn't attack him when he kept her from falling in the fire?

Back home.

Tobias's little face was before me. His smile when he was being sneaky, or when he woke me in the dark of morning, hungry for his breakfast.

The warmth inside the blankets was perfect. Then images of Karl and Tobias swirled together and the memory of Karl with his arms around me dissolved.

The wind was loud now, drowning out his breathing. Once again, I was alone.

It was morning. I could tell before I opened my eyes.

Karl sat on the other side of where the fire had been. "We need to put distance between us and that station."

I sat up and my back, my legs and everything hurt, my head worst of all. I spread my hands on the ground and closed my eyes, waiting for the world to stop spinning. "I sat up too fast is all," I said before he could ask and opened my eyes.

He came around the charred bits of wood and crouched close.

I swallowed and stood. I couldn't see, my head swam and I almost fell. I grabbed the tree and took a breath. Then I looked up at Karl. "I'm ready."

Karl slung on his pack then held out a canteen. "Thirsty?"

I stepped towards it and took it, my hands trembling so much it had to seem like I was pretending. I had to laugh.

"What's funny?"

But water was flowing down my throat, I didn't know how thirsty I was. I couldn't stop till I choked.

Karl backed up, something flickered across his forehead.

I wiped my chin. "Did I drink too much?"

"No," but he said it too fast.

"What did I do wrong?"

"Why assume you did something wrong? It's possible I did something wrong and just realized. You aren't always to blame," he closed the steps between us and reached for the canteen. "Do you want more?"

"No."

He strapped it to his pack, then started into the woods.

I followed his path when I could to keep out of thorns and vines that tried to pull me down. It was easier than last night, except now I was sore. I waited for the day to get sunny but it never did. We were alone in the woods and Karl wasn't talking.

What happened on the train?

Was it gestapo who questioned us?

Karl slowed his pace, walking beside me. "Do you like hiking?"

"I haven't hiked much."

"Not even in school?"

"No," it felt incomplete, almost untruthful. "I didn't finish school." My heart picked up, why did I tell him?

But he didn't press for more.

"Don't you want to know why?"

"You don't owe me anything," his pace slowed.

Water seeped into my boots, the puddle shallow so I hadn't noticed. A splash made me look at him. "Are you alright?" He was of course, but I couldn't help asking.

"Yes," he smiled. "I suppose it does get tiring to hear that so often."

"It's no trouble," I said.

Then his hand moved to his belt.

I looked away, hoping he hadn't noticed. "School was fine when I was young. I didn't love it, I didn't hate it," I shuffled a second, trying to lose the mud sticking to my shoe, it was heavy - weighing me down.

"Not the teacher's pet?" He asked, stepping away from a log and closer to me.

"No."

"Boy troubles?" He asked, teasing perhaps but it was hard to be sure.

"No. It was the other students, and the teacher. I'm jewish, and they treated me as such," I shrugged. "When I was thirteen I couldn't take it anymore."

"Your parents let you stop?"

I breathed deep in the foggy woods. It was cold but peaceful. Until now, when I had to think about why I quit school and why my parents let me stop. "It's complicated." There was no way he could understand. I didn't understand and I'd lived it. "Did you like school?"

He laughed. "More or less," he sighed. "It's complicated." He looked down at me.

I looked away. "Some things aren't easy to explain."

The afternoon got colder and darker.

"We need to get food," he said into the quiet.

I swallowed down a lump, shifted my bag and nodded. Hopefully he wouldn't notice my hands tightening on the strap of my bag.

"But we shouldn't go in together."

I was so surprised I looked up. "You want me to go in alone?" I felt safe with him. He scared me, but so did the trees and the dark and the wind and anyone who might hide in them. Going in alone would be scarier than going with him.

"No," he said before I could take my nightmare any further. "I think you should wait, and I'll go."

"Why?"

"If someone's after us, a single person won't fit the description. And I said if," he added. "I don't know that there is."

Wait outside. I could do that. "That's a good idea," now I wanted to sink to the ground. Of course he knew I was scared of the town. "But I can go if you think it's better."

He shook his head. "No. I'll go. You can probably handle sitting and I'd go berserk having to wait." He knew I was exhausted.

"I could stand a break," I looked up. "I don't think there'd be any trouble with me going berserk from a rest."

His pack was sliding down a bit.

"That thing looks really heavy. Are you sure you don't want me to go?" Then I wanted to slap myself, now he knew I was looking at him.

He laughed and stopped. "What's wrong?"

I stopped but didn't turn around. "Nothing. Why did you stop?"

"Because it's less than two kilometers to the next town. We passed the sign a few minutes ago."

"Sorry."

"You don't . . ." he paused, his lips pressed into a hard line. "Come this way, let's get off the road." He started straight into the woods, leaving the road, rough and little used though it was, it was a road.

I bit my lip and followed. I was used to following but this was scary again. Not that everything wasn't scary, but the shadows were starting to fall. The light, I couldn't say sun, was dimming, and waiting alone in the woods wasn't all that much better than facing people. "You're sure this is a good idea?" I asked before I could stop myself. "I mean, are you sure you can find me again?" How could I say that?

"We need food and we shouldn't keep being seen together. I'll find you," Karl paused then added. "Don't worry." After a minute of tramping away into the dense undergrowth he stopped.

"It's only a short way off the road. I'll find you."

"Alright."

He pulled a blanket out of his pack and held it out.

I stepped closer to take it, then glanced at his face and tripped. I caught myself before I fell but he'd reached out, catching my arm.

His hand tense.

Like always.

"I've got to hurry," he said and let go, setting the blanket on the pack. I listened to him go, but didn't watch. I didn't want to see. Then hurried footsteps came back.

"Don't follow me," he said a commanding tone he'd never used before.

"What?"

"Don't come after me. If it gets dark and I haven't gotten back, look through my pack."

I opened my mouth.

He held up his hand. "Go through my pack and use anything you can. There's a little food left."

"Is something wrong?"

"No," he shook his head backing away again. "But if I'm not back by tomorrow, you'll have to decide what to do on your own." Then he faded into the trees.

What if he didn't come back? Was he trying to be rid of me, tired of everything I'd put him through? The blanket in my hands brought me back. He'd left his pack and gotten out a blanket for me. He'd be back.

I pulled the blanket tight to me and sank to the ground,

leaning on the still warm pack. Warm from Karl. I stared at the tree in front of me. For all I knew he already had a girl. A wife. But that wasn't something I could think about. "He's a friend," I said aloud and let my eyes close. "He's just a friend."

NINE

I woke with a jolt. What woke me? Then I heard creaking wheels. Old wheels. It was almost dark, was Karl watching me sleep again? I sat up and looked everywhere.

He was nowhere to be seen. The noise of the wheels passed, not too far away.

What could have kept Karl? What if he'd been caught?

If I could see the wagon I'd at least know where the road was. The creaking got fainter. I struggled out of the blanket and hurried towards the noise, through the ferns and vines, fallen branches and massive trees, everything got in the way.

But I hit the edge of the road in time to see the back of a wagon, disappearing down the road.

I found the road, what now? It was dark so I sat behind a tree and waited for Karl.

The road stayed empty and the trees started blending into the darkness more and more. The forest on the opposite side of the road was a wall of blackness, the thought of entering made me shiver.

No doubt I sat in the same darkness, but I wasn't going to

think about that. I could have waited in the blanket, with the pack. Why did I have to come to the road?

The roaring of a car's engine made me start, but I leaned forward. There weren't many cars around here. Not this far from a town of importance.

It got louder and louder the closer it came, till I was holding my breath, staring down the road and waiting for it to appear out of the gloom. Then it appeared and rushed towards me, the closer it got the bigger it was.

Now I wanted to be farther away from those headlights, from whoever was inside that car. Speeding as fast as the rutted lane would allow, it blasted past.

It was gone and I sighed, taking in a deep breath. It was past, on its way to the town.

Karl.

What if it was someone looking for us, and they caught him? I had to warn him. I stood and rushed to the road, but it was empty and the car long gone, what did I expect to do? Run after it?

I could sneak in, see if I could warn him. I had to do something.

The clods of mud sticking to my shoes held me back, and he'd said to stay. Though he'd said to stay before he'd known someone would come. I ran up the road till I saw lights.

If I went around, if I could see where the main road was and stay off it, I could stay out of sight.

The dinner hour had cleared the street, thank goodness.

I hurried on.

The small fences around little yards were a blatant reminder that not everyone's lives were torn up and wrung out by this dreadful thing called war.

My legs ached and though it wasn't a big town, it was bigger than I thought. I crouched by a house, listening.

Supper time now, people were busy with eating. A child cried out and a stern reproach followed.

I crept around the side and peeked in, the mother was holding the little girl. She fussed, her curls bouncing.

I wanted to hold her, I wanted to hug her to me and whisper something to make her smile again. Forcing my fingers off the ledge I took a breath and looked around.

The car was nowhere in sight. It could be kilometers away now and Karl would be furious that I didn't stay where he left me.

"What business do you have here?"

The question brought me spinning around. The air in my lungs fled and I was left paralyzed. Unable to answer had my life depended on it.

Which more than likely it did.

"Why are you here?" The man stepped out of the shadows of the alley, his rough clothes out of place with his polished tone.

"I was looking for someone."

"In that window?"

"No," *think. Think.*

"Come with me," he reached for my arm.

I swallowed and backed away. "I'm going now. I won't trouble you again."

But his hand was still reaching for me. When his fingers closed around my arm, my mind went blank.

———

Jail, that's where I was. The bench I lay on was nothing but a board. I'd ignored Karl and screwed everything up.

"She freaked. I swear I didn't do a thing to her."

"Did you touch her?" This voice was low.

I held my breath so I could hear it better.

"No," the man said fast.

"Did you touch her arm at all, to bring her in for questioning?"

"Yes, I took hold of her arm, but I didn't hurt her. Why on earth are you focused on that?"

At least I wasn't the only one confused.

"I swear. I took her arm, nothing more. And she freaked, screamed her head off and fainted dead away."

Something scraped the floor.

"Sophie?"

Very near me, I could feel the heat from someone very close.

"Sophie?"

I dragged in a breath and opened my eyes.

Karl stood close, pistol in hand.

I looked around.

Another man sat in a chair across the room. He was staring at me

I shivered then looked back at Karl. "I'm alright."

Karl looked relieved. "Are you sure?"

"Yes."

The other fellow let out a long sigh.

I sat up and winced, my shoulder throbbing. "I'm sorry."

"Never mind," Karl said. "Can you walk?"

I moved my toes then swung my feet over the edge. The room swayed for a minute then settled into place. "I'm ready." I looked at the man. Why was he here and who was he?

"I'll explain later," Karl said without turning around, his jaw clenched, the words barely able to squeeze through his teeth.

I swallowed at that. I knew what to expect. I knew what I deserved.

Karl handed me the pistol. "Hold it on him," he said then went towards the man.

I held my breath. The metal warm in my hands, warm from Karl's hands.

"I expect you won't be needed elsewhere for the time being,"

Karl bent and tied his legs to the chair, his hands already tied. Then he tied a gag around his mouth.

The man sat still as the chair, his eyes on me.

Something shivered up my spine.

Karl left him and took the gun, his face set in rigid lines. "Let's go."

I followed him out.

The darkness was overwhelming after the closeness of the room, whatever sort of building it was.

"Who was that?"

He shushed me and strode faster. We were almost out of town when a dog starting barking. It was close.

"It doesn't hear us."

"How do you know?"

"He hears a rabbit or bird," Karl whispered. "If he heard us, he'd be after us."

Every breath pulled the stitch in my side deeper. It wasn't just the dog that was scaring me.

We were out of town now, no houses, no streets.

"Why?" His voice shook and he slowed his pace. Agitation at the very least. Anger - much more likely.

"Why what?" I asked, buying time though it would make him madder. I knew what he was asking.

A tree branch stood in my path and I sucked in a breath.

Karl knocked it out of the way, he didn't slow a step. "Why did you go into town?" He was walking closer, was it because of the trees?

"A car drove past, it looked official. Important," I tried to reason out in my head why I'd done it, how I'd thought it would help. "I wanted to warn you. Before they could find you because of me. If something happened to you because you're helping me. . ." I choked.

There was nothing else in my head. I had to warn him.

"So you ran into town to find me and warn me about a car

you saw?" It sounded stupider when he said it than when I did. "I can't believe you did that."

"I had to do something."

"So you ran into town?" He was yelling now. Not loud, but he'd never yelled at me before.

"You hadn't come back. What was I supposed to do?" I was angry enough to forget that he'd risked everything to save me. "How was I supposed to know if you were ok?" I added then caught myself. "I'm sorry."

But he didn't slow and he didn't look at me.

An owl hooted.

I jumped. I couldn't see it anywhere. There could be other animals close that I couldn't see.

Minutes passed and then more minutes. My side was beyond aching, the pain pulled more and more with every step, every breath. I couldn't ask for a pause now. But how had he found me?

A break in the trees and Karl's face was clear in the moonlight.

Every line so hard I could have traced my finger through them. I longed to smooth them out till I remembered why they were there.

He was mad at me.

When was he going to turn around and yell at me? Waiting was driving me mad. I stopped in the path. "Are you going to yell at me now or later?"

"I'm not going to yell at you," he said. He wouldn't turn around and look at me, but he did stop walking.

"Yes you are. You just haven't decided what you're maddest about yet."

Now he spun around and strode the few steps back to me.

"I can't stand the waiting."

He was glowering now, his hands fisted at his sides.

I wasn't even going to look up and see his face.

"Why do you want me to yell at you?" He asked. "Look at me. Tell me why."

I clenched my own fists and looked up, he was so close my neck was almost bent backwards to see him. "Because you're mad. And I can't wait any longer." I closed my eyes and could feel his breath on my forehead, fast puffs of air. I opened my eyes after a long minute of silence.

He was staring down at me.

My stomach curled around my heart, beating faster now than when we were running.

He moved closer.

I wasn't looking at his eyes anymore. His mouth was so close, I was staring at his mouth. My face turned a shade of heat I didn't know I had. I was burning up but he didn't seem to notice.

"Yes, I'm mad," he backed up a step. "But it doesn't mean I'm going to yell. What kind of animal do you think I am?" He looked over his shoulder. "We can talk later, we have to get out of here."

I willed my feet to move but they wouldn't.

"Can you keep going a while longer?"

I stood where I was.

"Did you get hurt?" He came back, reached out then stopped. "Did anything happen before you fainted?"

"What?"

Karl shifted. "He said he took your arm and you fainted. Did anything else happen?"

"I don't remember what happened," my hands were stuck in the folds of my dress. "I screamed?"

"We can talk later," he held out his arm and waited. He wanted me to go first.

I went, too tired to wonder why.

TEN

The crickets in the woods and our boots in the undergrowth weren't loud enough to cover Karl's breathing. He wasn't trying to hide it.

Every step I was ready, waiting for him to get closer, close enough to teach me my lesson. My neck was tense, my hands hot and wet. I spun around. "Why won't you just tell me?"

"Tell you what?" He asked.

Standing in the shadows I couldn't see his face. Just an outline, a man. Like my father, those men at the jail. They'd never told me anything either.

"No," I shouted, rushing at him, beating at this invisible man hiding something from me again. I wanted to beat them, all of them. But only Karl stood before me.

His hands closed around my wrists, stopping the pounding.

"Why won't you tell me?" I couldn't fight, he was too strong.

"Tell you what?"

I sucked in a breath. "Just leave me," I tried to pull away.

But he didn't let go. "Why would I leave?" His grip held my arms against his chest, his heart pounding so loud I couldn't hear anything else. Or was it because I wasn't breathing at all?

"Lena."

"Don't call me that."

His hands were strong on my shoulders now. "Why?"

"Don't call me anything."

He let go. "There's a barn ahead. We can get out of the rain for tonight."

I hadn't felt the wind blowing around us until now, but it was so loud, how had I not noticed? I circled around, looking for a barn.

"I don't see a barn."

"It's straight ahead."

We'd be sleeping in a barn. Somehow that was worse than outside. If that were possible.

"It's just a bit further," he was close behind.

Clouds covered the moon, I couldn't see a barn, or building of any sort. I couldn't see anything. "I don't see it."

"It's close," he stepped in front, careful not to brush my arm. "I'll lead the way."

It was raining now. The tracks Karl left were soggy, and splashes of water hit my legs with each step. The ground was uneven, and we were going uphill.

My legs were killing me. I wanted to be done with walking, I almost wanted him to carry me. The ground took all my attention to keep from falling. It seemed determined to trip me with holes and rocks and clinging vines. I glanced up but the stiff look of his back reminded me why I couldn't do that.

Why did I lose control and hit him? Rain ran down my forehead and into my eyes. I couldn't be more soaked if I jumped in a pond. A hole grabbed my foot and the next instant I was in the cold mud almost to my elbows. If only it could suck me down. If only I could give up.

"We're so close," a voice by my side, next to me. "It's right ahead."

I didn't move.

"I can see the barn. We should be able to dry off and warm up a little."

Warm sounded good. I shoved with both hands but the mud was thick in every direction. How could it be so muddy so fast? I sighed. "I'm stuck."

He crouched beside me. "I'll lift you out. Is that okay?"

"I won't scream."

His hands closed around my waist. "Am I hurting you?"

"No," I was out of breath from the fall and trying to get out up and from trying not to collapse into the mud and not to respond to his touch. But he wasn't hurting me. In a quick motion I was standing, Karl's hands still tight around my waist.

Then he pulled his hands away. "Do you see it?"

I looked up and saw the barn. It looked as dead as I felt.

He waited, so I went. There was nothing else to be done.

Huge berry vines, sharp and relentless brushed against my legs and my arms. They scratched my face and pulled at my dress.

The massive doorway gaped like a mouth and the darkness we'd been walking in wasn't dark at all. My feet froze to the ground. "Do you think it's safe? What if it comes down on us?"

"It should last at least one more night," Karl stepped around me and went inside. "It doesn't look as bad from inside." His voice echoed.

I swallowed and went inside.

"If we stay away from that hole the rest seems dry enough," he was right beside me.

I flinched but held my ground.

"I'm going to make a fire," he walked into the shadows. "There should be enough around here to get it going."

"Your pack," I was so mad with myself and then him and then myself again, but how could I forget his pack? "I forgot it."

"It can't be helped," he said, from the other side of the empty room. Or not quite empty, his arms were full now, of something.

"I'm—" nothing I said would make any difference. I couldn't fix what I'd done. A spark flicked in the darkness, I walked closer. "I'm really sorry."

"How's your dress?" The flame was struggling to take hold.

"What?"

"Your dress," he didn't look up. "I think it got torn."

I shook inside. I didn't want to understand him but I did. And I couldn't help running my hands over my shoulders, my sides. Something caught at the back of my neck but my fingers were too numb to feel much. "I think a little."

"I wasn't sure," Karl was still bent over the ground.

My eyes adjusted to the light but I still couldn't read his face. What he was thinking? "How did you find me?"

"It's dry over here."

I walked closer to the fire, closer to him, and sat down. I gripped my legs to my chest wet and muddy they were, but I had to hold onto something.

"I heard you scream. That's how I found you."

I shivered, from the inside and not because the room was colder than a moment before.

"You were still in town?"

"On the edge," he looked at me. "You have a loud scream."

"I know."

"You . . ." he shifted, his feet crunching on something. "You've always screamed easily?"

I dropped my face to my knees, I still needed to hide my face despite the almost darkness. "More or less. Why did you ask about my dress?" One bad topic to another, but I had to know.

"It's too wet to keep this fire going."

I bit my lip to keep a sigh inside. My teeth were trying to click together. I wasn't walking now, so the little warmth I'd been getting was gone.

"There's straw over here," he wasn't asking.

But it didn't matter, I was too tired to move anyway. "I'll sleep here," I said, rolling to my side.

"No. Over here," his footsteps came back towards me. He was standing over me now, and I held my breath. What was he going to do? "You'll be cold enough already. At least try."

Then something rustled on the other side of the barn. It wasn't close but it was inside.

"Something moved over there," I whispered, sitting up and pointing across the empty cavern.

He was already in front of me.

I wanted to grab his legs, just to feel that he was still here. That he was real and human and alive.

"Come on," he said reaching his hand back to me. "Let's get further away from whatever it was."

My heart was pounding but I reached out to him. I had to, I needed something to tell me I wasn't alone. His hand was strong and warm when I slid mine into it.

He pulled me up, it felt so effortless. "I can't see what it is. Stay close," something rustled under our feet. "It's just the straw. It should be here now. Do you feel it?"

I sank to my knees and traced my free hand along the dusty ground.

His other hand tightened around my other one. He'd either forgotten or forgiven me for ignoring him earlier.

There. That was something. The pile of straw grew larger the further my hand went. "Found it."

He let go and I sank into the musty pile. Wrapping my arms around myself I tried not to shiver. My stomach growled.

"I'm sorry, I lost the food," Karl said.

"It's my fault anyway. What was that over there?"

"Likely just a rat, something trying to get out of the rain," a click, a gun being cocked.

Karl was standing, still. Something small was in his hand but there wasn't enough light to say what for sure. "Are you," he paused, "familiar with guns?"

I clutched at something twisting in my stomach, this time it wasn't hunger. "A little."

"I won't shoot unless I have to."

"Why did you ask about my dress? And how did you find me if you were already on the edge of town?"

"How did that man find you?" He asked back. "Where were you?"

"I was in an alley. Trying to find you," I said. "How did you know my dress was ripped?"

The straw beside me rustled. But his voice when it came wasn't close. "He wasn't a nice sort of fellow who found you."

My stomach twisted.

"I heard you scream, so I ran back. But I couldn't see you anywhere. I was listening for another scream, for something hitting the ground, anything. Then I heard a door slam."

I couldn't see his face but I could feel his stress, hear his panic.

"I was only a street away from the slammed door I heard and I didn't know if it was you anyway."

The straw under me wasn't enough, I scooted further into the pile. Now he was telling me, maybe I didn't want to know after all. "You don't have to tell me, I wanted to know but-"

"I broke through three doors before I found the right one," it sounded like he was choking. "The snake was almost licking his lips. I'd have known it was him even if you weren't passed out in his arms."

I pressed my fists on either side of my face. I didn't want to hear this, a moan escaped my lips. And then I'd beaten him? "I'm sorry."

"You're sorry?"

My eyes were shut tight but I felt the air stir as he stood. "I'm sorry I lost your pack and the food," I sucked in a breath. "It's all my fault for coming after you. And then I started beating on you." I didn't want to hear what came in between. I didn't want to imagine it.

The silence was deafening. What had I stopped? What was he going to tell me? I couldn't stop shivering now. I held my breath, trying to hear any noise from across the wide silence, but the only thing I could hear was my own loud breathing.

Rain was pouring down both outside and in, but not on this spot. It was dry on this pile of straw and softer than the ground. Karl was right and for whatever reason, he was here.

Again I'd forgotten to ask him why.

———

The light in my eyes hurt, I rolled away. Then I took a breath and sucked in a mouthful of dust. Bits of straw covered my face and I tried to roll again. I couldn't. I was stuck. Something heavy held me in place. I opened my eyes.

It was Karl's heavy coat and I rolled onto the arm. That's why I wasn't very cold. I sat up and couldn't see.

Another hole from the roof and the sun was in the exact right spot to shine down on us. Us. Where was he? Where had he gone?

My heart racing in seconds, I took a deep breath. If I'd been left alone in the middle of the woods, at least I wasn't on that train. I sat up slowly and looked around.

Karl lay on the edge of the straw, his pistol in his hand. He'd covered me with his coat, sleeping all night in only his shirt. He rolled and the thin cotton shirt rolled halfway up his chest showing far too much skin.

I shivered and backed away.

In an instant Karl was on his feet, his hand swung in a circle with the gun aiming, coming to rest on me.

I held my breath. Why was he so quick with his gun?

"What happened?" He circled again. "Did you see something?"

I shook my head, then swallowed and nodded.

"What was it?"

"I didn't see anyone."

He lowered his gun and straightened, looking at me.

I dropped my head. "It was nothing. Really. I'm sorry I woke you."

He froze for a second, then shook his head and sat down.

The next instant my eyes were glued to his. "What's funny?"

All the buttons on his shirt undone, clear to the middle of his chest. At least he had his shirt on. "You face so much without blinking," he was tall next to me, even sitting down. He stared at me. "Why did seeing my side make you back away?"

Sitting with his coat in my lap and straw in my hair, a complete and utter mess, my face still showed everything. "It doesn't matter."

"Why do you scream when I touch your shoulder?" He asked, serious at once. "That's a much bigger question."

I held his gaze. "Why did you come back for me when I ignored your order to stay out of town? Why are you helping me?"

"Does it matter?"

"Yes," I stood and walked a few steps away. My shoulders ached. "It does."

"Why?"

"Because no one does anything without a reason."

"Sometimes things don't make sense."

For once I had the upper hand, standing while he was sitting. But he looked dangerous even sitting on the straw, no weapon in sight. I wouldn't scare someone if I pointed a gun at their heart. I shivered and gripped my arms to my shaking stomach. What were we talking about? "I don't understand."

"I heard you scream. Of course I came after you," he looked

away but his throat swallowed. "You're too good looking for your own good."

I wasn't good looking. I was good for nothing but getting in the way and making trouble. I backed away.

"You don't believe me," he grabbed his coat and stood. "But you are, and I wouldn't leave anyone to that fate."

I wasn't as innocent as I looked, how men acted didn't surprise me. But Karl looked the part of the perfect soldier and wasn't. "That's why you're helping me instead of turning me in?"

He just stood there, staring at me.

I backed up, the barn too confining all of a sudden.

"We should get going," Karl threw his coat on. "Whoever he is, he's not going to like what happened last night." He laughed but there was an edge. "Though we can hope he doesn't report it."

"Why wouldn't he?"

"He lost. That's embarrassing, don't you think?"

I shrugged. How was I to know how that man would respond. Had I lost my bag too? It wasn't on my shoulder. I spun around.

"It's probably in the hay."

I hurried to the hay and found my bag. I stood and threw it on my shoulder. If I looked half as worn, he must be lying. No one would ever want me.

ELEVEN

*T*he town appeared out of nowhere.

"Is it obvious we've been outdoors for long?" I asked then bit my lip.

Of course it was.

Karl looked down at me then reached for my face.

What was he doing? My heart thundered but I stared at his shoulder and didn't move.

He pulled a piece of straw out of my hair, then another and another.

"We look the part I think."

"The part?" I asked, pushing a strand of hair behind my ear. "Oh, yes, what's the story?"

"Newlyweds, our car broke down."

We started walking again, we were getting closer to the town. "What else?"

"I'll do the talking," he was walking close by my side when we stepped onto main street.

"You're not worried?"

"Should I be?" He asked smiling. He looked over at me.

Now the blood was pounding in my ears. "Last time didn't go well."

"Don't worry about last time. Today's a new day."

A child ran past, why was she out so late? A man followed. He glanced at us and hurried after her. She wasn't much bigger than Tobias.

How long had it been since I held him, a week? A month? I couldn't even count the days. Was he alright?

Had they discovered him? I clenched my jaw. Focus. We had to get food.

"Karl?"

"Yes?"

"I understand if we have to sell the story."

He kept walking, all at once his strider longer and quicker.

I ran to catch up, then fell against him when he stopped.

He caught me, his hands on my arms. "What are you saying?"

"I don't know. I just—"

"Did you think at all before you spoke?" His hands were shaking. "Are you telling me to do something I promised not to?"

"No. But we can sell the story without doing anything." I moved my shoulders, he dropped his hands at once. "There wouldn't be much in public, but I'm saying, if it's needed, you can put your arm around me or. . ." I shuddered and pulled my coat closer. Reminding me why we had to come into town. Karl's stuff was gone, all the blankets and food and everything he'd carried. "I'm sorry about your pack." I said keeping my eyes on the sparsely planted window box ahead.

Windows of an inn were lit up ahead, the only one around.

"Don't worry about it," he took my arm. "We'll get some supplies while we're in town."

"We should have gone back for it."

"There wasn't time," he said, his fingers on my arm tightened.

I could feel his gaze on me.

His hand slid down to my elbow, then he shoved open the dark, paneled door, and led me inside.

"I told you. A young couple," a woman said, her voice loud enough to be standing beside us, not across the room. "And here they are."

I looked around till Karl's fingers tightened on my arm. Oh, yes. We were that couple.

But why was she talking in German? I looked up at Karl and sucked in a breath.

He was smiling and walking forward, obviously pleased beyond anything to have found a nice inn with German-speaking hosts. He said as much and rattled off our story. He almost convinced me it was true.

Part of me wanted it to be true, till I took a breath and remembered why I shouldn't want it.

"Supper, of course," the big woman moved faster than I'd have thought possible, whisking a chair over to a small table and motioning us forward.

"Anything hot," Karl said to no one I could see in particular, unless it be the big woman herself.

It was so loud in the small, closed- in sort of room, I must have missed the question. My head spun. I leaned against Karl. Would he understand?

His hand settled on my back, but it was tentative, careful. He didn't want to scare me.

But I couldn't tell him it wasn't only him this time.

He leaned down, smiling. "Is this too much?" He whispered; his arm circled around me. He made everyone think he was being romantic, when his real purpose was checking how close I was to freaking out.

I leaned into his arm and smiled back, catching my breath at his eyes before I could speak. "You're fine. But I'm tired."

His throat worked in ways that sent my stomach spinning.

"And a little dizzy. I'm really—" I sucked in a breath and gripped his arm. My legs buckled.

"Let's sit," he said setting me in the chair and pulling his around so he was sitting next to me. Right next to me.

"I'm ok."

He leaned in close. "It looks natural, don't worry. Is that better?"

I nodded.

"Here you are," the woman was back with bowls of stew and a plate of bread. And glasses of water. Water, now I was thirsty.

"Thank you," Karl said, his arm around my shoulders.

I clenched my hand and focused on the pain on my palm. He was keeping me safe, our story. I reached for the water.

"I'll let you eat first," she leaned closer, almost in my face. "Then I'll see about getting you two a room."

How could someone trying to help frighten me so much?

"Let's eat," Karl said, his tone was strained as he moved the bowls looking for a spoon. He handed it to me. "Sophie?"

"I'm thirsty, not hungry," I reached for the water again. My hand shook but I couldn't get enough. Like I hadn't had water for days. Then I felt the eyes on me.

The others in the room found us more interesting than their own food.

"You should eat," Karl said leaning closer, he smiled but his eyes were worried.

I put the cup down and a thought came from nowhere. Do it. I pushed his face away. "Stop, you'll make me choke."

His arm slipped and he almost fell into me. He hadn't expected that.

I turned back to the food. "This looks really good," I dug into the stew and put a chunk of carrot in my mouth. The thought of meat made my stomach turn but if my mouth was full no one could expect me to talk.

Karl dug into his own food. He didn't say a word and he didn't touch me. Probably he didn't know how to respond.

"Why don't you kiss her for mouthing off like that?" Someone called in German. Was the whole crowd watching?

I looked towards the speaker, a man whose clothes looked as rough as his manner of speaking. He was no gestapo, but trouble enough. Others were calling for the same now, they wanted a kiss and it was my fault. And I told Karl to do what he needed to sell the story. Would he think this was needed?

"We're hungry," Karl said turning towards the speaker the smallest bit and shaking his head. "And I don't kiss my girl in public."

I took a bite, then another before I even swallowed. If my mouth was full I couldn't say something else even more foolish that Karl would have to deal with.

The loud woman came back through the swinging doors. "What's all the ruckus?" She looked around, stopping beside our table. "Something wrong?"

"No. Everything's fine," Karl said.

I stuffed another bite in my mouth. Chewing meat was reason enough not to be talking. I tried to swallow, then Karl put his arm around my shoulder. I held my breath.

"Something wrong?" The man was close now. "Aren't you going to kiss her?"

I wasn't blushing. I was too scared to be embarrassed.

"No, sir, I'm not," Karl said pulling my chair closer to his, "We want to finish our food."

"What's the problem? Afraid she wouldn't like it?"

Karl stood up. "How dare you speak of my wife in so rude a manner!"

I grabbed his arm. "We just want to eat," I dug my nails in, but he didn't seem to notice.

"So you've said," the man said backing up, watching us. Then he went back to his table.

What would they do if they found out? The laws about people helping us were anything but vague.

Karl sat down and looked at my hand on his arm. "I'm not getting into a fight," he was trying to joke but failed. At least in my eyes.

I leaned closer. "What'll we do?"

"We'll eat and they'll move on to the next person who comes in to eat," Karl took a slice of bread. "He's still watching. Finish while you can."

"I'm done."

"You've only had a few bites."

I looked from the empty bowls around him to my own. It was rather full.

"Just a little more. Anyone else would be starving after walking even a few kilometers through the woods."

"I suppose."

He smiled and took a bite out of my bowl.

That was something people did, people who were together. I took a bite and swallowed. We had to get out of here.

People were watching us. We were telling lies. Karl was about to get into a fight with some fellow and I wasn't his wife, I wasn't even his girl.

"Let's go now."

Karl's hand was by his pocket for the slightest of seconds before it he laid it on my arm. "I guess you weren't listening."

"Listening to what?"

"We're here for the night," his fingers on my arm shook though his face was calm. "I'm sorry."

"I understand," it was hard to imagine the comfort of a bed. "We can sneak out early tomorrow, right?" I wanted a nod, something reassuring. Anything.

But his face grew hard. A look that before I would have thought was anger. But now I knew better. Now I recognized it was his mask for fear.

"I couldn't help overhear," this new stranger sounded anything but sorry. "You're on your honeymoon. How lovely. Why not make it official before you take it upstairs?" She was too obvious, almost taunting us to prove our story wasn't just that. Small only in size, she was used to having things her way. And she was not scared of Karl the way the man had been.

Karl's hand tightened around my arm.

"What's wrong?" She asked from only a few steps away. A glass of wine balanced between her perfect fingers, she watched us. "You don't seem shy. Why don't you kiss her?"

Karl didn't twitch. He could pull my face to his without the smallest effort and end all this attention. All this dangerous questioning. Why didn't he? Maybe he promised to treat me like a sister not to reassure me but for another reason all together.

I stood and pushed my chair back.

Now everyone was watching.

My head spun. I bit my lip, shoving away the voice that told me to run. I had to do this. I had to try for Karl. I circled behind his chair, trying to decide.

What was worse? Let them wonder what was wrong, maybe tell someone? Or kiss him and hope we weren't discovered?

My hand clutched at his chair's arm, trying to keep from falling. Then I looked at Karl.

He stared at the table, a piece of bread in his hand.

I reached for his face, tried to look confident, but what if I was doing it all wrong? Everyone would know. I couldn't pretend we were together if I wanted to. I leaned against him and set my hand on his neck, my thumb crept up to his jaw.

He met my eyes.

I tried to ask, with my eyes. He'd always read me far too well before.

"I promised," he whispered.

I stilled. His skin so warm under my hand. "Why?"

"Why does that matter? I did."

"I can't let them catch you because of me," I whispered as I bent down.

He closed his hand over mine, pulling it off his face.

Maybe he didn't want me at all and this had been my worst mistake yet. After all he'd done for me and now I offended him. The room spun. I grabbed his shoulder and closed my eyes. My heart started beating so hard it hurt. Something warm on my cheek.

Karl was close now, very close. It was his breath that warmed my cheek. Then his breath was whispering in my ear. "Faint."

I let go.

Karl's arms were there, he caught me.

I was so tired. It was easier than pretending to be fine. It was too easy. Then through Karl's shirt, I felt his heart pick up. I was leaning against him and couldn't get away from the sound that he couldn't control.

What was I doing?

A few exclamations came, but staying limp was my only focus.

Karl caught me in his arms and now he stood, still holding me.

I was safe in his arms. *No. This was wrong. Why did I do as he said?* In an instant every bit of me was screaming to get away. I stopped caring about everything else and all I could hear was Karl's breathing so close. All I could feel was his arms so tight around me.

Then the swinging door brought a burst of greasy air that should have made me gag.

"What happened?" The woman asked.

"She fainted," Karl said. "It's been a long day, I'm sure she's just worn out and needs some sleep."

"Of course. Follow me."

Muttering came from several directions and I didn't care. Couldn't muster a fraction of my attention on anything but not moving. Not ruining this chance. How could I let him pick me up and hold me? Why did I allow it?

The stairs echoed. Last time we'd stayed at an inn things had gone from bad to worse. What would happen this time?

I focused on my hands, not clasping them together. On my feet, letting them hang limp. On my breathing, low and slow.

"This is the only room we have," the woman said. "It does have a nice bed though."

"Thank you," Karl said. "I'm sure it will do fine."

The seconds dragged out, each one longer than the last. Why was he still talking? Why was he still holding me in his arms? Why was I listening to his heartbeat calming mine? Sweat dripped down the back of my neck.

"And there's more blankets in the chest," her skirts swished, brushed past my head, and the door closed behind her.

I held my breath, I couldn't move. If I held still nothing bad could happen.

"We're alone," Karl said. "You can open your eyes if you like."

I did. "What's wrong?"

His fingers on my leg twitched. "I was afraid you'd really fainted." Then he pulled a smile from somewhere I couldn't fathom.

"I almost did," I looked away. "Are you upset?"

"At you?" His voice went up a notch. "Why?"

I waited.

"Look at me."

I closed my eyes, there was no way he was seeing me cry. And if I opened my mouth, I'd lose it.

"Why would I be mad at you?" He pulled me closer.

I shook my head.

All at once his hands were hot. Close. He was still holding me, so tight. Something moved in his chest, so close.

I could feel so much, too much. He was all around me. "Put me down."

"What's wrong?"

I pulled out of his arms and stood, grabbing the dresser.

"Are you mad I didn't kiss you?"

"No," it was this right now. For a moment, it was better with him close.

"What did I do?" He asked. "I said to faint, and you did. You got us out of there."

He must think I always pretended.

"It wasn't you. You kept your promise. I didn't know what else to do."

But that never would have come into my mind before. "But you aren't mad I almost . . ." I couldn't say the words. The edge of the dresser dug into my hands. "You never pushed and then I was so close. I almost. . ."

"Kissed me?" He stood and the bed creaked. "If you had any idea how guys think, you'd know I'm not mad about that."

I turned and faced him. "So, you're mad about something else."

"I'm not mad, will you try to believe me?" He came a step closer.

My knees locked and my teeth ached from clenching, but I held my ground.

He reached into his back pocket and held something out. In the blue darkness I couldn't make anything out but it had to be the picture. That one of his sister he'd showed me. "I made a promise. I won't break it."

"Like a sister," I said, the image of the little girl leaning against him still clear in my mind.

"As much as possible," he sighed, backing away. "I'm trying.

Everything I did was to keep you safe. And I'd do that with my sister."

The pressure behind my eyes grew till the need to cry was overwhelming, my chest ached from holding my breath. The shadows covered so much of his face. Did it cover enough of mine?

He walked past me and went to the dresser. A snick of a match and a candle flamed up, chasing away the darkness. Sending away the shadows so good for hiding. "A candle is a warmer light than electric, don't you think?"

A knock at the door.

I looked at Karl. "What do I do?"

He motioned to a chair and went to the door, pulling it halfway open.

"Yes?"

By then I was slumped over on the chair. He hadn't told me whether to be awake or to fake sleep.

"I must speak with you," it was a man's voice, that was all I could hear.

"My wife's had a long day," Karl said. "Tomorrow would be better."

My toes curled inside my shoes. He sounded so comfortable with that story, that lie. Did he have to lie often? Was he lying about why he was helping me? No, he couldn't have lied because he hadn't told me why.

"You need to hear this."

The door closed and I waited. To hear them talking in the room. Or outside the room. But there was nothing. I waited another minute then opened my eyes.

Karl had gone with the strange man. He was gone.

I walked to the door and pressed my ear against it, but I couldn't hear a thing in the hall. I straightened and looked around the room. Little to see and nothing unexpected. Where had he gone? Who was that man?

The window looked down into an alley and though the light from the front door spilled into the street, I couldn't see who came and went.

Footsteps sounded in the hall, I jumped, hitting my head on the window frame. Whirling around I looked for somewhere to hide. There was only the bed. I squeezed under, holding my breath till I cleared the frame.

Scooting to the wall I waited, trying to slow my breathing. It could be Karl coming back. It could be someone passing by to another room.

The footsteps stopped at the door.

I bit my lip and the sound of whispering made me bite down on it hard. A gust of wind made me shiver, the window. I'd left the window open, how could I be so stupid?

The door opened and boots walked in. Four or five pairs at least. We were caught.

"Sophie?"

My legs were going numb. Was it Karl?

"Sophie. We have to go."

It was Karl, I was almost sure of it. But who were the others? Then someone was on the ground. Kneeling, then hands joined the knees.

I held my breath. They were going to see me.

Karl's head appeared. "Sophie." He reached out to me. "We have to leave. Now."

I was too tired. I couldn't walk anymore, I couldn't move. "What's going on?"

He reached farther in. "There isn't time. I'll explain later."

I let go of the bed and crawled towards him. Then I stopped, trying to think. Was it a trap? No, he wouldn't do that. I kept going.

Karl pulled me up, but only touched my arms. He pulled me towards him, away from the others.

Then the candle was blown out, the door was opened, and

we were swept out of the room with the others. The hallway was dark, how late was it?

The cold air struck me almost before we left the inn, then we were in the woods, in the dark, moving at a pace closer to a run than a walk.

Were they taking us out to shoot us? No. They wouldn't take us this far for that. But I couldn't keep this pace up for long. The pain in my side and my legs and my head was greater now than fear of what they'd do to us. I stumbled, again, and almost fell into Karl. "I can't go much longer."

He moved closer and put his arm around my back, almost carrying me. "Is this too much?"

"No," a curve in the path forced single file, unless you were walking as close as we were. "What are they going to do?"

He glanced back. "They're helping us," he said, but his grip tightened on my side.

The man in front of us turned, and seeing the gap slowed his gait.

I needed sleep. My head spun, fighting. Anything to stop. It didn't matter what they did to me now.

Then Karl's arm tightened.

It wasn't just about me. There were others to think about. Always others. Was Karl tired like I was? How could he not be? I longed to ask how much longer, but I was afraid of the answer.

A low whistle and everyone stopped. We were all moving through the woods and a second later we'd all stopped.

I peeked over Karl's shoulder.

There was only one man behind us now and he'd closed the distance. He stood so close he could touch Karl. "Been awhile."

I started. The first words spoken in so long.

"Yes," Karl was more tense than I'd ever felt him.

"Is she worth it?"

"Don't," Karl pulled me closer.

The man was close enough I could see his nose turn down, the way his mouth twisted. "You're the girl?"

"Hans," Karl said.

The guy stopped talking and looked at me again, his appraisal brief. "Her?"

Who was this man that Karl knew? What was going on? I leaned closer to Karl. "Did they arrest us or help us?"

"Both," he said, with infuriating calm.

I just stared at him, waiting to hear what he said next. Waiting for some sort of explanation.

"He was one of us or he'd be dead already," a fellow said, ignoring Karl clearing his throat and the obvious fact that he didn't want me hearing it.

He'd be dead already? Was this common knowledge and I'd just been pathetically oblivious or was it a big army secret? Why would he be dead already? "What is he talking about?"

"You may have been right," he said. "You may have been safer alone."

I looked around the circle. I never said that, but what made him change his mind? "Do you know them? Tell them I lied to you. You didn't know who I was," I spun to face him, here in this clearing with soldiers all around. "This is your chance to get out of this mess."

Two strong hands grabbed me from behind, pulled me away from Karl.

"Get your hands off her!" Karl shouted.

The man pulled me into his arms. Sickening breath slithered down my neck and my throat swelled, trapping the acid burning to get out. I pulled away but he held me tight,

"How dare you grab her?"

"Are you claiming her?"

It was Karl again, but I couldn't see him now for the shadows. The man pulled my chin around, a memory flashed of another man pulling my face around. Someone screamed loud from somewhere close. Nails dug into my arms, how had they gotten so tight so quickly? "Give her to me!" Karl was shouting. "Or I swear I'll—"

"You'll what?" The leader was close now.

Another scream, so loud, so close. A slimy hand clamped over my mouth and it cut off.

"You're dead already. There's no point in threatening a Lieutenant."

"Have you forgotten who I am? How dare you turn your back on me?"

"You turned your back first."

"I had good reason!" Karl shouted. "I'm no coward. When did I ever shirk my duty or shy from any danger? Tell me that! Will you so readily shoot one of your own?"

"Tell us why you've turned traitor."

"Give me the girl first."

The hands were still holding me, the sweaty hands so close. Karl wasn't about to be shot. But the pain inside was too much. This strange man was too close. I dug my fingers into the arms holding me against his smelly, sweaty body.

Curses laced the air.

My heart beat so fast it hurt, I couldn't stop screaming. The strange man shook me, trapping my arms to my sides.

TWELVE

"*E*verything's okay now," Karl's said.

I was warm, the roughness of a coat against my cheek. Something itched my leg. I squeezed my hands together.

A finger brushed the back of my hand, I sucked in a breath.

"We've worked it out."

"You should have told them sooner," that wasn't Karl speaking, but the voice was familiar.

Did I imagine that I knew it? I opened my eyes.

"You alright?" Karl asked.

We weren't in the same place. I finally found Karl's face, right above me.

A jagged scratch up his neck made me want to puke. He shouldn't stick up for someone who was capable of such violence. "Did I?"

He saw where I was looking. "No. I had a skirmish of my own," he ran a hand through his hair.

"I'll say," the unnamed guy said, determined to keep that nightmare alive.

Karl ignored him, though his jaw tightened. "Can you sit up?"

I did, holding onto his arm. "What happened to the others?"

"They're gone. But I think Helmut would have apologized," Karl opened a bag and held out an apple. "He's the one who—"

"That's alright," I took the apple, rolling it between my hands. "I can guess."

"I'm sorry..." Karl stopped.

"You're something," the other guy said. "You must be. I've known Karl for a long time. And that back there?"

I turned towards this voice, this person so relentlessly intrusive.

He returned the look I gave, he didn't seem to mind.

"You should eat something," Karl said. "I'm sorry we have to hurry on, but we can't sit here much longer."

"I know," I bit into the apple. Didn't we always?

The other fellow chuckled. "My goodness, when you let Helmut have—"

"Leave it," Karl yelled, cutting him off. "Just leave it alone."

"It's left. Easy Karl," he looked at me and held out his hand. "I'm Max, and once upon a time, Karl and I were friends."

I looked at Karl but his jaw was set and he didn't meet my eyes. I looked back at my lap, my hands were sticky from the apple but I took another bite. He couldn't expect me to eat and talk at the same time.

"I can't blame you," Max said. "But I didn't mean anything by it."

"Leave it," Karl said through gritted teeth.

"What happened?" I turned to Karl. "Where are the others? How did you get hurt?"

"I'm not hurt enough for notice and they let us go," Karl said. "That's all that matters."

I fixed my eyes on him.

Max coughed.

"I told them you were my fiancée, there'd been a mix up," he met my eyes. "I told them you weren't Jewish."

"Helmut was disappointed," Max said. "Very disappointed."

What did Max know?

"I don't want to discuss it," Karl said, juice trickling from the apple in his hand. "They helped us get out of town. That's all the good I can say about it."

I ate my apple.

"Where'd you two meet?" Max asked.

Karl stood up and held out his hand. "Time to go. We slipped past the gestapo but we shouldn't sit here long."

I took his hand. It was shaking. Was he scared of Max? Wait. He said something. "The gestapo?" The blood in my veins froze. His hand grew hotter and hotter around mine.

He pulled me to standing. "They're hours away. And they didn't follow us."

We took off down the road, where we were it was impossible to keep track of. But Max was still with us. After we passed a few road markers I turned to him. "Who are you?"

"We fought together," Max said.

Karl's neck was tight again.

"You haven't slept at all, have you?"

"What's wrong?" Max asked. The road was wider here and he was walking beside us now.

Would I ever learn to hide my feelings from my face?

"What is it?" Karl moved closer, though he didn't touch me. He moved in between Max and I. "What's wrong?"

"He reminds me of someone," there was no use saying it was nothing. "That's all. I'm alright."

The mist crept along the ground as we came down a hill and into a thick wall of whiteness.

Dampness covered me and I spread my hands and tried to feel it, but it was just mist. It was morning, an overcast day but at least it wasn't raining.

"Are we far enough away from that last town?" I asked, looking at Karl.

"We can stop and eat," he said walking into the brush, away from the road.

I followed and dropped to the ground, leaning forward and resting on my knees. Was it only yesterday we were in that inn, was it just last night Karl was carrying me? I sucked in a breath.

Karl was beside me. "I'm sorry."

I finally saw the roll he held in his hand. "I can't." I tried not to sound like a child. And failed.

He shook his head. "You need to eat."

I took it and took a bite, trying to remember when I'd made bread myself. I missed making bread, the taste of it, the smell of it, the feel of it.

Max cleared his throat. "Man."

I looked up.

Max had said one word, but why? It had to mean something.

Karl coughed and looked away. Hiding something.

Then they both kept eating. In silence. What were they saying?

My dress was damp now and I stood up. Bothered by their secret conversation more than my soaked backside.

Both the guys stood as well, and we started walking.

The monotony was different today. Why was Max with us? "What happened when you left the room last night?"

They both stiffened, neither looking my way. The sameness of their response hit me. Was he simply another soldier? Was Karl ever like Helmut? No. That was impossible.

Karl walked with the strong set of his shoulders, so like the others in that clearing. His stance of power, more even than the others, what had they called him? Lieutenant? His jaw, his muscled neck and arms. Why was he helping me?

What made him different? What made him act as almost no

other soldier in the Wehrmacht would have? He'd ignored orders and instead of capturing me, helped me escape.

I stopped in the road. "Why was I followed?"

They stopped a few feet ahead and Karl turned and looked at me.

"I'm not afflicted with a false opinion of my importance. No one would notice if I disappeared," Tobias's little face flashed inside my head. "At least, no one of importance."

"They don't like being thwarted," Max said.

"And they don't like soldiers disobeying," Karl added. "It's me more than you." Karl slowed to my pace, walking alongside me. "So don't worry so much."

I shivered. Of course I was worried. "What are the others going to do?"

"What they said they'd do," Max said. "Nothing."

It didn't make sense but my feet were tired, so I closed my mouth and walked. It seemed like every curve was the perfect place to sit but we just kept walking. I opened my mouth to ask how much longer, then I shut it. I couldn't ask. If we weren't stopping in the next two minutes I couldn't keep going. My eyes jolted open, I'd fallen asleep. Was it possible? "When are we stopping?"

"For dinner?" Max asked. "We already did."

"That was hours ago, where are we?"

"We have a few kilometers to the next town, we planned to stop there tonight," Karl said, close enough to be both comforting and distracting.

At least we weren't sleeping outside. Karl said I was his fiancée to the others. What about Max?

"What's eating you?" Max asked, suddenly so close.

I jumped.

"Sorry," he said stepping away from my side. "Just trying to be friendly."

Karl was quiet on the other side. What part of what story had he told Max?

"I'm tired," I said. It was true.

"Want a lift?" He asked. "I'm not Von Liedersdorf, but I'm strong enough."

I shuddered before I could stop and clenched my hands.

"Easy, I'm also not Helmut."

I would've been uncomfortable with anyone trying to be so familiar, but his face and now his tone were hard to ignore.

"Enough," Karl said. "She's had enough hands on her for today."

"Were you going to offer? She's about to keel over," it sounded like a challenge. "Or is that pack enough weight for you?"

The lines in Karl's forehead were tight. "If she wants help I'm here. She knows that."

"I'm fine," I said touching Karl's arm. "It wasn't anything." I whispered knowing they both could hear. Hoping they both would stop.

We'd stopped in the middle of the road. The two of them standing opposite each other.

I was right between them.

The clouds overhead were gray now. Was it the weather that turned them against each other, or me?

"Please, don't do this."

They didn't move.

I hated it but I turned my back to Max and put my hands out to Karl. Stepping towards him I bit my lip and pushed him away. "Karl," I pulled on his coat. "Let's keep walking. If I need help, I'll ask you." I pulled harder, trying to break the line between them. Trying to stop the fight about to start.

A fight between them – that would be horrible.

I peeked over my shoulder and shuddered when I saw the anger in Max's eyes. I'd made it worse.

"Lena," Karl didn't meet my eyes. His hands were on my shoulders now and he pulled me behind him.

"Really?" Max's words were low. "Still think she's worth it?"

"No," Karl said.

My heart sank. Why did it matter so much? I'd told him to leave me so many times before, for his own good. It was the right thing.

"Then—"

"She isn't a catch," he put his hand behind his back, held it out towards me. "A girl isn't caught, she's won. And if anyone was ever worth winning, she is."

I put my hand in his. My throat caught when his hand tightened around mine. I couldn't see around Karl now, but I didn't want to. I shouldn't have believed Karl would turn on me.

"You're a fool."

"Because I see her as a person?" Karl said. "Or because I won't hand her over to you?"

Max's boots came into view, Karl's hand dropped mine.

They were only inches from each other now.

"When did this become you against us?" Max asked. "You're one of us, you were the best of us. Can you throw out everything you believe, just because a girl's caught your eye for the first time?"

The first time? Had I caught his eye? Max believed we were together.

"Think, Karl." Max softened his voice. "You've fought for this, you believe it. What about your family? Your father, what will he think? Can you face him after betraying everything he stands for?"

"I did believe in what I was doing. Just as I believe in what I'm doing now," Karl's back was rigid, his breathing quick. "She hasn't done anything wrong."

"Think about what you're saying," Max's persuasive tone was slipping away now, his frustration coming through. "Think about all the people who've died protecting our people. Rudolph, Hans." He paused. "Ernst."

I could almost feel the static zapping between them.

"Where they fighting in vain?"

I knew what he'd say next.

"Did they die in vain?"

Karl didn't say anything. Was he changing his mind? In the middle of the road they towered.

"Karl. You've always led us. We're fighting for our country, to make it great. It is great. We're respected again. Are you going to let this..." Max struggled with what to call me. "This girl ruin all that?"

"Think about it. She's never done anything wrong. Could you set her against a wall and shoot her yourself?" He walked forward.

Max backed away.

"Could you murder her with your own hands?"

"That's not what's happening."

"It is, except it wouldn't be you shooting. It'd be putting her on a train. Not everyone understands, but you and I do."

Karl never talked about this before. What was he talking about? I always tried to ignore rumors, stories, the whispers that went around. But he sounded like he knew something. Something bad.

"We don't know everything. We see some things but not the whole picture."

Karl closed the distance between them. "Would you let your cousin go on one of those trains?"

"What?" Max stumbled back.

"We both know Otto's grandmother is Jewish. Would you help him if you could or put him on that train yourself?"

"We don't know for sure."

"But you wouldn't, would you?" Karl jabbed him in the chest.

"Because you and I both know being Jewish doesn't make him less of a person or less deserving to live."

A pause followed, both of them standing there, staring at each other.

"Why didn't you go with the others?" Karl asked. "If you think you can change my mind, you're a bigger fool than I've ever been."

"They'll find you," Max whispered. "And you and I both know—"

The wind picked up, blurring out the words. Branches shook overhead.

I pulled my coat closer and watched them fighting about me and all the trouble I was causing. I should leave so Karl wouldn't have to figure out what was the right thing to do. I was a moral issue now. I'd ruined his life so completely that now Karl was fighting with his friend, the one fellow who hadn't left.

I would have to leave him later, but not with his back turned, not when he was fighting for me. I sat and waited, a random word or two getting to me now and then. Leaves were falling around me. I hardly noticed the raindrops flicking down from the trees.

"You'll go to hell."

Karl was coming towards me now.

Max stood in the middle of the road, his face livid, his hands fisted for a fight.

"Time to go," Karl said reaching his hand down to me.

I took it, biting the inside of my cheek to keep the tremors from taking over.

He put his arm around me and we walked down the road. "Don't look back," he said, our feet covering the rocky road so fast it didn't seem possible.

The sky turned dark in less time than it took them to stare each other down, it didn't seem real.

But who won?

"I'm sorry if I did the wrong thing," we were going too fast to say anything more. Getting a breath was hard, but we couldn't slow down.

After rounding several curves Karl stopped. "Which way should we go?"

"What?" He'd never asked me which way we should go before.

"Should we go on into the town, as we'd planned with Max, hoping he assumes we wouldn't do what we'd planned or should we go north or south?"

"Why are you asking me?" I shrank away from the intense way he looked at me. "I don't understand your question at all."

"I'm asking for two reasons," he swiveled his head between the road behind us and me. "Most urgently because he's likely to think the same as I and go where I'd go right now. So you need to make the decision."

"You want me to decide which way we go? Where we sleep tonight?" I said. "What if I lead us right into a group of partisans? Or soldiers?"

He tried to laugh. "I led us into a town swarming with gestapo. You can't do worse."

A warm bed sounded good. Too good, it had to be the wrong decision.

"Then south, I guess."

He looked at me. "Why do you say that?"

"Because that's not what I want to do," I blurted out then clapped my hand over my mouth.

"What?" He looked at me after another look behind us. "Why?"

"I'm not fond of being out of doors at night. That's why I thought it would be safer," I nodded behind us. "He'd probably guess I'm scared of the dark."

"That's what we'll do," Karl said starting across the road, running towards the trees.

"What?" I panted.

He was almost dragging me now.

"Why are we—" I heard a motor and almost stopped moving.

"Hurry."

And I did.

The line of trees was thick and we hurried into them. Branches slapped at my face, bushes and brambles. Tall ferns and fallen logs, the wood was full of things to trap me.

A motor roared behind us on the road.

We kept running. Or hopping, since running wasn't possible. Then Karl pulled me to the ground.

I landed on his hand before he slipped it away. Resting in the damp leaves I tried to breathe.

Karl was next to me, peering through the undergrowth his hand still on my back.

I swallowed but he didn't notice the movement.

He muttered under his breath. The only word I heard was "dogs."

I listened but couldn't hear the motor that had all but chased us into the woods. I tried to hear people but I couldn't hear that either. Then I heard something else.

Dogs.

"Come on," he said pulling me up. We ran through the woods. Karl holding my hand and pulling me along after him.

My heart was pounding before I'd gone ten steps. Behind us I could hear car doors slamming and dogs barking.

Karl was dodging branches and somehow finding a way through this pathless wood.

It was only dusk but in this dense wood, it seemed much later. The trees grew so close further in there were less branches, but it was darker. Less light got in from above.

"This way," he said pulling me downhill, towards a rushing stream.

I shivered listening to it, but at least it blocked out the barking.

He was going straight for the water. "Choose fast," Karl said his hand shifting to my arm. "Get soaked or get carried?"

We broke through the trees, the water was close enough to fall into.

I was shivering already but he couldn't pick me up right now. What if I lost control and screamed? That would bring them all the faster. "Get soaked."

He sighed but moved his hand back to my hand.

We were at the water's edge. Clenching my teeth together I stepped into the dark water, a rock jabbed through my shoe, I gripped Karl's arm tighter.

"Are you alright?" He asked.

I kept going. The water was up to my knees and every bit higher was adding more layers of tingling, searing pain. I thought I was cold before. Burning numbness had taken over my feet by the time we were in the middle of the stream. I held onto Karl with both hands.

"We should be past the deepest now."

I was shaking inside too much to answer. Another step and the water went halfway up my thighs. I bit my lip to keep from screaming.

The dogs, I could hear one howling. Had they found our scent?

I couldn't fight the shaking, it was deep in my bones. I didn't have anything left to fight it with. The bank was only a few steps ahead.

Then Karl turned us downstream. "Another step or two." We walked along the bank, still in the water. He dragged me out of the water.

My shoes were so heavy.

"I'd offer to carry you, but you have to move now. You need to get your blood flowing," he led us straight into the woods.

We didn't go fast, but my clothes were heavy and my feet were numb and I couldn't stop shaking. Walking was painful. My feet had become far too small for my shoes and my socks were wedged between my toes. "How much further?"

"Can you make it a few more kilometers?" he asked.

Kilometers? "I'll try." It was the best I could offer.

THIRTEEN

a breeze swept past us, through the woods and straight through my clothes.

I could have been naked for all the good they were doing. The wet had seeped up to my waist now, and I was beyond cold.

Gripping Karl's hand I kept walking, but I didn't warm up. "Isn't walking supposed to warm you up?" I asked cutting my question short when my voice shook.

"It doesn't always work," he said. "But we're almost far enough."

I closed my eyes and kept walking.

"We're here," his hand clenched mine. "We can stop now."

I looked around but there was nothing to see, we were deep in the woods in the middle of nowhere.

"You have to change. If you stay in those clothes you'll freeze."

There wasn't enough light through the trees to see his face. Was he joking? "I don't have any others."

He dropped his pack and pulled his hand.

But I couldn't make my fingers let go.

He turned around to me and with his other hand unfolded my fingers from his.

"I'm sorry," I couldn't clench my hands to keep calm, they were too numb to move.

"It's my fault," he ripped the pack open and dug through it.

"It was my choice."

"I shouldn't have let you," he said through gritted teeth. "If you get sick because of this. . ."

Finally I realized what he was doing. "That isn't your pack."

"I know," he said pulling out several things. A small shovel was on the ground. "But you can't stay in those clothes." He stood, his hands full of something.

I shivered, my knees knocking together.

He held them out to me. "It's better than nothing."

I was close to tears again. Why did crying come so naturally all at once?

"You have to change," he said coming a step closer.

I wasn't trying to be difficult. I didn't have the strength to move a step closer to take the clothes, let alone change into them.

"What is it?"

I forced my legs to move forward, my hands reached out automatically. I needed to change, then I'd be warm. That was all I could think about. I took the pile, but he didn't let go.

He met my eyes and swallowed hard. Then he backed away. "I'm getting branches. Not far but I won't come back till you call me," he waited. "Call me when you're changed." He stood, waiting for an answer.

"I'll call you."

He nodded and disappeared into the woods.

I was alone. I wanted to scream for him to stay. What if those people came? What if the dogs had followed us and they came when he was gone and they took me and he never knew what happened? What if I never saw him again?

Change and call.

I set the clothes down and struggled with the buttons on my coat. It took so long but I got it off. Dropping my coat I tugged at my apron, the ties knotted at my side. Blowing on my hands I held them under my arms. When they warmed enough to hurt, I tore off the apron and picked up the first piece of clothing.

The air was so much colder now, it didn't seem possible.

I was shaking and couldn't stop. Trousers, of course they were huge. It was too cold to think about anything else. Karl wasn't changing till I'd finished, I had to hurry. Unlacing my bodice was tricky. My fingers wouldn't behave. Finally I got everything off except my woolen undershirt and shorts, both somehow only damp. Then I pulled on the shirt and trousers Karl gave me.

"I'm done," I whispered. Standing up I peered through the trees, keeping a hand on the trousers to keep them from falling to my feet. "Karl?" I called, still quiet but more than a whisper.

It had been awhile. Maybe he was still far away.

Give him a minute I thought and bent, picking up my wet clothes piled around the ground. My hands weren't working right. They were too stiff, rigid with cold. Where was he? "I'm done."

The woods were dark and closing in more with every second.

His pack was next to me, he wouldn't leave his pack, would he? I shook my head, but then I remembered. It wasn't his pack.

I started into the woods, calling again. "Karl."

A crashing in the opposite direction made me spin around. I couldn't see anything but something large was out there. My heart was pounding so fast I almost couldn't breathe. I held the top of the trousers tight in my hand and backed away from the sound coming closer and closer. It couldn't be Karl. He would never be that loud.

"Don't move."

It was Karl, behind me. I froze. But the peace I felt just hearing his voice scared me. Why did I feel safe?

"Back up, slowly."

I backed up two steps and then his hand was on my back, he pulled me behind a tree. I couldn't stop shivering. "What is it?" I whispered.

"A bear, I think," he pulled me closer, the click of his pistol close.

His breath so close made me shiver, but he was warm. His hand moved to my side and he pulled me against him. His warmth seeped into my back through the linen shirt that kept trying to slip off my shoulders. "We're upwind, if we're still he might not smell us."

We stood watching and waiting for the bear to emerge. Now both Karl's arms were wrapped around me. "You're freezing," he whispered in my ear, as if it was a secret.

Minutes passed but there were no more crashes. No more noises.

My head started to spin.

"I think it must have gone somewhere else," he said.

I didn't have an opinion and I wouldn't have argued if I had. I waited for him to pull away, but he didn't.

Another minute passed.

I tried to see past the haze that covered everything. I pushed through his arms and pulled away from him. He'd never made a move, never taken advantage, but I was fighting a silent battle that only knew black and white. And being so close was very black and white.

"I'm sorry," he said. "I shouldn't have done that."

"Have you ever held your sister like that?"

"I heard the bear and was worried. Then I got here and I was more worried. And then you were so cold, and you where shivering. I swear, I had no intention of...doing anything."

"Like a sister."

"I've never had to rescue my sister from a bear. But I would have. I would've held her close to keep her safe."

"Alright." What else could I say?

"I'm sorry."

"It's alright, I believe you," I pushed away the haze with difficulty and looked up to see him holding something out.

"I found another shirt. You need another layer."

I took it and stepped back, still holding up my trousers. A branch caught my foot and I was falling. I flung my hands out and watched Karl lunge towards me but he was moving too slow to catch me. Everything was happening so slow. I could see his eyes widen then focus, he stretched out his arm. The tree branches came into view as I landed on my side.

All the air sucked from my lungs, I stared at the treetops and tried to breathe. I rolled away from a sharp rock poking my back.

Karl was right above me.

He was talking but I couldn't hear him. I blinked a few times, looked away from him and then back. "What?"

"Did you hit your head?" He had both hands on my neck, feeling up the back of my head and pressing along my shoulders. He was serious. So serious. "Does this hurt?"

I was glad of the darkness or he'd see the heat in my face. "A rock is jabbing my back, but my head's alright."

"Move your hands."

I did, holding them up. They looked small between me and the sky.

"Lena."

I looked back at him.

"Now your legs."

I tried but they were heavy. My head swam when I tried to sit up but scarcely more than usual. Less than I'd have thought after falling.

"Move them," he ordered again.

"I'm trying," I sat up. The pants had slid to my feet, that's why I couldn't move my legs. I wanted to cover my face and never show it again.

"They're just caught in the trousers," he slid his hand to my back.

I jumped, my breath hitched.

"I'm sorry. Is that where that rock hit you?"

The shirt came almost to my knees, covering far more than a bathing suit. But to be so exposed before him. So entirely at his mercy as never before, I stared at my hands.

"Why don't you wait here," he put another shirt in my hands. "I have to grab something." He said and went back into the woods.

What if the bear came back? I pulled the pants back up as far as I could, and lay back, pulling them past my waist. I was so tired. I could almost fall asleep if I wasn't so cold. In my lap was the shirt. I should put it on.

"You should put that on."

I jumped and looked up. His voice echoed my very own thoughts.

"I know," I tried to sit but my back hurt, I bit my lip and forced myself up, then stopped, waiting for my head to stop spinning. Then I pulled the shirt over my head.

His hand was there, reaching out to me. "I've got something rigged up, it's better than nothing." He'd propped a load of branches between a fallen tree and a live one making a little tent. "We can't start a fire I'm afraid."

I understood, taking the blanket he held out. Then I sat on the branches he'd put down in the tent.

"Hungry?" he asked, laying out the wet clothes. He'd changed too.

When did he change?

"Yes," for once I finally was.

Sitting a few feet away he handed me something. It was too dark to see what it was.

"What is it?" I asked, cold liquid oozing onto my hand. "Is it food?"

"I'm sure it is," he said taking it back and opening it, but it was too dark for me to see what it was.

"It's meat," he said wrapping it back up.

I smelled my hand and my stomach heaved. Thank goodness I didn't have anything to throw up.

"We can't cook it," he said.

I wasn't going to argue and I wasn't going to eat it raw. "I know." I pressed hard on stomach to stop the noise.

"We have bread," he said handing it over. "I'd just hoped there was something else too."

"Bread's good," I said, wiping my hand off before taking it. "I'm hungry for anything tonight."

"That's new."

"I know," I didn't have time for more of a response. I was too hungry to think of anything else or keep my mouth empty enough to say it.

Something rustled, not too far off.

"What's that?"

"Nothing big," Karl said, but he moved closer.

I kept eating, but the dark night loomed all around, the hours stretched ahead. Again, we were out here. Again, we were alone. The last bite of bread finally swallowed I turned to him. "What's Max going to do?"

Karl snorted, then sighed. "I'm not sure. But we can't stay here long. You should sleep if you can."

Maybe I'd warm up in my sleep. Scooting as far under the branches as I could I wrapped the blanket around me. I'd been dead tired before, but now I couldn't get my eyes to close.

"If I put my pack behind you it would block the wind," Karl said.

I wanted to say no. I wanted to stop him from coming that close, but he was only trying to help and he hadn't broken his promise. There was no reason to think he would now. "Thank you." I said rolling away from the branches so he could reach behind me. I almost screamed when the pack touched my back, but I bit my lip. It was still so sore.

But if he'd wanted to do something he didn't have to wait till now. He'd had plenty of chances.

The dark was eating into me.

The woods weren't silent. With the wind, the trees made plenty of noise with their branches. Suddenly I needed to know I wasn't alone. I needed. . ."Karl?"

"Yes?" From the darkness.

I relaxed, then stiffened. Why did hearing his voice make me relax? That wasn't good.

"What's wrong?" He asked, and I could hear him moving closer.

My throat tightened, but I had to answer before he got even closer. "Nothing. Bored is all," bored? I wanted to kick myself. I might relax hearing his voice in the dark, but when he got closer I was scared as ever. "Sorry I woke you."

"That's alright," he said. "You didn't wake me."

"Well, I'm glad." When the darkness loomed large again I listened for his breathing. Somehow I could hear his breathing over all the noise of the wind, and it was calm, relaxed. If he wasn't worried, then we must be okay. I closed my eyes and curled up against his pack. It did block the wind.

Branches tickling my face made me move my head. I was mostly warm, how did I get warm at all? I couldn't see much, my face still pressed into his pack.

But the pack was warm. Warmer than I was.

My legs tensed up and my jaw set. I tried to roll and an arm tightened around me.

Karl was asleep and his arms were wrapped around me.

Something took over. Screaming came from my mouth as I thrashed around trying to get away from the hands on me. Branches fell on me and a buckle on the pack dug into my side.

"Don't scream," the warmth was gone. "I'll explain, but don't scream."

I covered my mouth with my hand and froze. I lay with the branches all over me, the blankets in a lump and the cold all around.

"I swear I didn't do anything. Do you need a minute, or do you want me to explain?"

I shook my head. I couldn't hear anything right now.

"I'm backing up," Karl said. "But I'm still here."

I lay still and tried to focus on breathing slow. Tried to get any breath at all.

"Don't you want to know?" Karl asked.

I jumped. After hiking in silence for hours his question was loud.

"Know what?"

"What happened last night?"

If he told me what happened I'd have to explain my response. "I thought you said nothing happened."

"I said I didn't do anything. Not that nothing happened."

"If you didn't do anything, what's to talk about?"

Karl stopped in the road. "Maybe why I was asleep next to you? Don't you want to talk about it?"

Talking would lead to more questions. "No." I kept walking.

After a minute his footsteps caught up with mine. "The next town is bigger. We're going to make the train if possible."

"If possible?"

"It's bigger, more soldiers. More chance of being questioned," he looked over and met my eyes. "More chance of being recognized."

My feet turned to lead. "What if they do? Will they—" I stood like a dummy on the fern Karl had flattened.

"If I thought we'd get caught for sure, we'd go somewhere else," he turned back and held out his hand. "It's not safe in the woods either."

I shoved my feet forward, but I didn't take his hand.

"Are you up to it? Pretending with me?"

I shivered inside. It was so hard. Every time it got more difficult. "Of course."

"It won't be for long. We'll buy tickets and food and once we're on the train we'll pretend to sleep. Less questions that way."

A sign for the town loomed ahead, 3 kilometers. It would be nice to sit down. Except for being around people. And having to pretend we were together. And getting on the train. My feet got heavier and harder to pick up.

"We have to hurry," Karl said.

I hurried but he was faster. I almost ran to keep up. He wasn't this anxious last time.

The town was like the others we'd seen since crossing the border, boring in its commonness. Karl was right, it was bigger than the other towns we stopped in. People didn't notice us much. Karl walked beside me now and his hand found mine.

I held my breath. Why did he take my hand?

We walked past shops and the police station. Past a giant tree with a bench built round it and people, everywhere people. Some who ignored us and some who didn't.

"Lena."

I looked up. "What is it?"

"My hand."

I dropped his hand. I'd been digging my nails in; deep red marks lined the side. "I didn't know. I'm sorry."

"It's alright," he took my hand again. "It's easier to catch you if I already have your hand."

I looked away, across the square to the tailor shop. "Next time tell me right away."

"It's okay. I'm scared too."

Scared. He thought I was scared of the police. "Shouldn't we find the train station?"

He pulled me closer and laughed. "We're almost there. And it looks more natural to be talking anyway. So, it was good you gave us something to talk about."

I couldn't keep looking at him, so I looked around at normal people living their normal lives.

A heavy woman carrying her shopping home. She looked tired. A man drove down the road in an old beat- up car. A girl with a package walking up the street away from us and a soldier marching towards us.

I swallowed. Karl's hand clenched mine. I released his hand but he didn't let go of mine, so I kept walking. And walking. I turned my head to look.

"Don't," Karl whispered.

I looked at the flowers in the pot by the nearest door and the cart driving by as if I cared.

Karl didn't break his stride or lessen his hold till we rounded a corner. Then he leaned against the alley wall and closed his eyes.

I watched him, resting there.

He didn't look so strong in the shade, with his eyes closed. A thin scar under his ear made me swallow and the wave of his hair, my fingers itched to touch it just for an instant.

Then his eyes were open, staring into mine. He caught me.

I stepped back.

"You didn't speed up or anything," he reached for my face.

I couldn't move as his hand got closer and closer.

He took the strand of hair over my eyes and tucked it behind my ear. "I was afraid you were going to faint."

I'm not that weak. "I don't faint very often. And usually I'm a whole lot stronger. It's all the hiking I'm not used to."

He smiled at me, his hand dropping to his side. "Well, let's go end the hike for now, alright?"

I nodded not trusting my voice to answer.

The train station was empty, even to the station master. We waited at the desk for several minutes then Karl rang the bell.

"Two please," he said when the man appeared. "When's the next due in?" Then taking my hand we walked out.

Had the man even answered?

"We have an hour. Plenty of time to get food."

A soldier walked by.

Karl stiffened, his hand tightened on mine but he smiled down at me. "Come on."

"We can get food tonight," I said. "I can wait."

"No. We're eating now," he said, a determined set to his jaw. We went into the closest café and Karl ordered.

"It's nice to sit at a table for a change," I forced on a smile and looked up. He was working so hard to keep me safe. Helping with the story was the least I could do. "It's been awhile."

He laughed at that, but his eyes were searching the room. He could see everything from his seat and watch he did.

It happened too fast to understand. I was watching the waitress bring our food. I could see the steam rising. My stomach cramped at the smell. "You were right." I looked back at him. "It's…"

But his face had changed. In an instant he was angry and dangerous. A killer. And he was fixed on something or someone behind me. "I'm sorry." He whispered, tearing his eyes off of something and meeting mine.

My heart was in my throat. His hand resting on mine was

hard as stone and I couldn't move it if I'd tried. But I knew better than to look behind me.

"What do I do?" I mouthed. But he wasn't looking at me.

The waitress stepped up to our table and set our bowls before us as if nothing else was going on. Giving the usual small talk, if we want more or anything else or water. She finished and stood waiting. Staring at Karl.

"Thank you," I said.

He didn't even see her, he was staring at something or someone else.

I turned my head to look and wished I hadn't. It wasn't a soldier he'd seen.

It was the same man Karl knocked out when we'd left the inn days ago. When I turned back to Karl, he was looking at me.

"Eat. If we don't it'll draw more attention."

How could I eat now?

Karl was eating, spoon after spoon as if he was starving.

Even starving, I couldn't eat that fast. It could've been nothing but potato broth for all the flavor I got, but I ate.

"I don't think he's seen us," Karl whispered after a few minutes. "Don't turn around. I have an idea."

"An idea?" I almost choked.

He tried to smile but his eyes were worried. He looked at my plate, "Pocket the bread, we'll want it later." He stuffed his roll somewhere.

"What's your idea?"

"Trust me?"

I looked at the bowl of soup. Did I trust him? Should I trust him?

He leaned in. "Slap me across the face, then run out."

"What?" I backed away. "No."

"We don't have much time," he was serious.

"It won't work."

"Slap me now, hard. Then run without looking back. I'll follow once I've set the story."

It might work. But I couldn't do it. I couldn't hit him.

"Do it now," he leaned in, but instead of going for my ear, he zeroed in for my mouth. A fraction away and he breathed in my face.

I jerked away and slapped him. No. I stared at him, my hand stung. Horror filled me. I'd struck him after all he'd done to help me.

He nodded the smallest bit.

I jumped up, my chair sliding away and ran out. He'd done that on purpose, to make it simple for me. I stopped outside the door, inside the ruckus started. Someone laughed, another called something.

He said he'd be right behind me.

I ran to an alley nearby. Leaning over I gripped my knees. I had to catch my breath. And my wits. They scattered when he leaned in. I almost kissed him back. I'd started to, I'd wanted to. Then panic kicked in, fortunately, as he'd thought it would. How could that have happened?

What was happening to me?

FOURTEEN

*F*ootsteps came around the corner, but it wasn't Karl.

I backed away from the entrance to the alley. I kept backing till a wall hit me.

"Waiting for someone?" The man from that inn so long ago, it was so long ago now, but he remembered me, and he was coming towards me and this time he wasn't asking. He came towards me with intensity, with intent.

"You didn't knock me out," he slid his hand along his belt, towards his holster. "Is there someone you'd like to call again?"

The anger I thought I had deserted me, replaced by paralyzing panic. My blood instead of burning was frozen in my veins, and I could only watch him come closer.

"We didn't mean to hurt you," I said. Why had he followed me? "I didn't do anything to you."

"Didn't do anything?" A harsh imitation of laughter escaped him. "Knocked me out, left me unconscious." He shook his head closing the gap between us then stopped, just out of Karl's reach.

Karl gripped my arm and stepped in front of me.

I shivered at the tension coursing through him. We were here again so soon, Karl standing between me and very certain danger, but somehow I knew he'd come in time.

"Sneaking off?" The man stopped a few yards from us. His perfect German sent a shiver through me. "No rebuttal? No explanation?" His tone was menacing even if his words seemed innocent.

I leaned against Karl's back, gripping his coat.

"Give me one reason I shouldn't blow the whistle, one reason."

"I always followed orders," Karl's words were soft, but he let go of my arm and shifted towards the man.

"These are your orders?" His voice grew louder. "You disappeared and they thought you were dead. No one imagined this."

"I have my reasons."

"You didn't come back. You know what that means," he was standing so close, he pointed at me, his fingers so close to my face. "It's not just your career you're throwing away. You've been sucked in by her lies."

Karl grabbed him with both hands, his face scary close to the soldiers face. "Keep your hands off her," his voice was dangerous. His grip on the man tight.

I backed against the wall again. Didn't the man have any sense?

Karl exploded, brought his hand hard against his neck. He crumpled and Karl caught him, leaning him against the wall.

Shouting came from a few streets over.

Karl spun around and picked me up.

I sucked in a hard breath. His face was so close. Last time he'd been this close...I held my breath. And that man.

Karl was almost running and in a few minutes we'd left all the buildings of town behind. "It shouldn't be long now."

I couldn't help remembering how he lost his temper and downed the soldier.

Karl slowed down, lines etching themselves around his mouth. "I'm sorry. I shouldn't push you that hard. If we're lucky, we may find where he left his car. His sort tends to leave them out of sight." He set me down.

I breathed against the swirling in my head. I was fine. I wasn't going to puke. I wasn't going to scream; he was protecting me. "Stealing a car?" Food seemed different, because we had to eat.

"We'd be in it if we hadn't gotten away," he kept looking from side to side and watching the road as well. "I think we may be lucky today." A few more steps and he pulled me to the side of the road. He was right. It was a shiny black car. "We have to hurry. He'll be close behind."

Someone shouted.

Karl's eyes jumped to mine. "We can talk about the right and wrong of it later," he held the back door open.

I got in and he slammed the door closed behind me.

Throwing himself in the front seat the engine roared and the tires squealed a minute later. The shouting was close, they'd seen us.

I watched the veins in Karl's neck bulge. He was so tense. Ten minutes later, they were still tense.

"You should leave me," I gripped the blanket on the seat. "Just leave me and you go. It's no use."

"I'm not leaving you."

"They're probably at the police station, whoever they are."

"It doesn't matter," Karl said, his voice clear despite the noise of the car. "This car is full of petrol, and soon we'll be far away."

"We can't always get away."

He shook his head.

"I'm not worth it," I covered my face. I ruined his life. But how? I never meant to. Now he couldn't ever go back.

The car swerved to the side of the road, the jolt knocked me against the back of the seat, and I sucked in breath. The engine shut off.

"Why would you say that?" Karl said, his voice was loud in the silent car. "Look at me."

I shook my head.

"You're worth it."

I opened my eyes.

He was leaning over the back of the seat, his eyes dark so serious. And so very close. "Why can't you believe that?"

"Because I'm not," I blinked back the tears that always tried to make me weak. "Can't you see I only bring you trouble?"

He looked out the window in response to something I missed. Then he looked back at me. "I believe you're worth it. I don't waste my efforts and I never will," he turned back and started the car. He turned the key again and pumped the gas but nothing

The engine didn't roar to life.

After a minute he got out and looked at the engine.

I'd done it again, now the car wasn't working. I shivered and pulled the blanket tight around me. The minutes ticked by in my head. I gave up when I lost count the third time. I curled into a ball, slowly.

The door by my head opened.

"Lena," he sounded so down.

"I know. It's time to walk."

He clenched his teeth but there was nothing else to be done. "We don't have much choice. I'm going to push it off the road first."

"Maybe they won't notice."

"Why it had to quit here, the worst place ever," he was mad but held out his hand and shook his head. "I'm not discussing it."

Was he planning for us to stop soon or was he planning to carry me? "Tell me when you need a break," like he could read my mind, he answered before I could ask.

"I'm alright for awhile." I was doing okay, but how long could I? I was worn out already but having him carry me? For hours? That couldn't happen.

My legs were shaking but I kept moving, one step after another. Breathing was painful. I slowed further and leaned against a tree. "I'm sorry."

Karl sighed. "You just walked for hours."

"Yeah. Amazing," the acid rose in my throat. I needed my head to stop spinning but I couldn't get a deep breath.

"Exactly what I was thinking," he held out the canteen.

I dragged in a breath. My back screamed.

Karl unscrewed it and stepped closer, putting his arm out to steady me. Was it that obvious I was about to fall over?

"I think I'm alright now," I took the water. It went down my throat in a stream of cold. The sweat on my forehead made me shiver.

"Ready for a break?" He asked.

"I'm ok now," I said handing it back.

His eyebrows rose.

"I know we can't stop till we have too."

He didn't push.

"Do you have any siblings?" I asked the first question that came to mind when the silence was too much.

"Yes."

More silence. The soggy leaves underfoot sounded loud.

"Do you?" He asked.

The path was wider here and I hadn't noticed he was walking beside me now. I'd asked first, but what version should I give him?

"I had a sister," I watched the mist creep up between the trees.

"I'm sorry."

He'd heard what I said. "You get used to almost anything. Do you have any sisters?"

"Three."

I looked up. "Three sisters?"

"One older, two younger. When I was little, Elise got me in trouble all the time. "

"Did you ever get her in trouble?"

His shoulders dropped. "Not when we were little."

"I'm sorry," why did I always blunder into something personal?

"I'm not happy with some things I did in the past, but you have nothing to do with that."

I looked away from his intense gaze.

"I also have a brother."

That sounded safe enough. "Younger?"

He smiled. "Older. So naturally I got the blame when we got into any mischief."

"Mischief? You must have been very young," it was hard to believe he'd ever misbehaved.

"No, I was trouble for sure," he was smiling now. "My father had reason to be good with the strap."

I couldn't keep the shudder from coursing through me.

"I deserved it."

I looked over. He was too watchful.

"And I missed more than I got," he was trying to make me smile again but I couldn't.

Whippings.

"Whippings aren't—" he stopped and faced me in the path. "What is it? You couldn't have earned any yourself." He reached out.

I flinched. My heart picked up and I fought for control. "Not often," I managed to say and walked around him. I couldn't keep the memories out.

"You were whipped?"

I thought through different answers. "Yes," I said finally. "Tell me about your brother." I asked before he could ask anything else.

"Why?" He wasn't going to be distracted.

"The usual reason. To get my attention."

"That's not the usual reason. Whippings are punishment for willful rebellion. I have a hard time believing you deserved any."

"Well, I did."

"Why are you lying?" He said.

I kept walking though he'd stopped again. My side hurt and I was out of breath, and I didn't want to talk. Not about this.

"Who are you protecting?"

"Maybe I'm not," I sucked in a breath. "I was clumsy as a child."

"Clumsy," Karl said, it sounded like a curse. "You were whipped for being clumsy?" He stepped in front of me. "Is that what happened?"

I sighed. "It doesn't matter." I was too tired to go around him, so I just stood there.

"You're not afraid of me because of what happened in that jail," he said through gritted teeth. He wasn't asking.

My nails dug into my palms and I backed up.

He kept coming and stretched out his hand.

I flinched before I could stop, but he didn't touch me.

"Who? Your father?" He said.

I took another step back but tripped on a root. I swung my arms out but there was nothing but the air.

Karl caught me but I pulled away. I couldn't stop. I cringed away from him and sank to the ground. Hands still in the dirt I started sobbing. All the memories I'd buried, all the pain dredged up and then hands on me.

Karl cursed. "I shouldn't have reached out. I had no—."

I didn't hear anything else, if he said anything else. Curled in a ball, the chasm inside tore apart. Everything I didn't want to remember. Everything I did.

Gradually the sounds of the forest got louder. But nothing else was there.

I opened my eyes and sat up.

Karl sat nearby, staring at me.

I rubbed my hands together. I had to look frightful. "I think I'm just tired," I waited for some response. "What did you plan to do before I lost it?"

"I didn't, I mean--" He shut his mouth. Was he more mad I dissolved into a weak mess, or for holding us up?

I moved to all fours but getting up seemed too big a hill to climb. "Can you help me up?" I held out my hand.

He stared at it then stood and took it gently. All at once I was standing. He held my arm gingerly.

"Thank you."

He released me and backed up.

"You're going to leave me now?" I didn't believe it and it hurt to say but we couldn't stand here for the rest of the day. It was only midday now.

"No," he said, but he didn't make a move to come closer.

I reached for his arm, I was about to fall. We must have been walking for hours, every bit of me wanted to collapse. "I know you won't hurt me," I forced my head up to meet his eyes. "At least now you know it isn't your fault," I swallowed. "When I flinch."

"Every time, I didn't understand—" he couldn't finish his sentence.

I came the last step towards him, but I was so tired my legs were shaking. "It isn't you, or your fault." My head spun. I gripped his arm tighter and closed my eyes.

"You want me to carry you?" He held my arms as he kept me from falling yet again.

I took a deep breath. "Was that your plan before?" I opened my eyes. "We have to get out of here. And I really can't go on."

He looked at me, his eyes tight, thinking. Deciding. Then his jaw firmed up. He pulled his arm from my grasp and in the same motion picked me up. He was so tense, careful.

I took a deep breath and looked up. "Thank you."

His heartbeat picked up and mine followed.

The path seemed so smooth now, every step rhythmic, and I fought with my eyes. They were burning to close.

"It's ok," he was smiling. I could hear it. "You can sleep if you want."

I shook my head. "I don't want to."

He laughed. "You're awfully stubborn."

"Compared to?" Why would he say that? He was carrying me. I waited for the panic, I waited, but it didn't come. I swallowed hard.

"It's okay. I like stubborn."

Was I just too tired? Why was I able to rest with him? Whatever the reason, I was too tired to walk.

FIFTEEN

*S*omething loud thumped by my head. I froze. Then, there were arms around me. Karl's arms.

"Wait," he whispered close to my ear.

I opened my eyes, it wasn't dark, but it was getting there. The thumping was Karl's heart and he was staring into the forest. What was out there? All I could see was trees and more trees, like we'd seen for what felt like forever.

"Someone was in the path ahead of us," he said turning his head and peering intensely around. "But I don't see them now." He was kneeling on the ground behind a clump of trees.

I was in his arms.

He took a deep breath and looked down at me. "I think we missed them."

I waited for him to let me go but he didn't.

He straightened with me still in his arms.

"I'm awake," and I was ready to walk. Or at least, I was ready to not be in his arms. "I can walk now."

"I'm not tired."

"I've been carried enough. Put me down, please."

He put me down.

I stretched my legs and shivered. I was stiff and suddenly cold.

"Are you sure?" He asked, one hand still around my waist as if afraid to let go. As if once he let go, I wouldn't be here anymore.

"I'm sure," I started walking and his hand slid away. I clenched my fists.

And so we walked.

"How far to the town?" I asked when the silence was too much. "The town we're staying in. I don't think I'm up to hiking through the night." I was trying for funny but stopped smiling when I looked up.

Karl looked uncomfortable. "I'm not certain. Maybe a dozen kilometers."

I wouldn't make it that far. No matter how much I wanted to. And I couldn't let him carry me. "I don't think I can walk that far." Had I really admitted that?

"We're not going there tonight."

"Oh." Could he hear how nervous I was? Did he see my hands clench? A town right now, all the people who didn't mean companionship but individual reporters. But sleeping outside again, with Karl? He'd kept his promise so far. It was hard to remember when he'd gotten me from the bakery. Stern and tall he'd been then, but it seemed impossible that Karl was that man, that same man.

"We have to get away from the path, then we'll make a fire," he nodded through the trees.

I went were he nodded; he was close behind. Soon the dark closed around us and I kept tripping despite being so slow. Each time he caught me before I could fall, and each time I felt the jolt of current his touch always held.

"This is fine," his hand had stayed on my elbow the last few minutes.

My legs almost gave way, I grabbed a tree.

"You should have let me help you."

"You already do so much."

"Sit," he used my elbow to bring me to a stump a step away. Then kneeling under a big tree, Karl cleared the ground of leaves and dead branches.

I pulled my knees up and let my head down to meet them. Light made me look up.

Karl had the fire started and now he was cutting down branches. He was quiet, even for him. He dumped the branches in a pile then dug in his pack and held out a small package. He didn't meet my eyes.

I took it. "Aren't you hungry?"

He turned to work on the fire.

Was something in the woods? I looked everywhere but the woods were quiet. I shivered, was it a cougar? Wolves?

"There's nothing out there right now," he broke his silence.

I looked back towards the fire.

He'd taken a seat closer. Now that he wasn't working, his hands were distracting and imposing. And he was staring at me. "At least, nothing close."

"I have too much imagination."

"Are you going to eat?" He pointed to my lap where the food was, the bag not even opened.

I held it out to him. "No."

He took it, his fingers brushing the side of my hand.

I flinched, then hurried to smile but not fast enough.

His face hardened and he clenched the bag in his hand.

Would he always get mad now? I shouldn't have told him. I shouldn't have. I took a breath and focused on the fire. Anything but him. The fire was mesmerizing, blue streaks among the red. What kind of wood made it blue?

"Where is he?" Karl's whisper came from out of the blue. "Your Father."

"What?" Why was he asking that now?

142

He shook his head. "The town we picked you up from — was that your hometown or just where you worked?"

"I'd been living there for a year or two."

"I mean where does your family live," he stared at the fire, his hands still clenching the food. "Your parents, uncles, relatives, where do you come from?"

What degree of truth did I dare to give him? "The bakery where —"

He flinched.

"It's my uncle's. He took us in when my mother died."

"What happened to your father?"

I took a deep breath. "He left." The silence that followed was overpowering. Did I only think it and not say it aloud?

"What do you mean?" His anger was barely contained. "How could he just leave?"

"He didn't want to stay. He said we were…" the scene played out again, the small kitchen, Tobias screaming, the words Father shouted before he walked out the door that last time. "A new law made it simple."

"But your father?" He struggled to say the word. "How would any law change anything?"

"He's not Jewish."

"What?"

"I'm only half Jewish."

His eyes were dark as he stared at me. Then he stood and walked a few steps away. "Half."

"An outcast of two cultures, not one."

"So you don't know where he is? He beat you, and left you."

"I was younger when he punished me."

He was pacing now, his jaw set his eyes hard. "Your uncle took you in," then he stopped his pacing and stood before me. "You said, took us in."

I swallowed and looked down. I swallowed hard.

He knelt in front of me. "Who's us?

"It doesn't matter," I squeezed my hands tighter but my nails weren't sharp enough. It didn't hurt enough to keep my mind off Tobias.

"Why doesn't it matter?"

I closed my eyes. I needed any barrier I could use. He was too close.

"Alright," he backed away, his shoes snapping the twigs. "I'm going to eat. You should too."

Lying seemed so wrong. "My brother. They took in me and my brother."

"The boy at the station."

"We did it to keep him safe." My insides churned. How could I be telling him this? "It was to protect him." Saying his name, after so long, something snapped. How could I have left him? Every nerve inside ached to have him in my arms, I wrapped my arms around myself and bit my tongue. But pain covered so much of me it didn't make the difference I needed. The dreadful tears crept out the corners of my eyes.

"My little sister was always getting into trouble," Karl held out a hunk of bread. "She'd find a baby she liked and decide she wanted to keep it."

I took the bread.

"Once she had one in her room for most of the day before we realized. Half the town was looking for the lost child and Sophie had it in her room." He took a bite of bread and watched the fire.

I tore off a bite and looked at the fire too. At least we weren't freezing cold and we did have food. Somehow tomorrow would be another day and maybe he'd never ask about Tobias or anyone else again.

Maybe.

I clenched the sheets to my face, dragging in a breath, but my throat was dry, bone dry. What was wrong? Then I felt warmth and my stomach knotted. It wasn't sheets I was gripping.

"Are you awake?" So close. His voice was so close.

I spread my fingers, his heart was pumping hard beneath my hands. I pushed away from him and opened my eyes.

It was still night, and the fire was hot behind me, shining bright in his face.

He lay so still but his eyes were wide. "Are you awake?"

I couldn't mouth the questions.

Karl swallowed hard. "You had a nightmare."

"But you're—"

"You were screaming."

A chill crept up my spine. If I was screaming, he must have heard something. What did he hear?

"You grabbed me and wouldn't let go. I didn't do anything," he spoke louder now, faster. "I swear, I didn't do anything. But you wouldn't stop screaming till you'd grabbed me."

"What else?" I whispered letting my head sink onto the ground.

"That's about it."

But it wasn't. "What else did I do?"

"You hit me a couple times before you calmed down," there were raised red scratch lines tracing down his neck, a few smears of blood on his chin. Those marks weren't there before I fell asleep.

My hands, there was blood on my hands too. But I calmed down for him? "I'm sorry. I'm so sorry. You should have shaken me awake." It was bad enough he'd heard my nightmare. What had I screamed? I shook from the center of my bones. What did he hear?

"I'm not mad at you," he put his hand on the ground between us. A raised red welt, teeth marks.

"I bit you?" I looked up at him. "Why were you hugging me after I did that?" I couldn't believe it. I sat up and backed away.

"I didn't mean for you to see that."

"You didn't want me to know that I'd bitten you? What's wrong with me?" I dropped my head to my knees, sobbing. "What did I say?"

"I couldn't understand much," his voice was too gentle.

I didn't try to stop the tears. It hurt too much. Everything hurt and everyone I touched got hurt.

"I'll get you somewhere safe. Will you give me a chance to try?"

I sank to the ground and curled in a ball. They were after me. After us now. "You should let me go before I make things worse for you. It'll only get worse."

Silence. Maybe he would leave. Would he?

Then he pulled a blanket over me. That was all the answer he gave.

SIXTEEN

Cold bit my forehead, the only skin the air could reach. I moved my shoulders.

Karl was there, behind me. His body against mine, keeping me warm. Keeping me safe, like he'd promised.

I sighed.

He pulled his arm away. "Are you mad?" Then he wasn't behind me and the icy air replaced him.

"No," my voice shook.

He was in front of me now and he took my hands. "Lena."

I shivered.

His hands loosened but he didn't release me. "What happened?"

I looked away from his eyes, his intense stare.

"Are you scared of me?"

"Not much," I sat up. "We should get out of here. Didn't you say they were suspicious at the last town?" I peeled off the blanket.

Karl took the blanket and stood. He didn't say anything. Minutes later we were walking through the misty morning. The day was calm and soon he started talking again.

"So my sisters always got what they wanted and the two of us boys. . .not so much," Karl laughed.

"So now that you're all grown up now? How does that work?" I smiled. "Everyone has to grow up sometime."

His silence made me look up, his face was hard.

I bit my tongue. Why did I always say the wrong thing, even if it was on accident? "Sorry." I kept moving.

The colors of the trees weren't quite so beautiful now.

"No. You don't have to apologize," he sighed. "My older sister, she didn't ever grow up."

I looked at him. "What?"

"She didn't grow up, even when she got pregnant," he paused; his face grew a little red. "Pregnant when she was seventeen — before she was married."

I swallowed the lump in my throat and hoped he wouldn't look over. "Being a mother must have matured her a little. Was it a girl or a boy?"

He kept walking.

"What?"

"I don't know," he said, barely above a whisper.

How could he not know? Did the baby die? They still would have known what it was. "That must have been so hard. Losing her baby…"

"She didn't lose it."

A blackness covered my brain. Did his sister die? "I don't understand."

He faced me, his eyes boring into mine.

If the baby didn't die and she didn't die, why else wouldn't he know? "She gave it away?"

"Is that so terrible?" He said. "She wasn't ready to be a mother."

"Did your parents force her to give it away?" Maybe she felt trapped, with no way to support it.

"Does that change it?" The muscles in his neck tightened.

148

"You never saw the baby?" The pain filling me seeped into my words.

"She wasn't ready to have a child and she didn't want one forced on her." But he looked away.

"You don't believe that."

"What is it?" He stopped in front of me. "Why does it bother you that my sister gave her baby away."

"It doesn't matter what I think," I moved around him and kept walking.

"Is it a secret?" His words were too close to the truth. "Why won't you tell me?"

"What your sister did is none of my business," a branch slapped me in the face.

"But you have an opinion," Karl was right beside me now. "Would you have her keep a child forced on her?"

"It was still her baby."

"Would you want a constant reminder of that?" He couldn't get ahead of me, the path was too narrow. "Wouldn't you want to forget it?"

His ignorance dug into me. I spun around. "Would you forget if you gave away your child? Would you be able to go back to before? You'd be changed either way," I was in his face. "It was her child no matter how she came to be pregnant. Her bone and blood, he grew in her. She was a mother whether she wanted to be one or not."

Karl was staring at me. Just standing there, staring and listening.

I backed up, the forest was silent now. "I didn't mean to shout."

"I'm sorry."

"We shouldn't waste any more time," I pulled back from his outstretched hand, I couldn't stand his touch right now.

"There's only few kilometers to the train station," he said after a long silence.

What did I do? Surely he couldn't think I came up with that by chance.

"I'm sorry I got mad before," Karl said. He was apologizing to me?

"You shouldn't apologize to me," I said, hanging my head. "I get worked up sometimes, but everyone has to make their own decisions."

He pressed his lips together and looked away.

"I always say the wrong thing."

"No, you don't."

"I do. I'm always saying things wrong and I'm quick to make judgments. I'm sorry."

Karl grabbed my arm. I could feel each finger through my coat but it was gentle. "Don't apologize for having an opinion."

The town marker said only a few more kilometers but it was nearly dark. I looked away from his intense stare. "Are we too late?"

"Yes," he said letting go and walking again. "But we can get food before the stores close if we hurry."

I opened my mouth to ask then shut it, he'd say what's to be done next.

"I don't know where we'll stay. Outside might be the only option."

I couldn't see if he looked down at me or not. I was studying the trees to my side.

Who knows what I'd do if we were outside together again. Last night was burned into my brain. The little I remembered. What he hadn't told me, I didn't want to know.

———

The night was closing around us.

I could see the stars again, it'd been far too cloudy before. Seeing them made me feel smaller.

The sameness of everyday, walking and eating and sleeping and walking more. "What—" I stopped when he looked up from the fire.

"What is it?"

"Nothing," if only the fire wasn't bright enough to show my face.

"I'll imagine it's something worse," Karl said. "You know I will."

I sighed and looked away. "I was wondering where we're headed. What you're planning."

"If I've thought about anything at all?" Karl said.

"No."

"It's okay," he said, laughing a little and holding up his hand. "But I do have somewhat of a plan."

"What is it?" I clapped my hand over my mouth but it was too late. "Sorry."

"It's fine," he said standing up. "I keep having to change my mind. But now we're in the part of France that we, I mean," he stammered, "the part Germany doesn't control, it'll be easier to avoid notice."

"Avoid?" I took a deep breath. "You mean stay here?"

"I had thought to get you to Switzerland," he threw something in my lap.

I flinched but picked it up and smelled it. "Thank you." I said biting into the gingerbread. "When—"

"At the last stop. You like to know the why of things don't you?" He sat back down. "Switzerland was close, I thought you'd be safe there," he paused. "But we're so far into France now."

The silence was overpowering. Everything he wasn't saying shouted.

"How long do you think the war will last?"

"I don't know," Karl said, his shoulders drooping for the first time. "We were sure of a quick and victorious end. We conquered so much so fast. How could we lose?" He looked at me. "What if I was right?" He sounded scared. How could he be scared?

"It won't end fast," I shook my head. "It can't."

He pulled a letter from his pocket and sat staring at it, tracing the worn edges. Suddenly he was angry. He clenched it in his fist, closing his eyes. "What if I was wrong?"

Wrong to help me? Or wrong in what he did before? He was the strong one, the one with answers. I stood and walked around the fire towards him.

There was nothing to say, so I reached out and took his hand in both of mine. It was still clenched.

"Don't touch me," he said under his breath, pulling it away.

I staggered back. "I'm sorry. I just thought—"

"It's not you," he opened his eyes. "It's what I've done with this hand. You shouldn't trust me." He wouldn't look at me.

"Karl," I said desperately.

"Don't," he said putting his hand up. Finally he stood, finally he looked at me. His eyes were so dark. "I can't forget it. Any of it."

"You were following orders. What you were raised to do," I came towards him. "You didn't know."

"I was following orders, yes. I was saving our people, maybe," he backed away, talking fast. It wasn't like Karl. He was always calm and controlled. "But when do you use your own conscience? When is it too much?" He stood back, several steps away from me now. "I've tried to keep you safe but I haven't told you why."

I swallowed, the lump in my throat hurt. "No."

He walked towards me. "Do you want to know why?" He was only a few steps away now. "Do you?"

I swallowed. I wasn't scared of him anymore, but he didn't seem like himself tonight. "No."

"You've asked me why, over and over. Why don't you want to know?" He took a deep breath. "Am I scaring you now?"

Habit shook my head, then my face went hot. He was scaring me and I couldn't hide it.

"I am," he backed up, then he stood there, hands on his hips. "If I stop shouting, would that help?"

I took a deep breath and realized my hands were clenched at my sides. Of course he could see I was scared. I nodded, not trusting my voice.

He put another log on the fire and sat. "Now, do you want to know why I'm trying to help you get away?"

"Yes," I sat and kept my eyes on the fire. "I do."

"I'm trying to save you because you saved me."

The wind was sharp. Without the fear, I could feel it again but I looked up. "What?"

"I was sent to bring someone back after they ran from the train."

My toes curled inside my shoes. "I'm really cold."

He got a blanket and threw it around my shoulders, holding it tight for a moment before he backed away, his mouth tense.

"Thank you."

"You were a criminal," he whispered. "Bent on destroying our home. If you got away others would try."

I could hear the anger in his voice, but I'd lived with it for so long, it wasn't new. And he wasn't angry at me.

"When I realized it was you..." his voice was so low. "I got you from the bakery, I saw you on the train."

That didn't explain anything.

"What they said about who you were, what you were, I knew it was a lie. So I had a problem and I struggled longer than I'd like to admit. Whether to do what I'd been told, to follow orders," he took a deep breath. "Or not."

I knew what he'd decided, but it was still difficult to believe. "I didn't save you."

"I saw you arrested," his throat worked at that. "When those soldiers grabbed you, I saw what I'd been. What I was. And that's what decided me," he leaned towards me. "Everything they were doing or would have done," his jaw hardened, "was allowed."

The skin on my scalp tingled. "Are you asking something?"

"No. I'm trying to explain. I'm keeping my promise the best I can," he sighed and shook his head. "But I will keep you safe if I can."

He hadn't said why he decided to help me.

"I suppose you have a question?"

"You still haven't told me why," I turned back to the fire. He shouldn't be looking at me like that. I shouldn't want him to. "Why you threw away everything."

"I was following you. I'd been close for over a day when you got caught and thrown in jail. I knew what would happen if I left you, so I had to decide and live with it the rest of my life."

Someone had been following me.

"I'm sorry," he put his hand over mine on the ground. "I almost decided too late."

I closed my eyes and pushed away the memories from that night. His was hand heavy on mine, linking me to the present, but there were other hands on me too, rough hands. I could hear the voices. I bit my tongue, harder and harder till the back of my head throbbed and I shivered, letting go.

"I shouldn't have brought it up."

"I wanted to know. And you shouldn't feel bad it took time to decide. Few would have done the same."

His hand tight around mine, squeezing tighter and tighter, almost to break it. He stared into the fire, his eyes locked on the flames.

I pulled away but he didn't let me. "Let go."

He didn't notice. Didn't move.

My hand hurt more and more. What was I supposed to do? He couldn't hear me, it seemed. Would he feel something? I fisted my other hand and punched him in the shoulder.

154

He looked up.

"My hand. It hurts."

He wrenched his hands away, his eyes went wide. "I'm sorry. I'm so sorry."

"It was an accident."

"Sometimes I hear them, in my head. People screaming," he whispered. "Especially at night."

"What are you talking about?"

He shook his head, turning away.

I held my breath. He was so caught up inside himself. So tortured. So alone. If I hugged him, would he understand why?

"I'm not trying to atone for what I've done. I can't. But I couldn't live with more people getting hurt when I could have stopped it."

I wrapped my arms around him.

He shuddered but didn't push me off or say a word. Then he shifted under my arms and he was hugging me. "You shouldn't trust me," he whispered but his arms were gentle.

I wanted to pretend it was a hug and nothing more. That he kept me safe and nothing else, but I was only good at lying to others, not to myself.

"Now you know why."

Why would he say that I saved him? Why would he say not to trust him? A shudder snapped through me.

"Sorry," he loosened his hold.

I held on. For the first time in so long and as wrong as it might be, I felt safe. But what of him, his feelings? Was I taking advantage of him? I loosened my grip on his jacket. How did I end up in his lap?

"Don't move," his voice was low and so deep. "Unless you want to."

I had to get space before I ruined everything. I moved away from him, his hand on my back, he could feel my heart racing. Maybe he'd think I was scared.

"We need to find somewhere to stay," Karl put another stick in the fire. "It's too late in the year to be in the woods."

"I'm okay."

"We can't wander for months on end," he pulled his hand away. "And we shouldn't be so alone."

"Yes," I agreed, but I didn't say what part I was agreeing to. The woods were empty. I pulled the blanket closer and the wool scratched my neck. Easy to ignore, but I needed something to focus on.

"Is that ok?"

I looked up. "What?"

"The bakery I took you from," his hands clenched in his lap. "Could you work in one again?"

"Of course," I curled up near the stones around the fire and waited for sleep. Knowing Karl was waiting for me didn't make it easier. "You don't have to wait till I'm asleep."

"Why tell me that tonight?"

He always lay beside me now, once I slept, but after that first time, we never discussed it. Such a thing had never crossed my mind but I'd freeze otherwise. What I'd say if he asked, I couldn't imagine. "Tonight didn't change things for me. Not really."

He didn't move. "I wish I knew some other way to keep you warm."

"Why?"

"I've never done this with my sisters."

"Were they ever chased through the forest in the middle of winter?" Staring at the fire made it hard to think. "Sometimes life doesn't make sense. You can only do your best."

He put another branch in the fire, but didn't get up.

I couldn't keep my teeth from chattering, my feet were freezing, all of me was freezing and tonight I couldn't get to sleep. "Karl, you don't have to if you don't want to," I swallowed. *Just ask.* "Is there someone waiting for you?"

He cleared his throat. "No."

I took a deep breath, the icy air shot down my throat. That was something. "I'm so cold tonight."

He stood up and put several more logs on the fire. He looked at me then, his eyes sharp. "Are you sure?"

I nodded and closed my eyes. Did I ask him to lie down with me?

Karl wrapped his one blanket around me and lay down behind me. After a moment he put his hand on my side and pulled me tight against him. His heart was beating right behind my head.

I took a breath, the blanket he added trapped the air around my face but it shut out the light from the fire. I was so cold I couldn't think about how wrong this must be. About how much I'd regret it tomorrow. About the fact that a month ago I'd have thought this the last thing I'd ever ask a man to do.

"Try to relax."

"I am," but I couldn't feel his warmth and the only thing that kept me from shattering was the tension locking down every muscle. "I'm so cold."

He sat up, the air crashing in and he pulled the blankets off. "Take off your coat."

Something like fear welled up but worse, shivering hit the base of my skull. "What—"

"Trust me," he pulled me up and pulled off my coat as if I were no stronger than a limp two-year-old.

I couldn't move. Was this my fault? Did I bring this on myself?

He pulled me close and piled on the blankets.

My dress was thin and his shirt was thinner and there was nothing else between us. His arm held me tight to his chest. How could he be so hot when I'd had almost all the blankets?

"When I was little my brother and I liked to sleep outside. One time…"

I held my breath.

"Want to hear what happened?"

I needed something, anything to think about. "Yes."

"My sister's only a few years older, but she liked to be in charge. She seemed to like getting me in trouble too, but I probably made that easy."

Warmth surrounded me, seeping into every pore almost against my will. There was so much, I couldn't fight it.

"One night we were outside, and my brother fell asleep right away," he shifted and pulled me tighter.

Warm, he was so warm and his heartbeat steady as a clock. Or it had been, now it was speeding up, something was wrong. "What is it?"

"Nothing. But you were missing my story."

"Sorry," I moved my head so I could listen. "I'll stay awake."

"I won't hold you to it," he said. "Well, I was outside her window, howling and howling."

"What? Howling outside of whose window?" I asked. "I missed something."

"Not much. Elise annoyed me; I was annoying her back."

Branches creaked from every side, but I wasn't cold now and sleep fought to take me.

"I turned and saw Father standing there and I knew I'd get it. Elise was screaming inside, there was no point in trying to deny it. I stood waiting for him to order me to the woodshed," he was breathing fast again.

"It's alright," I whispered. "Tell me."

"He came right up to me," Karl stopped.

"You're dragging this out on purpose."

"Then he got down on his hands and knees and howled along with me," he laughed, shaking us both. "It took me a long minute to believe what I was seeing, then I got down and howled with my father."

"Your father, was howling?"

"Yes. And though I didn't understand, I looked at him differently after that," his arm tightened. "When he punished me, often I could see it from his view. And I didn't get in trouble half as much as before."

The light was fading and so was his voice.

I fought to open my eyes but couldn't. A breath of warmth touched my face and I shivered, but not from cold or fear. Not this time.

SEVENTEEN

"*Y*ou awake?"

It wasn't like him to wake me. "Yes."

He pulled me closer. "Sleep longer if you want."

I pulled away and looked at him. "You woke me up to tell me to sleep longer?"

He propped his arm up, his eyes bright. Something about his mouth, he was excited about something. Maybe I was imagining it.

My heart beat faster, but I couldn't get any air.

"Don't worry," Karl pushed the hair out of his eyes and stared at the dead fire. "I'm not going to do anything," his arms circled around me and he lay back down. "Just because circumstances throw us under the same blanket—"

I pulled the blanket over my face.

"I have some self-control. And I promised you Lena."

My name sounded so different when he said it. I sat up, keeping my face to the fire.

Something snapped in the trees.

Karl was on his feet in seconds, a pistol in hand. He had the pistol in the blankets? He walked around me, searching the woods. "Get the blankets."

I grabbed them. "Where's your pack?" It was here last night. Who was in the woods?

"It's there, behind you."

It was right behind my legs, I yanked it open and shoved the blankets in. "Now what?"

Karl held out his hand. "Give it here," he whispered, staring into the woods. In a fluid motion he flung the pack on his back as he turned in a wide circle, his pistol pointing at the invisible foe with one hand, the other he held out to me.

I shivered but reached for it. Two minutes out of the blankets and my hands were ice.

"Come on," he pulled me behind him into the woods. He hadn't met my eyes once.

Then we heard it. Right behind us, in the space where we'd slept, a branch was dropped to the ground. "Hello?"

I froze but it wasn't a choice. The blood in my veins stopped and my feet turned to lead.

A curse slipped from under Karl's breath.

"I'm not a soldier," the stranger called.

Karl looked at me, he shook his head.

"Do you need help?" The man called again.

Then Karl leaned in, his lips so close to my ear they almost touched. "What do you think?"

How was I to know a good idea from utter disaster? I shook my head. "I don't know."

He pushed me behind a huge tree, his hand on my shoulder. He waited till I looked up. "Stay here unless I call you," he put his pack at my feet and backed away, his eyes on me.

I swallowed and pressed my hands into the bark, gripping it. Why was he staring at me like that?

Then Karl turned away from me and walked towards the stranger.

"Do you need help?" The stranger sounded nervous now, he must have seen Karl.

"Who are you?"

"No one of consequence. I'm just passing through."

"And yet you offer help. Why?"

"If someone's out here in November, chances are they'd need help. But if I'd known it was a Lieutenant I'd—"

A strangled noise cut off his words.

What was happening? I pressed my hand over my mouth, but Karl wasn't in danger, not from one lone stranger. I couldn't see anything. I'd have to move from behind the tree and staying here was the one thing he'd asked.

"How do you know I'm a Lieutenant?" Karl said. "Tell me now. And who are you?"

A cough and a thump. What was going on?

"I—"

"The truth," Karl said. "And I'll know it when I hear it."

———

I dropped to my hands and knees and peeked through a pile of ferns.

Karl had a man pressed up against a tree, his massive hands around his neck. "Talk."

"I was a soldier too."

Karl's hands loosened. He almost looked back at me, he started turning his head but stopped at the last second. "What are you doing now?" Karl let go and backed up.

He was half a head shorter than Karl now, once his feet touched the ground. "I got a job."

Karl moved a few steps away, his back to me the whole time. "How far to the closest town?"

"Two kilometers east, shall I show you?"

"No questions for me?" Karl spread his feet. "Why I'm here

perhaps?"

"A German soldier, alone, in this region? I'd guess you're running from more than forced labor as a hostage and I'd rather not know."

I sank back on my heels and rubbed my hands together, though it did little to warm them. But what did he mean? What zone were we in?

Then the stranger looked straight towards me.

I must have made a sound. Should I duck or freeze? Why didn't I stay where Karl put me? Why couldn't I stay quiet?

He came towards me, but Karl stepped in his way.

"I heard something."

Karl nodded. "My wife."

The guy backed up. He wasn't getting between the Lieutenant and his wife.

So, we were married now.

"Sophie," Karl called. "Come out."

I stood and picked up the pack. Did he really want me to come out? I walked closer and closer to this unknown man and Karl. Breaking through the trees I was behind Karl the whole way, he hadn't seen me at all. I reached out and touched Karl's arm.

"He's going to show us to the closest town," he pulled me forward, drawing me close against his side. Very close.

He smiled. "My name's Louis."

Karl's hand on my side tightened. I looked up and he was smiling too, but he was anything but relaxed.

"Gustav," Karl said with a nod, sliding his gun into a sheath I'd never noticed before. He took the pack from my hand and threw it on his back.

"This way," Louis said and started into the woods.

"I'm sorry," I whispered once he'd put some space between us.

"That's alright," Karl wrapped his arm around me. He

seemed content with the charade he'd started. How long would we be keeping it up?

"Married?" I mouthed up at him when I caught his eye on me.

He grinned, this time it was real. Amused.

I looked away because he was right. It was the only thing he could say. We couldn't live together if we weren't married. I looked up at him, his light hair was getting long, almost in his eyes. He was right, no one would believe us siblings. But what was his plan, to live together—for how long?

"How long have you been hiding?" Karl asked.

Louis stopped and looked back at us. "I'm not hiding."

"What do you call it? Change your name, hiking out in the middle of nowhere, and you're helping us. You don't know who we are."

"You don't think you can trust me?" Louis asked. Why wasn't he mad?

"Should I?" Karl asked. There was a knife in the hand he had behind my back. "You could give me a reason too."

"You'd be hard to convince."

They faced each other, both guys staring at each other, so different from the standoff with Max.

"I'd give him something," to whom I was speaking I couldn't have told myself.

Louis looked at me for a second then cleared his throat. "I know who she is."

All at once I was behind Karl, my head still spinning from the sudden movement.

"It doesn't matter to me," Louis turned and kept walking. "And I won't say anything."

Once again we were walking, Karl's knife no longer hidden at my back. "Who is she? Who are you?"

"There's work in town," the man said. "If you're looking to settle."

The blood rushed to my head, but I sucked in a breath and forced my legs to keep going.

Karl's hand on my waist tensed. "What sort of work? How much is the occupation felt?"

"Little has changed," he said. "For the most part."

A road under our feet stopped the conversation and we walked the rest of the way in silence. Once we hit the town it felt like a spotlight followed us.

I pushed the hair behind my ear, pine needles fell out.

"Breathe," Karl said.

Louis led us down a side street and stopped at an unassuming building that I couldn't decide whether to call a house or a shop. "You can warm up here while you make plans."

I was cold, and tired too though we'd walked less than an hour.

"I share it with a few fellows," Louis closed the door after us. The front room held only a large table crowded with chairs. "There's one room free if you don't mind sharing the kitchen."

My heart stuck in my throat. We were married, I had to remember. What would a married person say or do now? We were going to live together, for how long? But right now it didn't matter, I was ready to drop. I leaned into Karl and gripped his arm he'd kept around me.

"I'm sorry," he pulled out a chair. "Here, Sophie."

I sat where he placed me, hoping Louis wouldn't think it rude.

"I hope you don't mind," Karl said. "It's been a long trek."

"No," he said. "But I must check that Fernand hasn't let the room to someone else in my absence."

"Mind if we wait here?" Karl asked.

"Of course, I won't be long. He works next door." Louis left, and the door swung shut behind him.

I slumped onto the table.

"What's wrong?" Karl whispered.

"I'm tired, that's all," I sat up, sucking in a breath.

He was crouched beside me, his face so close.

I wiped a smear of grease off his cheek. Where did that come from? "You shouldn't worry so much."

The dark of his eyes widened, his breathing picked up.

I pulled my hand back. What possessed me to touch his face? That wasn't something I would have done, that wasn't instinctive, was it?

"Lena."

"Sophie," I whispered, looking around the room. I could feel the eyes on us from every corner, even if there was no one to be seen.

"Don't worry," he pulled a chair over and sat beside me. "I won't misunderstand when you do things like that."

"Are you sure this is the right town?"

"We have to try somewhere."

Wasn't he looking for a place that I'd be safe so he could go back home? "I thought…"

"What?"

I swallowed and looked away. "I didn't know you were staying in France."

"What did you think would happen? I'd leave the second we stopped being chased?"

The door opened, throwing a blast of chill air over us.

I pressed my hands together. They were rough and the edges of a scratch on my hand itched. When did I get that scratch?

Karl stood, dropping his hand to my shoulder.

"My name is Fernand," the newcomer said, measuring Karl in one quick motion then falling back a step. "Louis tells me you're looking for work."

"I am. Is the room available?"

"Unfortunately, we let it to someone yesterday. But I might be able to help with the work."

"I understand," Karl said. "We'll be in town for a few days. If something comes up, I'd appreciate it. There's an inn?"

"Of course," Fernand looked at Louis. "Louis has things he must be getting to, but I can point you in the right direction."

"Thank you."

Louis nodded and left. What was so urgent?

Fernand opened the door. "We don't get many strangers here."

Karl slung his pack on and took my elbow, helping me up. "I see that."

We stepped outside and the cold stung. My feet had started to thaw while we waited inside, now needles bit worse with every step. I held onto Karl's arm and wished for the numbness to return.

The door shut behind us. "Back to main street, take a left. You can't miss it."

"Thank you," Karl said.

We walked up the street past houses like in every other village, with people who were watching like everywhere else. "Are you alright? Am I going too far?" Karl asked once we were away from him.

"No, we have to be convincing," but his hand on my side was all I could think about. I wouldn't admit to him or myself how much I'd gotten used to it. How much I leaned on him when I was close to collapse.

"Just a few minutes more," Karl paused at the door. It opened from the inside and a mountain of a man came out.

He looked from Karl to me, then held open the door, clearing his throat.

The deep sound made me shiver. My heart in my throat I leaned into Karl, as far from the man as I could get.

Karl pulled me close with one arm, nodded to the man and

took the door with the other. "He isn't dangerous," Karl whispered.

I couldn't answer.

A moment later a man hurried up, his face red and round and he nodded while he bowed. "You're very welcome."

I looked around the room, at the boring tables and chairs.

It was clean enough and though light from the windows tried to make it bright, smoke lingered in the corners from the last fifty years.

"We need a room for a few days. Do you have any free?"

"I'll get you a key," the little man hurried off.

"They do have a room, but we have to walk up the stairs to get to it," he had both hands on me now. "Are you ok?"

"My feet hurt," the whine would come out though I tried to hide it. Now we were in a warm room again, I couldn't ignore how bad the thawing hurt. "I'm sorry."

Karl swept me up in his arms, a few people at the tables laughed.

The smell of food making my stomach cramp couldn't distract me enough to calm down. Why was his closeness so frightening now?

His arms were tense, and he held me tight.

I bit my lip and closed my eyes. Could he hear how fast my heart was trying to run away?

Then we were moving through the people talking. The stairs were steep. Karl wouldn't let my head hit the wall, but I held my breath. I couldn't help it.

Listening to Karl's heartbeat was safer then thinking about the swaying as we ascended. It was okay to rest while we went up the stairs, it wouldn't matter if I just lay here. How long was this staircase? How long would it take to get to the room? And what then? We were walking down a long hall now, how big was the inn? More stairs.

I sank into the swaying. Karl wouldn't mind.

EIGHTEEN

*T*he light from the window was overcast, hard to say how late it was in the day, but it wasn't early. Something was wrong.

I sat up and looked around. What was it? I pressed my hands into the bed. It was soft, I was almost sinking into it again.

The window let in light, but the room was dark, only a candle sat on the dresser against the wall. Karl's pack leaned against the bed but he wasn't here.

I stood up and looked around the room. "Karl?" I called then slapped my hand on my mouth. How could I forget? What if someone heard? "Gustav?" I tried but the room was empty. There was no one to answer.

I walked to the door, my shoes must have shrunk. The laces were loose, yet somehow they were far too tight. My feet ached but that didn't matter now. Opening the door I held my breath, almost sure something would be on the other side to jump in and scare me.

There was nothing in the hall save a small mirror on the wall opposite.

I listened and tried to find Karl's voice in the noise below but I couldn't. Would he want me to stay up here? I swallowed, my tongue almost stuck to the roof of my mouth. Where was he?

A light on the stairs ended any thoughts of going down.

I backed into the room, pushed the door to the crack and held it there. I couldn't close it, they were too close. They'd hear the click if they stopped talking

It wouldn't do to trip on Karl's pack now. I looked back then caught my breath. I couldn't see his pack because this room had no candle. I was in the wrong room. I backed away from the door and waited for the inevitable.

But the footsteps and the talking faded out.

Now what? Should I go back to the room? I swallowed and remembered the reason I left the room to begin with. I needed water. If Karl was worried about something he'd have stayed or woken me.

I took a deep breath and walked down the hallway, down the stairs, through another hallway and down more stairs till I stopped at the last step, in the last of the shadows before the light and noise and energy of the suppertime dining room.

"Sophie," Karl called through the noise.

I looked around the room and back again. He wasn't the sort of person that could hide well in a crowd, but I couldn't see him anywhere.

"You're awake," he stood close, how did he get so close? "Did you get some sleep?"

I looked up and let out a breath I didn't know I'd been holding. I felt safer with him, how did that happen? "How long did I sleep?"

"Dinner to supper," he said, leading me to a little table by the back door. "I ate earlier, but I'm hungry again."

My stomach caved at the smells all around.

"I'd have woken you soon," he pulled out a chair. "I'll be right back."

No one seemed to notice us now, they were all eating and talking and going about their business.

Karl brought bowls of soup and sat across from me. He seemed more at ease.

I picked up the spoon, stared at it. "What are we going to do?"

The noise swirled around us, but Karl went still, he knew what I was asking. "We're going to find somewhere to live, for now. And then when things are more stable, you can go whenever you like. I'll even take you back to Karlsruhe."

"Somewhere to live?"

He nodded. "For now."

I swallowed and looked at the soup. A line of cream showed along the edge. Would I be making soup for him?

"I swear, nothing between us will change," he leaned forward and took a roll but left his hand on the table. "It's make believe, to avoid notice."

"I know," I looked up. "Thank you."

He nodded. "There's a bakery an hour south and they need someone right away."

I put a bite in my mouth and held it there.

A bakery needed someone now, at the moment we came along and needed a place. No doubt there'd be a house connected with the bakery, that was of course, vacant.

Karl dug into his food, bite after bite. He downed his bowl in two minutes. "We'll leave tomorrow."

Traveling together was difficult, how would it be living together?

I swallowed the soup and the hard lump in my throat together. It wouldn't be easy, that was all I knew for certain.

———

Weeks had passed since settling in the bakery.

Karl insisted on doing all the carrying and lifting and mixing when he was around and dealing with people, which was the hardest part by far.

I did the planning and shaping and baking of the bread. And I had to admit it was going well. But living with him grew more confusing by the day, it was strange to have someone so worried about me.

I tried to avoid conversations about anything beyond buying more flour and when to be home for supper, conversations that could lead to anything serious. But I didn't always succeed.

"You were in that town?" I stared at the wall. "I think I saw you."

"What?" He stayed in the doorway, but his feet shifted, he wanted to come closer. "When did you see me?"

"In the alley across from the station," I winced at the memory. "But I didn't know it was you, maybe it wasn't. But there were two soldiers, fighting."

"I was still trying to decide, trying to make a decision I could live with. And I was following you until I had."

"You shouldn't have done that for me," I turned to face him. "It's not worth your having him on your conscious, and now it's on mine too. "

"He isn't dead."

"What?" I took a breath. "I saw what happened."

"You saw me, you saw him. But you didn't see me kill him. He's still alive."

I stepped back.

"I knocked him out and tied him up. I could have killed him, should have and believe me it wouldn't be bothering me. But I didn't."

"Why would you say should have?"

He ground his teeth. "Because he's out there. And he knows you're free."

I shook my head. "I'm glad you didn't. It's been in my night-

172

mares, seeing that soldier kill the other. It's nice to know it didn't happen."

"You had nightmares about that?" He came closer.

"Maybe I won't now."

"That's not what your nightmares are about," he came another step closer, his eyes searching mine. "They're not about a soldier being killed."

"Sometimes they are," the blood in my veins turned to ice, but I refused to move my feet. Refusing to put more space between us. After all these weeks, of course he knew something about my nightmares, the question was how much. "I don't always have the same dreams."

"I've been trying to keep you safe," his shoulders straightened and his hands fisted. "But you needed that a whole lot earlier. Didn't you?"

He wasn't asking and I couldn't answer.

I reached for the broom. I had to have something in my hands, something to hold between us. "The flour gets everywhere."

He dropped back but he knew. I was hiding something and I didn't want to talk about it and so he'd pretend he didn't notice. "I'll be gone tonight. Don't forget to lock up."

Lock up. No one had followed us here. Had they? A shot of fear singed nerve. There was no way to know. Though he had to know locking the door wouldn't do any good. "I won't forget."

"Thank you."

The charade of who we really were never slipped when people were around, but now Karl did it in private too. Talking about things as if we were together. As if we were a real couple and he worried, so lock the doors.

"I was wondering."

He looked at me back at me. "Yes?"

The broom handle dug into my hand, I fought to remember what I had to tell him. "Can we not pretend when we're alone?

"What?" His surprise sounded real.

"You and me, when we're alone. Can we not pretend?"

He stared at me.

"I'm trying, but you're so good at pretending," no, that wasn't what I meant. "I mean, it's difficult and when no one else is around. What we are, or aren't..."

"I'm sorry," he put his hands behind his back. "When we're alone, I'll treat you like my little sister. And if I was going away at night, I'd tell her to lock the door."

No matter how unreasonable I was, he found a way to make things alright. How long could this last? "Thank you."

He nodded.

But the words were empty, so I held out my hand. Perhaps he'd see how grateful I was. Perhaps he'd know I didn't take him for granted.

He took my hand in both of his. Then he raised his eyes to mine. *"Liebling."*

A shudder ran through every muscle in my body.

He started and dropped my hand like poison, backing away. "I'm sorry. . .I don't know what happened. . .I'm sorry."

I held my hand over my mouth.

He turned and bashed his shoulder into the wall, but he kept going, shutting the door behind him.

NINETEEN

Curled in bed I lay still and sick to my stomach. The tension was eating me alive.

The back door opened and closed.

I waited for the creaky board outside the bedroom door.

There it was, a creak and then a pause, then Karl tapped the door frame with his boot. He always did that before he came in the bedroom.

It was a small bakery, and this room behind even smaller.

Karl slept in the front room for the first week, giving me the privacy of the bedroom, but after three people came in for bread it was clear that wouldn't work. We couldn't chance people wondering. So Karl took a few blankets and said he was more than comfortable on the floor of the little room.

Not that I had any other idea, but I always felt sick thinking about him on the floor. I listened to him close the door and pull out the mat from under the bed. Was he aware of me the way I was of him? How long were we going to do this? How long could we? "Are we going to talk about it?"

His eyes were on me when I sat up in bed.

"About what?" He stood at the door. "Why you're scaring me half to death when I thought you asleep?"

"Why you're doing this? Why you gave up your family, your future. Everything. To hide here," I swallowed. "With me."

Light from the sliver of moon was enough to see his face set in hard line. "I couldn't let you be taken away."

"Why not?" I shoved the blankets off. "What made me different from everyone else on that train?" The blankets were still in the way, tangled around my legs.

"I just couldn't."

"Why won't you tell me?" I leaned forward, grabbing the footboard. I searched for reasons but came up blank, like every other time.

"I saw something I couldn't ignore," he broke his statue stance at the door and came towards me. "And you deserved to be saved."

"I don't understand," I lost my grip and fell back on the bed, wondering was eating me alive. "You don't know me. And you certainly didn't then. It doesn't make sense."

He put his hand on the bed, so near my foot I could have kicked him.

The moon was too bright, he could probably see the blood flooding my face.

"Who said life makes sense?" And he pulled his blanket off the bed, like every night.

Since stepping inside this house he'd been more than careful, almost never touching me, never coming close except a few times when people were around and even I could see it was needed to keep up our story.

And yet I froze up now, paralyzed by the fear that this time would be different. That this time I did something wrong and he'd surely take something back.

"Would you really want all the answers? Would you really

want to know what's going to happen in a week or a month?" He shook out the blanket and lay down.

I stared at the space he'd filled before he lay down and shivered in the dark. My sweater was thin, it wasn't enough to keep me warm.

What if I never had a chance alone to say something to him.

I crept to the edge of the bed, but couldn't make myself look over. "Karl?"

"Yes."

I peeked over the edge.

His eyes met mine.

"I have to tell you something."

He put his hands behind his head.

"Thank you," I hid my face. "For saving me."

The room was silent.

I listened for one minute, then another. Then I looked over the edge again.

He was waiting. "You're worth it. And you're braver than you think."

"I don't think so."

"You're sleeping in the same room with me. That's pretty brave," he laughed low and serious. "Not everyone would."

I laughed a little, but choked at the end. "That's true."

"But staying awake all night and sleeping five minutes between shifts of bread can't work for long," worry had crept into his voice.

"I sleep," I lay back and waited for sleep to take me. Wished for it. Exhausted though I was, it didn't come. Not to me, and tonight, not to Karl.

He was still awake when the clock chimed.

I sat up in the bed and the cold pounced, in an instant I shivered from head to toes. I grabbed my clothes and tried not to trip on the frozen board floor. Maybe he'd sleep once I left.

A few minutes later I was dressed and shoveling out the oven, quiet as I could.

The dark of the morning was broken by the one candle, though I couldn't see into the oven anyway. The bucket was full of ashes after a few minutes and I was starting to warm up from the effort. I laid the fire, struck a match and held my breath till the kindling took. Still on my knees, still leaning halfway into the oven I held my hands over the little fire.

Then I got the bowl of dough from the storeroom. Karl must be asleep, or he'd have brought it before I could. I gritted my teeth and hefted it on the counter. It was heavy.

The window straight across from the counter couldn't be more perfect if I planned it. Every morning I watched the mist fade as I cut and rounded the loaves, dropping them into the cotton lined baskets. Today I sighed and took the first loaf back out, floured it and put it back in.

Forgetting to flour the baskets, when did that ever happen?

Lack of sleep was not enough excuse to forget that.

"Helena Weismann?"

I stepped back from the counter. "My name is Sophie, I don't know anyone by that name."

The woman stared at me then came closer. "Your uncle sent a message."

I bit my tongue, forcing my mouth not to move, not to give away that I was feeling something inside. "If there's nothing you wanted to buy, I must be getting the bread out," I turned away.

Everyone had an uncle.

"They have Tobias," she whispered.

I couldn't have heard clearer if she'd yelled. It felt like she had.

"They have Tobias," she said again.

The pain that filled my heart was followed by a dreadful numbness that made breathing worse than any pain I'd yet felt. I turned and faced her, was this a trap? "Who does? How did you find me?"

She looked towards the back.

"We're alone," I said. "But who are you?"

She leaned across the counter. "Come tonight and I'll tell you what you need to know," She looked at the loaves sitting on the board. "How much?"

I handed it to her. "Where?"

"Here," she said, backing away.

"Wait. Karl will be here later. He's," heat poured into my cheeks. "He's a friend."

"Jewish?"

"No," I swallowed. "A German soldier. He got me here."

"Behind the church then, after dark," she looked at me hard. "Come alone." The door closed behind her.

I had to be at that church. Think. How could I get away from Karl?

"What's wrong?" Karl said from behind me, standing in the doorway from the storage room. He was always watching, keeping me safe.

I shuddered. I needed it often enough, but now? "I'm tired," I forced my face up then turned away. "After a little sleep tonight I'll be fine."

Then Karl was standing behind me, his hand on the counter a fraction from my side. "You can tell me," he said. "Anything."

I tried to swallow the lump in my throat but I couldn't. And I couldn't tell him. I let my head drop back against him. "Thank you."

His hand circled my waist, holding me against him. "You're awfully warm," he brushed at the hair plastered on my forehead, his fingers so gentle. "Are you sure you're okay?"

My stomach dropped, my heart hammered, and I pushed

away from him and his questions and the safety I felt when he was close. "I've been at the oven is all, I'm fine. I have to get the bread out now."

I grabbed the peel and listened for the big door to slam when he went out. It always slammed even when I held onto it. At least we didn't need a bell.

TWENTY

*D*inner was quiet, but at least he didn't ask about earlier. Maybe he believed what I told him. And I was tired so it wasn't a total lie. I bit my lip, it was a lie, I was lying to Karl.

"Are you sure this isn't too much?" Karl asked.

I looked up from my stew. "What?"

"Running the bakery."

"It's fine."

He stared at me.

I stuck a bite in my mouth, the lump wouldn't let me swallow. I choked and still it wouldn't go down.

He sighed. "We can find another way to do this."

I forced the bite down. "To do what?"

"To hide. I'll find you someplace safe."

I sucked in a breath, the apron strings were suddenly so tight. "I don't understand."

"I want to make this easier, not harder."

"Why change it now?" I pulled the salt shaker closer, then put it back. I stirred the stew, mushing the carrot against the bowl.

"Lena."

I took my bowl and left the table. It hurt when he said my name like that.

If he knew me, all about me, he wouldn't be so kind. He'd be running away.

I was a coward to keep it from him, but I couldn't tell him everything, I couldn't. I did the barest of supper chores then escaped to the room.

Standing by the dresser I took a deep breath, tried to slow my breathing.

A knock at the door.

I jumped. "Come in."

Karl always knocked, always waited for an answer. "I'm going out for a few hours."

"Thank you," I didn't turn around like usual. The door closed and my heart picked up speed. I was lying to him. Lying. But I didn't have a choice.

A minute later the front door closed. He was gone.

The woman said after dark, but how dark? How long would she wait for me? The clock struck eight and I stared out the window. What if she was there now and left before I arrived?

If Karl was anywhere close, he'd hear that door.

I grabbed my coat and snuck out the window. I hurried along, staying in the shadows, but there were so many. Ten people could follow and I'd never know. But the church wasn't far.

A cart rumbled by.

I froze under the eves of the roof overhead. My heart stopped along with my feet, but the church was close, only one more block and I'd be there.

The cart went by and soon the street was quiet again.

I waited a moment then hurried on, through the darkness and the old snow and didn't stop till I was behind the church.

The silent, empty church where people gathered and prayed and looked for peace.

I sat with my back to the wall, watching the darkness and the woods. Watching the stars come out and the snow start to fall.

Was Karl home? Did he know I was missing?

"It's good you made it."

The shriek that followed didn't even sound like me, but it was cut off when a hand was clamped over my mouth.

A man was close. "Tobias." He whispered.

I stopped struggling and the hand came off. "Who are you?"

"You're here to meet a woman who brought a message from your uncle. I work with her and I'm here to help," he backed up. "If you can refrain from waking the entire town."

I couldn't see him well in the darkness, but though he spoke German his accent was French. "She said she had a message from my Uncle."

"Yes, the message is that they've taken Tobias."

"Where? Where have they taken him?" I was here, what more would I lose by asking?

The man stood and looked around. "To a detention camp in the south. Close to Oloron."

"I don't know where that is." The bigger question was why did they take Tobias, and why did these people come to tell me?

"It's near the Pyrenees. Gurs is the town, though it's hardly big enough to mention. "

I stood up. "How far is it?"

"It could be a trap."

"I don't care," and I didn't. Tobias in a camp without me. Anywhere without me was dreadful enough, but alone in a camp? He was just a baby.

"And your soldier?" He asked. "The officials are still at the camp. If he's caught, he'll be shot."

"I know," I whispered. "He can't come."

He stepped closer. "If you leave without telling him — in the middle of the night — he won't know where you went."

I laughed but it caught in my throat. He was standing too

close. My hands were shaking but I fisted them. "Even if I got away, he'd find me."

"Are you sure?" The man asked. "Maybe he'd want to help."

"No. I'll get him to let me go," I took a deep breath. "Is there some way I could get into the camp?"

"Yes. We can drive you there and get you in."

I stepped closer. "I'll do anything."

"What about this soldier?"

I backed up against the wall. "I'll take care of him. When can we go?" Tobias, alone. The ache in my chest burned deeper and deeper."When can we go?"

"Tomorrow night."

"I'll be ready."

He backed into the woods, then turned and hurried away.

I collapsed, the ground rising up to catch me. Sobs coming from deep, so deep inside I pressed my hand over my mouth. I couldn't breathe. All this time I'd been wrong. Tobias wasn't better off without me. What did he think when I never came home? When he was taken from his home and everything he knew?

The quiet of the night surrounded me. I couldn't get caught now, I had to be strong, I had to save him. I drew in a breath, a cold breath of freezing air and walked back to the bakery.

The lights were still off inside, but that didn't mean Karl wasn't back. I pushed the window open and climbed inside. My dress was soaked to my knees, my shoes as well. I pulled off my coat and overskirt and unlaced my shoes. A puddle of water poured out of my shoes when I pulled them off.

The floor outside the room creaked. He was back and I couldn't get in bed now, it was far too loud. There was nothing to do, I was caught.

"What's wrong?" Karl had opened the door without a sound.

I turned to face him, gripping the bed frame to keep my shaking knees from caving in. The energy that helped me run through the streets to get back deserted me now. "I couldn't sleep."

He walked towards me, stopping a few feet away. Until this afternoon he'd been careful about no contact but now I could feel the longing. Or did I wish it to be there?

He sighed and backed up a step. "What's bothering you?"

The man said to tell him about Tobias, but I couldn't tell him and I wouldn't think about why. "I'm worried about them catching us," I turned away from him. "Worried about you."

"Don't worry about me," he said. "We have a good cover here. We'll figure out whatever comes our way." He sounded so confident. So sure.

He said our way, what did that mean? Two months I'd known him and he was still impossible to understand. How could he say that so lightly?

"Can we talk tomorrow?" I clenched the post. "I'm tired now."

"Of course," he pulled the blankets from under the bed and lay down. "Goodnight."

"Goodnight," I went to the corner opposite his and unbuttoned my dress, pulled it off and slid into the cold bed. My feet beyond freezing, curling in a ball helped only a little. I pulled my head inside the covers and held my hands under my arms. I pulled my feet up and tucked them in my slip, but I couldn't stop shaking.

Karl shifted on the floor.

He needed to be free of me, especially where I was going. The camp would be more dangerous for him than for me.

The feather bed was heavy, but it didn't warm me up. I refused to remember when we were out in the woods, waking up with Karl's arms around me, keeping me warm. I wouldn't think about his hand covering my face on frosty mornings, warm all along my back. He'd always been so careful. And now we were in the same house, sleeping in the same room, his head was three steps from my feet but we were never farther apart. I could never think about him, and after tomorrow, I'd never see him again.

"Are you asleep?" Karl whispered from the floor.

"No."

He whispered more now when we were sharing a house than when we slept in the woods or the inns. Now he waited for me to talk.

I waited for him.

"Are you waiting for something?"

I pulled the blankets tight around my neck. "What?" We both waited in the silence. I sighed and gave in. "What do you mean?"

"Seems like you're shivering a long time tonight. Must be my imagination."

I swallowed hard. He could hear me shivering?

The night was half over before I got warm. I stretched out, my toes reaching for the edges, but I couldn't fall asleep. The clock struck four and I climbed out of bed.

Karl didn't look up, but he was awake.

What was he thinking? He must know I lied. But why not come out and ask?

I grabbed my other dress and went to the kitchen to pull it on. Then I tied on my apron, built up the fire and starting blowing on the flame. It was so locked in habit, nothing forced my brain to think.

The shaping went too quickly today, and all the baskets were on the rack before I could decide how explain to Karl why he should let me go with strangers.

I opened the oven and added the bigger logs, the fire was growing strong. Karl always had plenty of dry wood and kindling ready, even the fire laid half the time.

"You're up early," Karl said. "Or is it me that's early today?"

I hadn't even heard him come in. I held onto the door handle. "I'm not sure." I opened the baking oven and wiped out the bricks. It was nearly too hot from the fire below.

"Do you need more wood before I leave?" He poured a glass of milk. "Or anything else? I don't know how long this job will take."

"Will you be back for supper?" I spun to face him then stopped. That was far too concerned for a meal.

"Should I be?" He spread his hands on the counter, ignoring the flour, ignoring the seconds ticking away in my head. He knew it wasn't dinner we were talking about.

The door opened with a clang.

My heart jumped.

Karl flinched.

"I know you can't have got a blessed thing out of the oven yet," Madame Forney hurried up to the counter. "But I'm going to Bridgette's and I thought you might have a few loaves from yesterday."

I tore my eyes from Karl's and turned to face this nosiest of neighbors. "How many loaves?" There were too many rumors that her gossiping wasn't all innocent.

She paused and looked from me to Karl. "I'm so sorry. I'm interrupting," but she made no move to leave. "Is this a bad time?"

Karl always fixed the awkward pauses, but now he stood stiff and silent.

"I was letting him know when to be home for supper."

Karl unfolded at last and as though the frost had melted, he smiled, his face a huge grin. "Of course I'll be home," he put his glass on the sideboard. "Don't work too hard."

Madame Forney was watching us closely, her beady eyes taking in every detail.

I looked at Karl, hoping my face didn't show how torn I felt. One step away. Could he hear how fast my heart was beating?

"Be careful."

"My goodness," Madame Forney said. "Not even a hug goodbye?"

Karl's smile froze. No one ever questioned before.

"There's shy and then there's ridiculous," she said. "You're in your own home. Kiss her goodbye."

I should have hugged him perhaps. That might have been enough. But a kiss was something else completely. And Karl wanted this to be real. Though he'd never said the words, I could feel it. He wanted it. And tonight I was leaving him.

"A minute more won't make me late," she put her coin purse on the counter and rested her elbow on it. "I'm an old lady. A kiss from two newlyweds would be something to think about while I'm taking that long drive."

Karl slid his arm around my back and pulled me to face him.

I couldn't look up to face him. It might have been different before, but now?

"Sophie?" He said his other hand sliding up to my neck.

I opened my eyes and found him looking into mine. "No." I shivered under his warm breath.

"What do we do?" He whispered. He bent closer, his eyes on mine.

I couldn't talk, I couldn't. I closed my eyes. If it was just about me, I could kiss him now. But to kiss him, then leave him when he wanted it so much? How could hurting him more be the right thing?

He was so close I could feel the heat of his face. "Faint," he whispered.

And I did. My legs buckled and I went limp, not a hint of worry if he'd catch me —I knew he would. His arm around my back tightened, he pulled me close.

"Oh, my goodness, what happened?" She asked. "The poor dear, what's wrong?"

Going limp was easy. Listening to Madame Forney and not respond was hard. I heard Karl's heart beating so close, felt his hands on me again. I'd missed this, I caught my breath. How could I have missed this? It didn't make sense, how could I be doing this?

"She's tired," Karl bent and lifted me in his arms. "She's been working too hard."

"Does that happen often?" She asked coming closer, or was he was going closer to her?

"Once or twice now," he said, a bit of humor behind the stress. "She's been working too hard."

And everything he said, apart from the end, was true.

"It scared me the first time," Karl said. "But she'll be alright once she get some rest."

"Oh yes, of course," she said. "Well, I don't want to bother you."

"Your bread?" Karl turned towards the shelf, a half circle and my stomach heaved.

"You see to her and never mind me," she said. "I'll take what I need and leave the money on the counter."

"Thank you. Good day," Karl said, pushing through the back door and into the storeroom. We waited on the other side, listening to her bustle to the shelf, the clatter when she knocked over the only pan.

Karl stood so still.

"I'm okay," I whispered.

His arms tightened. "Lucky for me you're good at fainting."

"Lucky for me you're good at catching me."

Finally, the clank of coins on the table, what was taking her so long? I'd been holding my breath, I let it out and opened my eyes.

He was staring down at me, his throat moved.

189

The pit of my stomach dropped.

The door closed behind that woman, that troublesome woman who'd done this to us. Who'd made this last day worse than I could have imagined.

"I promised," after all the times he'd carried me, his arms were comfortable. "But if you don't want that promise kept, it's up to you. You just have to say it."

I pressed my lips together then stopped. "I just have to say what?"

"Is anything different for you now than when I made it?" He asked. He was looking at my mouth now. "Anything at all? Or is it just me?" He whispered pulling his head away. Distancing himself even while he held me in his arms.

I closed my eyes and found my hand reaching up his neck, sliding through his hair. I wanted to do that so long. *No.* My hand stilled, two parts inside of me tearing apart. I should tell him the truth and let him choose, and I wanted to tell him. I wanted him so much.

"Tell me," he whispered. "What is it? No matter what, it won't change how I feel."

But it would. Maybe I should tell him and then he'd want to let me go. I opened my eyes.

"I promise," his eyes locked onto mine. "It won't change the way I—"

I pulled his head down.

He stopped, his breath caught, his eyes widening. He came closer, his lips so close I could taste his breath.

I closed my eyes and wrapped both hands around his neck. My lips met his and he came alive around me.

His hands held me tighter to him and his breath came fast, as fast as mine.

I pulled away to get a breath.

"I'm so happy," he whispered. He wanted to say he loved me,

somehow I knew that. But he didn't want to scare me. He thought saying that would scare me.

I sank against his chest, under his chin, tears getting away from me. "I know." The worst reply there was. I might love him back, but telling him would only make it worse, because it wasn't enough.

He sat down on the floor, holding me close. Letting me cry, letting me realize what I did. He was so happy, I could feel it.

And I just wanted to die.

TWENTY-ONE

$\mathcal{I}$t was still dark outside and the dough only a little over- proofed.

Karl didn't want to leave. "The work can wait today."

"What were you going to do?" I asked, my mind rebelling against what I was going to do and against what I'd just done and what I was. "Are you going to tell me now?"

"No," he was serious again. "You'll be here when I get back?" He pulled me back into his arms.

We were in the kitchen now and I was trying to get started on the bread. I didn't want to make things worse, if that was possible. "Where else would I be?" I kept my face where he couldn't see it. Earlier I had considered leaving without the painful and confusing goodbye. But he deserved better than for me to simply disappear.

"Just checking," his arms tightened. He kissed the top of my head and disappeared out the back door. Then he came back in, his arm full of wood. "It's cold out there today." But he didn't look cold.

I sliced off a loaf amount of dough and shaped it, my hands

moving without any help, my mind too scattered to care. Badly shaped loaves weren't the end of the world.

Tonight was the end of the world.

Once I finished shaping all the loaves, and setting the last rising basket on the rack, I picked up the bread knife and went to work scraping off the counter. Karl wouldn't leave me till I'd forced him.

Everything was off today. One batch of bread almost burned, the other went in late.

People wouldn't be happy. They liked things on time.

"Why aren't the baguettes out? It's past ten now," the woman always came at ten sharp. Usually there were three different batches of bread cooling by then. Including the baguettes.

"I'm running a little late today, I am sorry."

She stood waiting, her bony elbows cutting the air beside her, her hands on her hips. "What's the trouble?"

"Just a bit behind," I threw open the oven. The sooner I got them out, the sooner she'd go. "If you'll give me a moment, I'll have one out for you."

"No," she snapped. "I'll be back later."

"I am sorry." I turned with the peel in my hand, still full of bread.

But the door was already swinging shut behind her. "Watch out," she yelled. "Lazy oaf."

I looked through the window and she was striding down the street, her steps sharp. A man was going the other way.

I shook the hair out of my face and hurried back to the oven, trying to forget her rudeness. Loaf after loaf I pulled out, loading them on the boards covered with linen. I stretched for the last loaf, but it was too far. It was burning and I couldn't reach it. Why had I shoved it so far?

"Need help?"

I whirled to find a man standing close, on the other side of the counter. "What?"

He pointed to the oven. "Getting that last loaf. I have longer arms."Long arms he might have, but he wasn't very tall. Taller than me, but nothing close to Karl.

"Thank you," I'd never had to have help before. But after this morning, and that dreadful woman, I'd been far too distracted to pay attention. I handed him the peel. "It's very kind of you."

He shoved the peel far into the oven and pulled out the last loaf. Then he handed the peel to me and started for the door.

"Don't you want some bread?"

"I did it to be neighborly," he said. "Not to be repaid."

"Why did you come in then, if not to buy bread?" I sounded mad. "I'm not upset, I just don't understand."

He stood at the door, one hand on the handle. "I was thinking on it, but hadn't decided."

I pulled a long torpedo from the rack, one with a perfect crisp golden crust. "Please take this," I came around the counter. "I was clumsy and shoved that loaf in too far but you saved me from a mess to cleanup, the waste of a loaf, and the dreadful smell of burnt."

He came towards me and took the loaf with both hands. "Then thank you," he said and hurried away.

Kindness was never easy to understand.

Karl had never been anything but kind.

A shiver shot down my spine. I wanted the decision taken out of my hands because try as I might, it was a choice. Either way I was losing something that I couldn't ever get back.

The thought of Karl's eyes filled with pain made me close mine, but that only made it worse.

I pulled the last batch of rising dough out and began kneading in the herbs. Only yesterday I picked them, ignorant that my life was catching up to me. I never could run fast enough.

The dough stuck to the bowl, with both hands I pulled it out and dropped it on the counter, sending flour flying everywhere, including all over me.

Customer after customer came, so many and it seemed so much earlier than usual. As if they knew I was behind today.

"Hello," one woman said, her smile the slightest bit wooden. That was all the German she knew, but I could say the few sentences needed to ask which loaf she wanted and tell her how much it cost. Today she was distracted, her eyes looking at everything but me.

She bought her bread and paid but today didn't leave...no doubt Madame Forney had spread a word or two about us before she left.

It was almost funny, most times I'd be amused by all the gossip. Karl and I had roused suspicions and now they were curious. Was it because we never kissed or hugged? Some people were shy, couldn't that be answer enough?

I looked up when the door opened. This time it was a girl not ten years old. "Mama wants two rye batards."

I only made the batards in rye, but no one seemed to realize that yet. I pulled down two plump loaves. "Do these look alright to you?"

"Yes," she nodded and held out her basket. "Where's your man?"

"He's out right now," was that all anyone cared about? "Is there anything else you wanted?"

"No," she shook her head and left, the room finally empty.

I groaned when I saw the next customer, but I left the rolls and wiped my hands off. "What can I get for you today?"

"Are you alright?" Madame Durand asked. "I can come back later."

"I'm fine, thank you," I said. "Everything is out but the rolls."

"Rolls," she said, "That's what I wanted." She always looked at three loaves before finding one that would do. And she never got rolls.

"I'm sorry."

"I'll have to come back," she turned to go. "When will they be out?"

"An hour I should think," I smiled but stayed at the counter, she'd have at least one more question.

"It's no hurry, I can get them tomorrow," she said. "Take a break soon, alright?"

I shivered at her train of thought. Why wouldn't she just leave? "Is there anything else?"

"No," Madame Durand said then came back to the counter and stretched out her little hand. "But if you need anything from me, or help, let me know. You're working so hard and you're so young..."

I held my breath. If anyone was going to come out and say it, it would be now.

"And in your condition."

Her assumption was obvious, but to hear it out loud, now I was close to fainting for real. "Thank you, I really am fine."

She nodded, though she didn't believe me. She still thought I was pregnant. Madame Forney probably told her first. "I'll be going."

I'd fainted, I looked tired. What else could it be?

"I'm not pregnant," I said before she could get out the door. "If that's what you were thinking."

She spun faster than I'd thought possible.

"But I appreciate your kindness. If I were, I know how much I'd need someone like you," though it was embarrassing that everyone thought I was with child, she was trying to be kind. I could see that.

"I wasn't sure. But you're new in town and we are close." Close? I delivered a loaf to her house, one time.

It was a kind thought, I could thank her for that. "Thank you."

She left quietly and I stood there.

Pregnant.

That's what everyone in town thought was wrong with me now. Clutching the counter, I waited to get myself back together. I had my work to do and it didn't matter what they thought. It didn't matter.

A shadow passed by the window.

I looked up, but whoever had walked by was gone. No surprise there. Why was I so jumpy? I hurried back to the counter and grabbed the dough knife, then went back to cutting rolls.

There was no reason to wonder why today had been so horrible. This morning I gave Karl the most positive encouragement possible and tonight I had to leave him. I had to make him let me leave.

I shoved the rolls in the oven, looking over my shoulder every moment, dreading when Karl appeared behind me yet still hoping for it. I had to get supper but I was tired, I was so tired.

The smell of crisp bread brought me around and after glancing at the clock I grabbed the peel. Opening the door I sighed, at least they weren't burned.

Would he be relieved? He liked me, I couldn't deny. But how much of that was because he felt responsible? "No," I said aloud and the emptiness struck me. Without Karl, this room and the entire bakery was empty.

Food. I had to buy something for supper. The little mirror by the back door said only too well what a dreadful mess my hair was. I worked at it, tucking strands into the knot at my neck. I was such a mess, it was better for his sake that I left. I found my coat and went out the door. If I were pregnant I'd be tired, right?

"It's nice seeing you," the butcher said, looking at my stomach. "It's been awhile."

I forced my hands to stay still, not to move to hide my stomach. "The bakery keeps me busy."

"Of course, I see your husband, he's a good man."

I knew that better than anyone. At least, anyone in town. "Yes, he is," I swallowed hard. "But I do have to hurry, I left the counter untended."

A few minutes more to get the meat, then I hurried back into the chill wind, the afternoon shadows already growing long.

I slipped in the back door. No matter when I left the bakery, someone was waiting when I returned. But today the front room sounded full. How many people were out there? I sighed and grabbed my apron, hurrying to the front room.

"I'm sorry I kept you waiting."

I helped person after person but only one left, the rest kept chatting while I helped the next. The wind blowing outside made me shiver. Was Tobias cold? How could I wait till tonight to go after him?

"How are you settling in?" One lady finally asked. She came in regularly, but I'd yet to learn her name.

I wiped the flour off my sleeves. "It's a lot to keep up with, I'm still getting used to it all."

"Of course," she stepped back, her basket on her arm.

Now she'd be wondering how to ask if I was pregnant, or how to mention the local midwife for no apparent reason.

"Have a good day," I said, taking up the scraper and leaning into the dried dough I left on the counter earlier. If I looked busy, perhaps they wouldn't have the guts to keep trying to ask more questions. When I finally looked up, the room was empty. It worked.

I grabbed the meat from the sideboard and set it on the little table where Karl and I ate and pretend to be married. Where we pretended to like each other. Where this morning I kissed him and tonight I'd leave him.

Pulling the pot from the cupboard, I kept looking at Karl's chair. It was almost like he was sitting there, waiting for me to say I loved him back, waiting for us to be a couple for real, waiting for me to kiss him again. But I couldn't lie to him. I had to be fair to him.

I slammed the onion down. Hadn't I lied to him already? I was in a relationship, as complicated as it was. As confusing as it was. We knew each other, to some extent, and I trusted him. At least, I trusted that he wouldn't do anything to me. But did I really trust him if I couldn't tell him the truth?

I unwrapped the meat and put it in the pot, sliced and added the onion and some carrots like always, then put the lid on and shoved it in the bread oven where it was still hot. There was no sense starting another fire in the cook stove.

"Are you ready?"

The whisper made me jump, I nearly grabbed the oven door, but it was the woman who came yesterday.

"What's wrong?" I grabbed her arms. "Is it Tobias?"

"No," she said. "You said you'd be ready tonight."

The man stood a few feet behind her. "Is there a problem?"

"No. Of course not," I found the words hard to get out. "I thought you meant after supper. I haven't had a chance to tell Karl."

"I thought you weren't going to tell the soldier," the woman asked.

"I'm not telling him why I'm leaving, just that I am." He deserved that much at least. I didn't even know their names. Was it a trap? But I didn't have a choice.

"We'll be back later," he said. "Be ready."

I watched them go, their quiet steps such a contrast to the chaos they brought.

A draft of cold air hit me from behind. I closed my eyes, I didn't want to see him yet. I wasn't ready.

"Who were they?" Karl asked. "Friends?"

I wasn't ready for that question or for any question at all. "Is it supper time already? I didn't expect you for a while."

"Is there a problem?" His voice shifted as he circled me. Careful now with his questions, he didn't ask why my eyes were closed.

"No," I dropped my head. Even with my eyes closed I felt exposed. He could see too much in me. "I wasn't expecting..." I had to give him something else to think about, anything else to think about. "Everyone thinks I'm pregnant." I opened my eyes.

Karl was leaning back against the wall, his arms crossed.

After this morning I'd have thought he'd stand closer. "When I went out to the butcher shop, and everyone who came in to buy bread—" I felt my face grow hot. "Everyone thinks we're ..."

"I know," he said. "I was congratulated."

"You were?" I found my hand was at my throat before I could register how cold it was. It was cowardly but I couldn't tell him yet. "The butcher was eyeing my middle. I don't think one faint is reason enough to suspect anything."

Karl pushed away from the wall. "We could fix that, if it's problem." He was smiling but his eyes were serious.

I stepped back, my head shaking hard so hard I couldn't see him.

"I've been thinking," Karl said. "We could take a drive, go for half a day and find a preacher to marry us."

My hand on my throat was closing, clenching.

"Take your hand down, I'm talking, that's all."

I pulled my hand away, staring at it I swallowed past the soreness. I'd been holding on so tight.

"It's just an idea, we're safe here, we could get married," he flung his hand around the room. "And if we get tired of this town," he leaned down, his lips right by my ear, "we can pack up and disappear in the middle of the night. If we're together, that's what matters. Right?"

I swallowed, hard. The lump hurt and made the back of my head ache.

I had to tell him now. "Can we talk?"

He stepped back and dropped his hands to his sides before I could blink. "Talk."

I grabbed my coat. "I mean outside."

"Why outside?" He asked but he wasn't arguing. He just followed me out the back door, into the woods. A few yards in Karl caught up, slid his arm around my waist and pulled me to face him. "Whatever's bothering you..." his hand rested on my back, tipping me back till I had to look up at him, straight into his eyes. "Whatever it is, we can face it together."

I bit my tongue hard, so hard, but it wasn't enough. The pain behind my eyes demanded release, but I couldn't, I wouldn't cry in his arms.

"I want to help, no matter what it is."

I closed my eyes.

"Lena, tell me. It's killing me that you don't trust me."

"I do trust you," I said. "Don't you know that? Can't you tell?"

"Then why won't you tell me what happened last night. Why you're sleeping less than the little you normally do, and most of all, who those people are?"

"I can't do this anymore," I tried to sound strong despite his arms around me, holding me up. Holding me in one piece if only for one more minute.

"Is it about this morning?" He asked. "I'm sorry. I didn't mean to let that happen."

Gone was the fear of him. How did that happen? I'd have thought it impossible, now my goal was not to hurt him more, but that was inevitable. "This morning was me, it's not your fault."

He stood still, the wind was blowing around us but there wasn't any rain.

I thought if I was cold and had a coat on, it'd be easier to talk. I wouldn't be thinking about kissing him again, but I was wrong.

Dead wrong.

"This is killing me," he pulled me close again, running his fingers through my hair. "Lena, I—"

I pulled away and turned my back to him. "I'm mad at myself for this morning, not you."

He came around me again, and kneeling in front of me he took my face in both of his big hands, hands that had saved me so many times. "Kiss me," his hands were gentle but his eyes were pleading so hard it hurt. "Please."

"I have to say something," I said, fighting everything in me not to bend my head the few inches to his face. "You'd rather hear this first."

"If it's only for my sake that you want to wait, I don't care what you say after," he begged. "I promise. Just kiss me first."

"You'll hate me, Karl. You don't want me to kiss you right now," I was desperate for him to stop staring at me like that. To stop begging me, his hands trembling against my skin.

"I won't," he whispered, standing up, his hands on my face the whole time. "I promise."

He promised.

I couldn't keep fighting with myself, with him. With everything. My chest was tearing in two and he was begging me to kiss him before I left him. I tipped my head back and watched his eyes light up. Reaching up around his neck I swallowed hard. I was shaking so, would I even be able to kiss him?

"Don't cry," he said, and he stopped letting me pull his head down.

I was crying?

"Never mind," he pulled my hands away from his neck. "Don't cry. I won't ask again."

"I didn't know I was crying," maybe a kiss didn't mean the same thing to him that it meant to me.

He stilled, watching me, his eyes worried now instead of excited. He was worried about me. "I'm sorry I asked, never mind, tell me what you want to tell me. But only when you're ready."

I wiped my cheeks with the back of my hand and took a deep breath. If he wanted a kiss, he deserved a good one. I leaned into him and dug my hands into his hair.

He closed his eyes and his arms were close around me again.

I pulled his head down till his lips were a touch from mine and let out a breath.

His arms tightened, tighter than I thought possible, and he shook from his core.

I pressed my lips to his, letting my mind run wild. I pulled him tighter to me, my hands grabbing his hair tighter as he kissed me back. He kissed me so hard I couldn't breathe.

Then I was on my feet, a few steps from him. The cold hit me where a moment before he'd been so very warm.

He stared at me, his eyes wild. His hands clenching, dragging in ragged breaths. "Tell me now," he backed up another step. "What is it you think will change everything. That you've been trying to tell me since yesterday."

Breathing in and out I blinked, trying to lose the tears still lingering. *Tell him the truth.*

"Just say it," he said. "It can't be worse than what I'm imagining."

"I'm leaving."

He spun around, his back to me. Next would be the anger. Confusion.

Something. Anything. "Why?" He asked, so quiet it was hard to hear.

I shook my head.

"Lena," he turned to face me.

I shook my head and backed from the look in his eyes.

"Lena, I'm—"

"No," it came out loud. "Don't say it."

"You don't know what I'm trying to tell you."

"It can't be good. I can't hear it."

He kept coming till my back slammed into a tree. He was still too close, he was getting closer and closer. He stopped in front of me.

"I love you, Lena," he said, never taking his eyes off me.

I felt my mouth drop.

He took the last step towards me, reaching out a hand.

I closed my eyes. This couldn't be happening. It seemed that kiss did mean something to him. Of course it did.

His hand didn't reach me. He was close, I could feel the energy snapping between us but he wasn't touching me.

I opened my eyes, dragging in a breath. "I didn't want to know."

"Don't be upset," he touched my chin, gently, with one finger.

I turned my head away. "Karl," I felt his heart jump when I said that. Swallowing I tried not to imagine what I'd see if I looked up. "I can't do this."

"Can't do what?" He wasn't sad or upset, he still didn't understand.

"This. Us," I took a breath and I didn't say his name this time. It hurt too much. "I'm sorry, you have to let me go."

"Why?" he said turning my face towards his. "Why are you sorry? Why do I have to let you go? I love you."

"No."

He dropped his hand to my shoulder, his grasp was tight. "You love me."

I shook my head.

"You do. I know you do."

I ducked under his arm.

"Tell me why, why do I have to let you go?" His huge hand held my wrist, touching me but not keeping me.

I pulled out of his grasp and walked away. I had to go. I had to leave now.

"Lena. Please," the torture in his voice was killing me.

I stopped. "You have to let me go. You don't want to know who I am. What I've done."

"You haven't done anything."

I couldn't say it. I couldn't tell him. I ran into the bakery and jumped when I saw the man from earlier standing in the center of the room.

"Now. We should leave now," I said, grabbing the bag I packed earlier.

We climbed in the car outside and it flew down the road.

"Are you sure you want to do this?" He asked.

I choked, but nodded. "I have to save Tobias."

"Are you sure about the soldier?" The woman turned from the front seat. "You could ask him."

"He won't want me if he finds out about Tobias," I said hugging my knees to my chest. "I don't want to talk about it." I couldn't talk about it. To leave Karl I'd torn out a piece of my heart and I'd never get it back, he'd always have it. But I had to save Tobias.

The road weaved around a bend and I imagined when he found I'd already left. The moon came out while I tried to decide what he'd do next. I fell asleep imagining I'd said "yes" instead of "no" and that his arms were around me now instead of gone forever.

TWENTY-TWO

$\mathcal{I}$ sat up, the car had stopped beside the road. "Why are we stopped?"

"We're here," the still nameless woman said.

"I slept the whole drive?"

"You needed sleep," the man said, turning in the front seat. "It might be awhile before you can rest again."

I shivered at this but nodded. "How long till we get there?"

The woman looked at him and he looked at her.

"What is it?" I looked out of every window in the car and there was nothing to see but the road.

Though that meant very little. Someone could be hiding behind the stone wall a few steps away or behind any of the trees.

"Our task was to bring you," he put his hands back on the wheel. "But that's all. We live too close to get involved, we might be recognized."

I took a deep breath. "No. I remember now, you explained it last night. How far do I need to walk?"

"We're less than a kilometer from town. We brought you as close as we could."

"Thank you," I got out and the woman got out too. "I'm grateful for your help."

"Save him. That is thanks enough," she gripped my hand for a moment then got back in the car.

I backed away and they were gone in an instant.

I took a deep breath. I could do this. The story was clear in my mind. The latest story. Soon I crossed the wide bridge over the river, right into town. Finding the right people shouldn't be too hard, convincing them to let me help, that might be the difficult part.

The truck was so slow, I wanted to get out and run. How far was it?

"Not long now. A few minutes and we'll be there," said Beatrice, the woman who seemed to be in charge. And she'd found me a place to stay with a few other volunteers. "It's good of you to come. These people need all the help we can give them. And the children…" she shook her head. "We have to get them out."

One woman across the bench was watching me, her thick brows knotted as she stared.

I crossed my arms over my stomach and looked out the other window. I had to keep my feelings inside.

There it was, the camp. Barbed wire fencing stretched as far up the road as you could see, and the guards at the gate watched everything.

"Don't worry. We're allowed to come in," she whispered.

"The guards are French?" I left Karl so he wouldn't get caught. "I thought it was a German camp."

"French, yes, though there were some German officers here for a time."

It was so big. We were inside the gates now yes, but there was barbed wire everywhere. And so many cabins.

"There's so many people." How would I ever find Tobias?

Beatrice put her hand on my arm. "Don't think about what you can't do, think about what you can," she pressed a bag into my hands. "Find the children. Give one roll to each."

The children. She wanted me to find the children.

One of the other volunteers took her arm. "She can't handle this. Look at her."

They both looked at me.

"No. I'm fine," I straightened my shoulders. "I want to help."

Beatrice looked at me, her eyes softened. "Hurry then, we can't stay long. It's only been a few weeks since they allowed us inside, I don't want them to change their minds."

I followed the others down the main path through the camp. Barbed wire separated the blocks on both sides, each filled with too many cabins to count. I picked one and the guard let me through the gate.

"Are there children in any of the cabins?" I asked.

He pointed straight ahead. "*La cabine des enfants.*"

A cabin for children? I couldn't stop to think about why. "Thank you." The instant I left the main path the mud pulled me in past my ankles. Was Tobias in the children's cabin? Was he even here?

I went to the cabin he'd pointed to and knocked.

A woman opened it.

"I'm with the…" I wanted to cry just looking at them. How many children were in this hut, with the wind whistling between the boards it was almost as cold as outside. I couldn't say how many children there were. Finally one little girl came up to me.

"Hello," I said and handed her a roll. In an instant I was swarmed.

"Careful now," the woman said. "Josef, only one."

I handed each child the small roll, if only I could do more. "I'll come back if I can," I said towards the woman then knelt down, searching again in the littlest faces. If I didn't have a reason to be strong there was no way I could come back.

The woman nodded. "Thank you for coming."

I nodded and left, was there a kind woman taking care of my little boy? I went to the next hut. Or whatever you call these buildings unsuitable even for summer in this rainy place, never mind the freezing winter.

Beatrice said it rained more days than now and the mud was proof of her words.

A flap of tarpaper whipped against my legs and a girl ran towards it.

She stopped when she saw me.

"Here," I held it out.

She came forward, step by step. "And I brought you some bread," I gave her a roll, so glad I still had some. "Do you know where any little boys are?"

She took it, hesitant at first. "In there," she pointed to the children's barracks behind me.

"Yes. I've been there," I smiled. "Can you tell me, are there any other children?"

She backed up. "Most huts have some." Then she ran off.

I looked around. Most? I stepped along the walk and made my way to the next one.

"I'm with the Swiss aid unit," I explained to the first man I saw. "I'm giving bread to the children."

He didn't say anything.

I stepped up inside.

He sat there, staring at me, then let out a sigh and looked away.

"You might try the next hut over, I think there's a boy. Lots of energy somehow, he's a loud one."

I swiveled around to see the voice.

The woman was so thin, so very thin, but her face was kind.

"Thank you," I said and backed out.

"Thank you for coming," she whispered.

I wanted to look back but the tears in my eyes didn't let me see anything. And I had to hurry. The time was passing. Flying by.

At the next hut I stopped before coming in. "I'm looking for a little boy," I said.

"There's three who stay here," a woman came to the doorway and peered down at me. "But they're out right now. Why?"

"I'm here with the Swiss aid unit. I'm trying to give all the children some bread," I opened the bag. Would Tobias get any? Could I even find him?

I handed her three rolls. "Here, I can't wait. Do you know where any other boys are, I mean, where other children are?" I backed up a step, careful to keep on the board swimming in the lake of mud. A person could drown in that.

"Most cabins have at least a few children," she stepped closer and looked around before leaning in close. "Who are you looking for?"

I swallowed and looked around. "Just children to help."

I hurried to the next cabin and gave bread to two little girls, thin and pale but their faces were washed. Their clothes were somewhat clean though how their mother managed it, I couldn't begin to imagine.

"Thank you," she said as I walked out the door. She looked fragile. Was their father here too?

Stepping closer I slipped a small piece of bread into her hand. "I'm sorry I can't do anything," I said, blinking back tears.

She reached out and hugged me. "You are. You've shown us we aren't forgotten."

I swallowed and backed up. This was likely the camp I was heading towards all those weeks ago, I was supposed to be here too.

"God bless you," she said.

I couldn't look back. How many cabins were there? I was

still in the first block. But there were no children in the next cabin, or the next.

The next cabin wasn't as full but the women were more withdrawn. No one looked up when I came in. "Excuse me. I'm with the Swiss aid unit. Are there any children in this hut?"

One old woman finally looked up. "Antonio," she called still looking at me. A little fellow came out from behind some people. He was covered in mud, mostly dry, but the expression on his face hurt me the most.

I knelt down and held out the bread to him.

He took it in his hand.

"The mud is everywhere," the woman said. "And he can't always stay inside all the day. We have been here some time." Her French was broken, her dark hair half gray.

His hair was almost black, and his skin was dark. But his eyes, when I looked into his dark eyes, I wished so much that they were gray, that there was a little scar on his chin and the smile I saw in my dreams. Where was my little boy?

I tried to smile. "Hello, Antonio."

He just stared at me, clutching the roll in his hand.

I reached out and pulled him close, mud and all, holding him tight for the smallest moment before I let him go. "Be good for your granny," I said standing up again.

He took a bite of the bread.

She came closer. "Thank you."

I shook my head. "I'm sorry I can't do anything," I hurried out and my boot caught on the door frame, throwing me to the ground. I sank to my elbows in the freezing mud.

Strong hands pulled me up and I stood, gasping.

The woman was familiar. "I have some water you can use," she kept her arm around my waist, and we walked to a cabin nearby. "Who are you trying to find?"

The chill that filled me had nothing to do with the mud.

"I might be able to help you," she whispered, pouring a small stream of water over my hands.

"I'm just here to help," I said. "Thank you for pulling me out."

"Is it a boy? Your brother perhaps?" She leaned closer. "Your son?"

The blood was loud in my ears and my heart beat too fast. I looked away. "No. But thank you for the water."

I hurried away and made my way down the path and back to the truck.

The others were still walking up, several covered in mud like me. Climbing into the truck it was clear to see who'd been here before and who'd just experienced it for the first time.

"So dear," an arm around my shoulder. "Are you alright?"

I focused on the weave of my skirt. "How do you mean?" I asked carefully.

She squeezed tighter. "Try to remember we're making a difference," she sighed a little. "However small it is."

"Yes, ma'am," I said then sat in silence as the truck's loud engine started.

We went through the gate and drove down the road.

I hadn't found him, and I didn't want to think about what I had seen.

And if I did find him? A deadness settled over me. How could get him out? The guards searched the truck when we came in and out, and there was a careful head count.

The guards had checked the truck, but a small child could be hidden. The question was the others with me, what would they do? I looked up, most of them were staring at me now. "Is something wrong?"

They looked away, the silence now almost worse than the staring.

I pulled my coat tight and kept my face towards the window. My telltale face.

At least Karl wasn't here to read it now. He'd know how scared I was and never let me go back.

TWENTY-THREE

*T*hese huts were their homes, I couldn't walk in uninvited. And they had enough trouble keeping the mud out without me bringing in more.

Five days now I'd been coming and while I'd seen hundreds of people and so many children, I'd yet to set foot in half the blocks, each of which held numerous huts.

"I'm giving bread to the children. I'm here with the Swiss aid unit," the words spilled out while I looked around. I knew what to expect now but it didn't get easier. Each time I knew it could be Tobias, and that thought made each freezing, windblown hut a new picture of misery.

This must be one of the men's blocks. The last three cabins were filled with men and only men.

"There's only one little fellow here," a man said. "But he's asleep." He got up and came over to me. "I promise I'll give it to him when he wakes."

"Is his mother here?" I spotted a lump on the bed and my heart sped to a dangerous beat.

"No."

But somehow I wasn't surprised, something told me to push further, to ask more.

"He came without any family, so I've been looking after him."

I handed the bread to the man, then for some reason the latch on my bag demanded all my attention. "Could I ask his name?"

"Tobias."

I bit my tongue. There were plenty of other children named Tobias, it was a common enough name. But something told me it was him, it had to be. I wanted to push past the man, run across the room with ceilings too high and blankets too few and clasp Tobias to me.

"Is something wrong, miss?"

I looked up to find the man staring, his eyes serious. "I'm sorry I can't do more," I pulled my hand off the door frame and turned away.

Staying on the plank took all my concentration till someone stepped on it behind me.

"Can you mail this for me?" The man held out a letter with a coin. "My friend doesn't know where I am."

I took the letter but not the coin. "I'll take care of it."

"I can't let you do that."

"Yes, you can. There's so little I can do. Let me do this for you," I couldn't help but look behind him to the hut where Tobias lay sleeping. "You're so kind, taking care of that child."

He looked at me and the lines around his eyes deepened. "Do you want to see him?"

I backed up. "I have to go." If I didn't leave now, if I stopped to think about leaving Tobias for one second more, I wouldn't be able to, I had to have a plan before he saw me. What would he do, seeing me and then having me leave again?

I got in the truck and closed my eyes. All I could see was Tobias on the bed. So small, so alone. Was it him? I knew it was. As much as I wanted to wish it away, it was true.

And I'd left him in that hut, next to starving, inside the barbed-wire fence.

———

It was two days later that I stepped inside that hut again and stopped in the doorway. "Tobias."

His little head swung around and he searched the room, his chin puckering like it always did when he was confused.

I walked further in. "Toby."

He saw me and his eyes grew wide.

My heart lurched, he did recognize me.

He jumped up and ran towards me, closing the distance so fast.

I fell to my knees and he jumped into my arms. I pulled him to me, his head tight against my neck. I breathed him in and sobbed. He was here, he was ok, he remembered me.

"Where did you go?" He was still in my arms, but he pulled back to see my face. "I waited, but you didn't come." He brushed at the tears running down my face.

"I didn't want to go. I was trying to keep you safe," I held my breath. I couldn't scare him after being gone for months.

"You need to get out of here."

I jumped at the voice and held Tobias tighter. Then I looked up.

It was the man from before, the one who told me Tobias was here.

"Is someone coming?"

"No. But you'll be noticed in this block," he came over and patted Tobias on the shoulder, though he was still in my arms. "And the truck you came in won't stay forever."

"I know saying it isn't enough," I sucked in a breath. "But thank you."

"Just get him out," he let go and backed up. "Get him safe."

I followed him to the door. Could it really be this simple?

The man stopped at the doorway and spun around. "Get in the back corner, quick. And cover up with the blanket."

"This way," Tobias pulled me down beside the bed. "Shhh."

The bed was only a straw filled sack, but I lay beside it. Now I couldn't see a thing.

Tobias curled up in my arms, he stayed so still. When did he learn to be so quiet?

I pulled him closer.

His fingers traced the scar from the palm of my hand up my arm, he'd never seen it before.

I needed to ask the man his name before we left, so when Tobias was older I could tell him about the man who'd taken care of him.

The door slammed open. "Have you seen any strangers this week?" At least the guard was French. That was something. "Anyone who doesn't belong?"

"I don't know everyone here."

"We believe someone got inside that doesn't belong. The Kommandant is most determined to find them."

"Why would anyone try to get in?" The man asked. "And what has that to do with me?"

"We're searching everywhere."

How did they know I was trying to get in?

Toby patted my face and smiled up at me, though he didn't make a sound. He still loved me even though I'd left him.

I hugged him to me.

"They're gone," the man was standing at our feet. "You'd better hurry."

"They're already looking for me," I said crawling out.

"No. Not you."

I looked up, was he trying to make me feel better? "I heard what he said."

"Not all it would seem. It's a soldier who tried to sneak in," he shook his head. "A German officer."

The hollow in my chest filled with lead. "If they caught him, why are they searching?"

"They're trying to find what he came for. Who he risked capture for," his gaze was intense, even in the dim light of the cabin. "Do you know any soldiers?"

"Poppy's scared of soldiers," Tobias said.

It was true, though I'd tried to hide it from him.

The man looked around then back at me. "Is or was?"

I sank on the bed and pulled Tobias to me, searching the man's face. "What do I do?"

He looked at an old man sleeping a few yards away, then sat on the sack opposite. "What is he to you?" He whispered. "If it is the soldier you suspect."

"He saved me," I whispered over Tobias's hair. "And when I came to find Tobias, he must have followed."

"Does he love you?" He asked.

I swallowed, remembering how we'd parted.

"If he loves you, he'd want you to be safe," he put his hand on my arm. "He'd want you to leave."

It was so different from when Karl touched me. I bit my lip and forced myself not to pull away. He was trying to be kind.

"He would want you to get out. To leave."

Tobias was standing now, watching us.

"I have to know," I whispered, wrenching the very center of everything I ever stood for in two. To risk Tobias, it was unthinkable. And yet I was, for a soldier. There was nothing that made sense anymore and yet I couldn't leave without knowing. What if Karl had come for me?

He nodded. "I'll find out."

"I can't let you do that for me."

"Better me than you," he dropped his hand to Tobias's hair, looking straight at me. "Tobias needs you."

Never would I have picked this plain man to be a hero. I'd only seen him twice but I owed him a debt I'd never repay. How could I let him risk more?

"How long till the group leaves?" He asked.

"Not long."

"What's wrong?" Tobias asked, his fingers picking at my sleeve. He looked from me to the man.

I still didn't know his name.

"I'm not sure yet," I looked back at the man. "Do you know where they'd keep him?"

"At the front. They have a small place of confinement near the guards' barracks and the Officers' buildings," he stood up. "I'll hurry." Tobias looked from the empty doorway to me.

One minute later the man stepped back into the room.

"What's his name? This soldier."

"Karl Von Liedersdorf. He's a Lieutenant."

He gave me a hard look, then left once again.

Please don't find him, I begged. Let it be someone else. I smiled at Tobias.

"Do you have more food?"

"What?"

Toby smiled. "He told me a nice lady left me some bread. Was it you?"

I gave him the cheese I brought, then held him close while he ate. He was so thin, how long had he been here? The wind blew through the cabin. I opened my coat and pulled Tobias closer, wrapping my coat around him. "What's the nice man's name?"

"Uncle Fritz. He tells me stories," he whispered, cuddling up in my arms, his head resting on me once again.

I tried not to see the tar paper on the walls, peeling off. To wonder where Uncle Fritz was. Had he found Karl? I shook my head. Karl would hate me if he knew why I came. After all he did to help me and then I just left? No, he hated me already.

Soon Tobias fell asleep, his hand clenched around a wad of

my shirt. I brushed the bits of cheese off his mouth, traced the scar on his chin. I pulled him tighter. How did I ever leave him?

Footsteps in the doorway made my stomach churn. I was sick inside, worrying he wouldn't get back before the hour was up. Sick he would and I wouldn't like what I heard.

"Lena," Uncle Fritz said, standing in the doorway.

"Did Tobias tell you my name?" I knew he hadn't but I wished it. I hoped it was so.

"No."

"Tell me it was someone else. Anyone else," I stared up at him as he came closer. "Please."

He leaned against the wall and turned to me. "I wish I could," he nodded to my arms. "For his sake, as well as yours."

"You saw him?"

"Spoke to him," he crouched down, his hand on the straw sack. "He wants you to get out. Now. He wants you to take the boy and leave and not come back for him."

My heart was exploding. "He knows about Tobias?"

"Listen to me. Follow your plan and get Tobias out."

"I can't."

His hands were on my shoulders now and he shook me. "You can. You can get him out. Staying here won't help."

"How did you talk to him? Is it hard?" I was trying to think, but my brain was frozen, thinking about Tobias and Karl. What if I couldn't save them both? What if I couldn't save either?

"It doesn't matter. You have to leave, while you can."

"What aren't you telling me?"

"Just go, Lena. Go like Karl wants you to."

He was right. I couldn't save Karl by staying. I stood up, pulling Tobias higher, his legs were longer than when I left him.

He buried his head closer but didn't wake.

I took a deep breath and walked out the door towards the block gate. It was obvious I was holding a child. Would I get him through, what if we were caught now? But the guard nodded and let me through. After days of walking past him, he'd grown accustomed to seeing me.

Now that I'd decided to go I wanted to hurry, but I couldn't attract attention.

The main road between the block of all the huts never seemed so wide and bare and long.

The guards saw me, but didn't seem to notice I held a child today unlike all the other times they'd seen me. Was I really going to walk to the truck with him?

Tobias had grown, he was heavy now.

Or had I gotten weak? *'stay asleep,'* I begged silently. How many more times would I be begging today?

Almost to the front of the camp now, one more block to go.

I turned and walked between the blocks. Still barbed wire on both sides, but less in the open. Soon it would be nothing but open space between me and the truck.

Hands grabbed from behind.

I screamed and clutched Tobias closer. A hand covered my mouth and I couldn't fight, Tobias was almost more than I could hold up already.

"It already left," someone whispered. It was Uncle Fritz.

I gasped for a breath but his hand still covered my mouth.

"I'll move my hand but don't scream," then he moved his hand.

I sucked in a breath, trying to hold in the shaking. "How did you find me?"

"He wasn't joking. You do scream easy."

I pressed my lips together to keep from shaking. I got Karl locked up, and he was still trying to protect me.

"Where have you been? The truck left without you."

"I left you at the hut and walked to the truck. How could it have left?"

"He's gotten heavier, hasn't he."

The moment he said it Tobias felt a hundred kilos heavier. "Yes."

"Hopefully the people you're working with are here tomorrow and don't make a big fuss," he looked around. "It wouldn't do for the officers to take notice."

They'd won.

I was trapped and now both Tobias and Karl were trapped with me. "What am I going to do?"

"Come with me," he said. "You're going to stay out of sight till that truck comes back."

I took a deep breath and followed, ignoring how dark the clouds had become. Ignoring the guards who were also ignoring me. Ignoring everything but the fact that I was holding Tobias and he was okay and so far no one had noticed I was inside the camp.

In a few minutes we were back at the hut and I sat down on the bed.

Tobias stirred when I sat and looked up at me. "Why'd you scream?

He'd been awake, but knew he had to keep quiet? No. He's too little for that. "I was startled."

He yawned and stood up, staggering back a step. He caught himself and smiled. "I almost falled over."

I wanted to grab him and hold him tight but hugged myself instead.

"You're getting so big," and he was. But he was still my baby.

TWENTY-FOUR

*I*t was dark and late and I could only hope the whole camp was as deep asleep as Tobias when I left him curled in the bed.

The guards paced along the outside walls, between the wire, and others along the main center road. But they didn't come through the center much.

So I crept from block to block, climbing through the wire and trying to keep from falling or getting stuck in the wire or worst of all — making a noise. I couldn't think about what would happen if I did.

I had to talk to Karl.

The front gate was close now, and the few buildings ahead had real walls and roofs, unlike the shacks everyone else was in made half of tar paper, half of air.

Where were the guards?

I circled the last hut and looked to the other end, still nothing. There was no other way to get to those buildings and that's where they had to be keeping Karl.

I sucked in a breath, climbed through the last wire fence, and walked straight through the open space, waiting for a shout, a shot, or a ringing blow to the head. Reaching the first building I sank into the shadow.

Fritz had talked to him. He must be in a room with a window.

I walked around the wall till I came to a window. I straightened bit by bit till I could see in.

A desk and filing cabinets, that was all.

At the next building I looked in the window and lost my breath. Inside the room a soldier was walking away from me, rifle on his shoulder, pistol at his hip. He was almost to the door opposite.

I sank to the ground and held my breath. Karl's gun had never scared me but this one did. I crawled to the far end of the building and went to the next. There was the next window. I stood up, ready to peek in, then stopped.

That soldier was guarding someone. How many people did they have to specially guard?

I went back to the building with the guard, going around the other side. Another window was close, I took a step towards it, then another. It wasn't glass panes but bars on this window. I took a deep breath, no mistakes tonight, then I looked through the window.

There, on the bench, staring at the ceiling, Karl was sitting. He was here because of me.

My eyes blurred and I pressed them tight together, holding onto the bars to keep from falling.

A hand cupped my face.

He didn't hate me. I opened my eyes.

Karl stood close. So close, his hands through the bars.

"I had to see you."

"Lena."

My throat closed and I turned my face away.

"You were supposed to leave," he wiped the tears from my face. "With Tobias."

"You know?" I whispered.

"Yes," his hand was on my neck, strong, gentle. "I know you have a son."

"What else do you know?"

His hands pulled my face closer till I was resting against the bars. He watched my face as he came closer. Then he kissed my forehead.

What did he see that stopped him from doing more? Or was he afraid I'd scream from him touching me? I was so far from fearing his touch now. "I'm sorry."

He shook his head. "I understand why you didn't tell me," his hands on my neck trembled. "And there's something I've never told you."

I leaned closer to him.

Footsteps sounded outside his door.

He pulled his hands away. "Go."

Without his grip I sank in a heap then crawled along the wall till I came to a bench and curled underneath it. I held my breath, I had to hear inside that room. Did I get him into more trouble?

"Lena," the words came as low as the wind.

I crawled out from under the bench and walked back. A lone brick caught me and I fell on my face.

He clenched his teeth, sucking in a harsh breath but no sound he made could scare me.

The clouds had cleared away and I could see him now.

His forehead was full of lines, his hands reached out and held me against the bars. "You have to leave now."

I swallowed. "Karl."

"No. You have to go," his eyes were so deep, so strong.

I was staring up into his and I couldn't move. I knew now just how far he'd go to protect me. He didn't know all my secrets, but he knew I had a son and didn't seem to mind at all.

His fingers on my neck, on my head, my stomach clenched. I rested my hands on his arms.

"I need you to be safe."

"What did you need to tell me?" A scuffle at the door.

"You have to go. Promise me you'll go," but his stern tone didn't scare me the way it once had. He pulled his hands away.

"Karl," I reached for him. "Please."

He turned his head away, then looked at me. "What?"

There were no words. I was helpless to save him. "I'm sorry."

He shook his head. "You have to be strong now. Promise me you'll take Tobias and go."

I shook my head.

He stuck his hands back through and pulled me as close as the bars allowed. "For me? Will you go for me?"

I sucked in a breath, a breath of him, and reached my hand through the bars to his face. There was a welt on his forehead.

His eyes darkened and he lowered his head.

I reached as high as my toes would take me.

Then he stiffened and let go. "Go. Now. Don't come back," he shoved something in my hand then backed from the window and sat on the bench.

I slid to the ground, my feet impossible to stand on.

The door inside the cell opened and boots tramped in, then out again.

I crawled across the narrow walkway to the building opposite, then walked across the big space to the first block that somehow felt safe.

At any second someone might shoot me, I half expected it. But no one did. I got through the fence, found a shadowy corner and curled in a ball.

He was here, locked up, because of me. And whatever came next, it wasn't good.

I sat in the dark, wracking my brain for some way to get him free. To get Tobias and Karl and me all out of this camp, it was impossible. But so was falling in love with a soldier.

My hand clenched, then I saw I still had what Karl gave me. It was bread, Karl saved bread for me.

He knew I'd come.

I walked back to the cabin, bit by bit, and held my breath when I opened the door. I made my way to the bed where I'd gone to sleep with Tobias. I sat down slowly, bit by bit, then lay down and pulled the thin blanket up.

Tobias cuddled into me like I'd never left. His head was right below mine. I could feel his heart beating and I pulled him closer. I couldn't lose him, I couldn't leave him again. I wrapped my arm around him and breathed him in.

"What did he say?"

My whole body locked up.

Tobias shifted, pulling away from the tension in his sleep.

I turned my head.

Fritz half sitting in his bed. "It was him, wasn't it."

"Yes."

"What did he say?"

Karl loved me, he wanted me to be safe. "We didn't have much time before a guard came."

He sighed. "What are you going to do?"

I wanted answers, not questions. "I don't know."

"But you aren't going to do as he asked," again, it wasn't a question. "You're not going to take the boy and leave."

"Why did you tell him about Tobias?"

"I didn't," he whispered. "He knew you came for your son."

I flinched.

Someone across the room rolled over. Thank goodness most of the men in this cabin were old.

My mind hurt. There was too much to think about, but I couldn't leave Tobias. And I wasn't going to leave Karl here.

"You should get Tobias out before you do anything else."

I dropped my head to the bed and listened to his even breathing. "I know."

"I'll do what I can to help, but a child shouldn't be locked up in here."

The moonlight was dim, but there were cracks on all sides and a few were close enough to see his face. "Do you know anyone outside?"

He shook his head. "Do you think he'd still be here if I could've gotten him out?"

I swallowed. He must have believed me when I said he was mine. "I'm sorry. I just mean —"

"Go to sleep," he turned away.

I sank down, pulling the blanket closer.

Tobias rolled over, facing me now. I picked up his little hand and pulled it back under the blanket, kissing it and holding it to my face.

He was tugging at me, in his sleep. Showing me he needed me, begging me to keep him safe.

I swallowed. The feeling of Karl's hand curled around my neck, his lips pressing into my forehead, his desperation burned into my mind. He needed me too.

But who needed me more?

Something was off, something felt wrong. I held my breath. What was it? Then I felt a little person burrowing in my arms. No, it wasn't wrong, it was so very right. I pulled Tobias closer.

He held my hand, moving it back and forth. "Are you awake?"

I didn't move. I didn't want to change anything about this moment.

Tobias was in my arms.

He scooted forward and blew in my ear. "I saw your eye move. You're awake," he poked my mouth. "I know you're awake."

Happiness so out of place here, but I wouldn't stop him, I didn't want to. I pulled his little face to mine and kissed him.

Then I opened my eyes, Uncle Fritz. I needed to find out his real name.

But now he stared at us, at Tobias and me, his face such a mixture of emotions I couldn't decide what he thought of us. Was he still mad from last night?

"Good morning," I sat up, hugging Tobias to me.

"So that's what you wanted in the morning," he came over and patted Tobias's head. "It takes a mother to get that right."

I shot a look around the hut but no one seemed to care that I joined their group. No one seemed to notice a girl in this block of only men.

"What are your plans?" He asked, his tone light but his eyes dead serious.

"I have a present from a good elf," I said and handed the bread to Tobias.

His face lit up and he started in on it.

I sat and watched him dig his little wooden car out from under the bed. "I don't know what to do."

"The Swiss aid workers will be here in an hour," Fritz said. "And you need to get on that truck."

And leave Karl here? I shuddered. "How did you found out who was locked up yesterday?"

"Just take Tobias and go."

"No."

"Lena."

"No," I couldn't even pretend to be calm. "I can't leave him. I have to think of something."

"Listen, take Tobias. Find him somewhere safe. And then…" he stopped.

"Then what?" I asked.

He yawned. "Hope that the letter gets through."

The others in the room started moving again, they'd been listening.

The lump in my throat grew. What if there wasn't time to get anything figured out before the truck came? What if I'd lost my chance to get Tobias out?

"And you should decide if you want him to stay here or join the other children."

"What?" I looked up.

"I waited while we looked for you," he was talking for the others now. "But there's a children's hut in every block where he'd get extra food and some schooling. Mighty little but it's something."

"I'll think about it. Come Tobias, let's go outside. It's not raining," Which was reason enough to go out, as it rained here more often than not.

"Just go," Fritz whispered as I passed him.

I didn't look around. Tobias held my hand and we walked out to the cloudy day.

"When are we going home?" Tobias asked looking up. He narrowly missed the edge of the board. Mud was on either side, waiting to suck him in up to his knees.

"The guard at the front, Louis, he's sympathetic," Fritz whispered, he pressed something into my hand. "If you find him in the town, he may help. Good luck. And don't come back."

I looked down, Tobias's car. We really were leaving. I held Tobias's hand tight in mine and we walked, block after block and not a guard stopped us. Did they still believe I worked here? There was talk of taking the children out of the camp. Did the guards think I was doing that? I held my breath when we passed the latrines.

In the clearing I watched for the guard we met earlier, and there he was, standing at the truck. I didn't let myself look towards the building, the only building that mattered, the one that held Karl.

We were close now, I held my breath. Was Fritz telling the truth about the guard being sympathetic?

I lingered at the side of the truck, holding Tobias's hand,

willing him to behave. I caught my breath when the soldier looked up.

He caught my look and kept turning till he was facing the opposite way.

I didn't have time to think about whether it was a trap or not.

I lifted Tobias into the truck, gripped the side and jumped in. There wasn't anything to hide under. Tobias scuttled under the front seat bench.

He looked back at me. "Hurry."

"I have to stay out here," I grabbed a blanket and covered him, hiding him as best I could. I stroked his face. "Try to keep quiet, okay?"

He nodded.

"Here, hold your car," I said covering his face, then sat in front of him and picked flecks of straw off my dress. The sleeping mats were little more than bags of straw and it wouldn't do for that to be noticed.

Beatrice would be here soon. Would she believe my story or would she be suspicious?

Footsteps hurried up to the truck.

I gripped a handful of my dress. But the woman who appeared wasn't Beatrice. It was one of the others.

"What are you doing?" She asked.

I hadn't opened my mouth and she was mad at me.

"What is it?" Someone else asked from around the corner. "Who's there?"

I dreaded that corner more and more.

But this time it was Beatrice. "What happened?" She climbed into the truck.

"I went too far, and when I got back here the truck had left."

"I thought perhaps you hadn't come yesterday. I would never have left you. But why didn't you tell someone? One of the guards?" She hugged me to her as more people filled the benches.

"I was afraid they wouldn't believe me. Couldn't they put me in jail?"

She shook her head. "The guards are doing their jobs, for the most part," her lips tightened. "There's plenty for you to do in town, no need for you to come back into camp."

The truck engine started up.

I was leaving Karl here. And he was here because he'd come to save me.

"What a brave thing you are," one of the older women said, handing me a blanket and patting me on the head like a child. If only I was a child.

"I'll stay closer next time," I pulled the blanket close though I wanted to wrap it around Tobias, I wanted to make sure he was ok. But I couldn't. "I came here to help and that's what I want to do."

I heard a hiccup and froze. I looked from face to face but no one responded.

Then the truck stopped, the guard at the gate spoke with the driver. At last he waved us on.

I started to breathe again. I kept my eyes closed, my head down, and prayed.

Get Tobias safe. Find the guard. I chanted it over and over. Was it the right thing to do? Maybe I could find the underground.

Uncle spoke of the French underground once, two years ago.

I sank further into the seat. How could I even find them, let alone convince them to help free a German officer? I might be outside the camp with Tobias, but we were out of luck.

TWENTY-FIVE

A few more blocks to go and we'd be back to the rooms we were staying in.

"Are you alright?" The question dragged me from the fuzzy into the urgent. She was trying to be kind, but I needed her to be oblivious.

"I need to walk around," I whispered, hoping my expression was confused. pr serious, anything but dishonest. "You know, a little freedom after…"

"I understand dear," she nodded. "But don't get too tired."

I nodded and pulled the blanket down from my shoulders. "Thank you for the blanket."

I waited to get out last then dropped my bag on the floor. I knelt down. "Stay here," I whispered.

Tobias nodded and clutched his car.

I jumped from the truck and followed it from across the street, hoping no one would notice. I walked after it till it was out of sight. Down the road and out of town. I ran now, past a few tired houses and an ancient apple orchard.

Where was the truck going?

A house loomed ahead, larger and finer than the others. And there, the tail end of the truck stuck out behind it.

I swallowed and went for the trees bordering the road.

Who lived here?

I gripped the nearest tree and stared at the house. In this moment, nothing mattered more than finding a way to get Tobias out.

A door slammed.

I moved along the edge of trees, getting closer to the house and the truck and whoever was between me and Tobias.

The thought of someone discovering Tobias, of him getting caught and taken back or worse. I bit my finger and waited.

He wasn't found yet.

The driver stood at the back steps and a woman stood above him near the door. She tried to pull him inside, reaching up to kiss him. For one moment they kissed, a short gentle kiss I'd always dreamed about, my gut twisted.

Sometimes life hurt too much.

Then he pulled away and went to the truck and the woman went back inside.

Shadows crept up, I crawled closer.

He was on the other side, but he'd still be able to see me.

A child shouted.

The next instant I ran through the trees, towards Tobias. He'd been found and it was my fault. I should have thought of something else, some other way to get him out. Another cry, this time I was closer, but it wasn't Tobias at all.

Then the driver came around the truck, between me and Tobias, a little girl his arms.

I dropped to the ground at the edge of trees. It wasn't Tobias and now the guard was close. He could see me, if he had a mind too.

The woman called out the door and the man went inside.

He might come back. He might have more to do once the

child was settled. I waited, for what I couldn't say. The night was closing in, how long would Tobias stay quiet? I ran forward and crouched by the truck, listening, waiting.

Hands on the ground I looked under the truck. Nothing to surprise.

I climbed into the truck, ran to the back and dropped to the floor.

"Tobias, hurry."

A slight shuffle and he wriggled out from under the seat. He'd been still and quiet for so long. He leaned against me and shivered, holding tight. "Where are we?"

"I don't know. But you were such a good boy," I said, hurrying to the front of the truck.

A door slammed.

I dropped to the floor of the truck, pulling Tobias with me.

The man walked by.

Tobias curled into my side, trembling. Of course he was scared. A little finger tapped my arm.

I looked down. "Yes?"

"Is he looking for us?" There was light enough to see his wide eyes full of fear.

"He doesn't know we're here. Ready to run?"

He nodded.

I looked out again. Should we run or wait? I crawled forward and Tobias followed.

Then footsteps came down the walk. The sound of footsteps had become an omen and I hated them, I hated them tonight more than ever before.

The man was close now, he'd see us if he looked.

I was waiting, holding my breath, I couldn't hear him at all. He hadn't gone inside, I would've heard that, but we couldn't sit here all night. I sat up inch by inch till I was staring straight at the driver. Staring at him as he stared at us.

I was ready to beg.

But he didn't move, he was staring at a paper in his hands.

I sank down and tried to breathe without making a sound, pulled Tobias to me and hugged him close. I waited to hear an order, feel a rough shake. I strained my ears to hear it.

But nothing. Counting the seconds was painful, just sitting there waiting to be caught.

Then shuffling footsteps walked to the door, it opened and closed. Something shook him, and it was good for us, though it probably wasn't good for him.

I jumped from the truck and reached back for Tobias.

He was climbing out, but it wasn't fast enough for me. I grabbed him and ran to the woods. A few steps in I put him down, grabbed his hand and ran.

I slowed when he needed a break and then stopped. I looked in one direction, then another.

"Are we lost?" He asked.

I pulled him to my side. "I'm not sure," I said, trying to sound calm. I got him out of the camp only to get lost in the woods.

A light ahead, that was something.

"This way," I started towards the light. Branches and bushes blocked our way, slapping our faces. These woods didn't get many hogs foraging. I'd need to carry him soon. "I think we're close."

"Poppy, I'm hungry."

I reached into my bag and gave him a roll. How long had it been since I ate? I'd need to eat something soon, but there wasn't much left.

He ate fast, still gripping my dress with one hand. "I'm tired."

He was tired and I was tired and we were lost. Karl wouldn't give up on me, there was no way I was going to give up on him. If only I knew where to go or what to do.

Tobias smiled and in the pale light his face was never more beautiful. "I love you."

My heart twisted and I hugged him tight. "I love you,

Tobias." If we were caught the next minute, at least he heard me say it one more time.

"I'm glad you came," he whispered.

"So am I, baby," I hugged him tight then pulled him around to my back, settled him carefully and started towards the light.

Soon a path opened and I followed it.

It had to go somewhere.

My legs were shaking, I was so tired.

The path grew bigger and the next moment it was a road. The guard that Uncle Fritz told me to find. How was I to find a single person in a town, no matter how small? And this wasn't a small town.

But Tobias, if he could have a bath and a bed to sleep in, if I had food for him when he woke up. I looked both ways along the road, but they looked the same.

His head rolled to the side, he was so peaceful in his sleep. I pulled him up higher and took the road to the right. At least in choosing one I had a chance of making the right call, even though I didn't know what to do once I got somewhere.

Walking at night, with a child, alone, it wouldn't be good to meet up with anyone. I tried to keep an eye on the ditches. If someone came along, I wouldn't have much time to hide.

A dog barking ahead made me start, I heard it before I could see anything. I tripped to the side and leaned next to a bush, hoping Tobias didn't wake. I had a lot of hopes these days.

A sharp command shut the dog up, the speaker didn't seem to see me.

And I'd come to a town, though which one I couldn't say.

Tobias snored, I was so glad to hear it again. But my arms ached, and my back was pulling in so many places. A few more blocks in the dark moonlight and I found the center of town. Was it the same town? I circled, trying to decide.

I sighed in relief when I recognized the bank. It was the same town, and this was close to the inn I was staying in.

New energy helped me cover the last two blocks quickly.

There it was, the door to the inn. I stopped short. It was painful really, I could almost feel the hot water of the bath, feel the warmth. And the food, I was so hungry the hurt in my chest was gnawing at my spine. But going in the front door with Tobias was asking for trouble.

Surely there was a back door, and a back staircase I could use to sneak Tobias up to the little room they'd found for me. And tomorrow I could find a way to help Karl. If I could get a little sleep, I could think of some way to get him out.

I walked up the street till I came to the turn that had to be the way to the back alley. There weren't any lights shining from windows here, it was all dark. The dark was good, easier to hide in, but it made me shiver.

Tobias shivered on my back, and I shivered too.

There were plenty of doors, but which was for the inn?

Peering into the windows I tried to see anything that would tell me what I needed, anything to say it was the inn, not just a house.

I reached the end. So I went back and looked again.

This one, it might be it. Was it? I went up the few steps and took a breath. Holding onto Tobias with one hand, I opened the door with the other.

It was too dark, I couldn't see a thing. Stepping in I waited for my eyes to adjust. I made out a table, a few things on the counter and I drew in a breath, this wasn't a kitchen. Those were doctor's instruments.

This was the doctor's house.

Then the door closed behind me.

I spun around, backing into the table.

"What are you doing here?" It was a man, tall and thin. "Why are you here?"

"I was looking for the inn and came in by mistake. I'm very sorry."

He stood still, but the shadows hid his face. "Why were you out with a child so late?" His voice was hard to read, was he mad, was he suspicious? He was asking the right questions. "I'm not going to hurt you."

I backed up and the table dug into my hip. What was that supposed to mean anyway?

"You're from the internment camp?"

My chest was tight, how did he know that? I shook my head, but my lips wouldn't work.

"Not everyone approves of what's going on," he said. "Many oppose it."

The quiet of the room made my breathing louder. "I'm looking for the inn," I moved towards the door. "I'm very sorry. We won't bother you further."

He moved away from the door. "They're looking for you." Now that his face was in the light, I could see a mustache and graying hair. It was hard to read him though, because I wasn't good at reading anyone.

"Who is looking for whom?"

"The guards from the internment camp are looking for a girl who stole a child," he said. "A three-year-old boy with light brown hair."

I backed away from him and clutched Tobias tighter. The blood in my veins beat faster, it was painful not being able to fight back.

"What I'd like to know is why someone would steal a child from the camp. It sounds easier to steal one from, well, pretty much anywhere else. Unless it's a particular child," he took a step towards me. "All the inns will be searched. You have to know that. And the woods too."

"Why are you telling me?" I asked. "If it is me, I must be the worst sort of criminal, stealing a child."

Tobias stirred.

"I can help you," he came closer and looked out the window beside the door.

I wanted to back away but there was nowhere to go, we were backed against the wall already.

"We were all out looking for you," he looked at Tobias. "If it is you."

My legs were starting to shake, this must be a trap. How did I end up in this house? "Who's we?" I tried to think, to use my brain, but I was so tired.

"Will you let me help you?" He held out his hand.

I looked around for some kind of sign. Some sort of telling thing to let me know what to do. But I didn't really have a choice, did I? "Thank you." I breathed and pulled Tobias around to my front.

"You must be exhausted," he locked the back door and led the way into the house. "It's a fortunate thing you came here."

I prayed under my breath that it was true and followed him to the next room that was lit and warm, Tobias sat up.

"You must be hungry," the man said. "I won't be gone long." He disappeared through a door opposite.

I sat in the chair and took a deep breath. "The man has food for us," I set Tobias on the floor.

He looked around; his eyes wide. "Where are we?"

If only I had somewhere to take him. Somewhere safe. "I don't know."

The door swung open. "Here's something," the man came in, setting a tray on the table. A younger man followed with a basket of bread.

I pulled Tobias to me. Who was this?

But the younger man stood at the door without saying a word.

"Who are you?" I asked, when the gray-haired man turned from the table. "Why are you helping us?"

"I'm a doctor. I like to help people," the older man said. "Would you like to eat while we talk?"

That wasn't reason enough but Tobias pulled towards the food. My hands still on him I could feel his stomach growl.

"Thank you," I nodded and went to the table, pulling Tobias into my lap. "But I don't understand why you're helping me."

The younger man served out soup, handing me a smaller bowl.

"Maybe you're helping us," the gray- haired man said. "I am Monsieur Basil Laurent."

"Poppy?"

I looked at Tobias.

He pointed to the sausage. "They have sausage."

I placed the soup in front of him. "Here's some soup, Toby."

The men both shifted, the younger almost dropped the last bowl he served. Then he sat down and ate spoon after spoon from the steamy bowl.

"Eat this first," I put the spoon in his hand. "It's warm soup."

He took a bite and then kept eating, not spilling a drop. How could three months make so much difference?

I set down the second bowl he passed me but I couldn't make myself eat. It looked safe enough, the younger fellow started eating before I'd handed Tobias the spoon, but I couldn't swallow over the tension in the room.

"We needn't wait to talk," I looked at Tobias eating the soup while he watched the sausage. Looking from to the other I waited for one of them to say something. "You found his name significant."

The younger man choked. But the soup was smooth, there was nothing to choke on.

"We were looking because we heard you'd gotten in," the doctor said.

"And out," said the younger.

"Heard of me. From who? Who are you?" I looked at the younger man.

He took a piece of bread. "I'm Louis."

The doctor held out the basket to me. "He's your son?" I flinched, but smiled at Tobias when he looked up at me.

He smiled back and went on with his soup.

"It went around, what you were trying to do," the doctor nodded to Tobias. "Getting in and . . ."

The soup smelled good, so good. My stomach cramped. "What was I going to do? If I was indeed that person."

"Save the boy," he whispered. "Though it meant you had to leave the soldier who saved you."

Now I choked on the soup. I closed my eyes and bent my head closer to the soup.

"Well?" The doctor asked.

"I ate it all," Tobias pointed to the plate of sausage again. "Can I have sausage now?

"The soup is all I want," I looked at Louis. "Would it be alright if has a small piece?"

He put one on Tobias's plate and one on mine. "There's plenty."

And shockingly enough, it was true, there was more than enough food on this table. Why was there so much? "Thank you."

"You should eat," the doctor said. "We'll talk in a bit." He nodded to Tobias.

Tobias yawned, his hand clenched the sausage. He took another bite but his chewing was slow.

The soup was smooth and creamy, I couldn't think of eating anything else. The men were eating too now, almost ravenous.

Tobias lay his head on the table. His hand clenched around his last bite of meat.

I ate his potatoes. We were all eating fast now, in this small room without windows. These two men I'd just met, Tobias and me.

"We have to know where you're going."

I looked up.

In an instant it seemed, they were through eating and ready to talk.

Tobias asleep in my arms now there was nothing to stop us. "I don't know," I paused, looking from one to the other. Why would they, why would anyone risk anything to help a German officer?

"What is it?" The doctor asked.

Louis leaned towards him and whispered low and quick. I could only pick out a few words. Soldier and love.

"He was trying to save me, again," they knew already, likely, perhaps they would believe me. "I can't leave him."

"The only German soldier being held is there because he never returned from an assignment," the doctor said. "Louis knows one of the guards, the German police are sending someone to investigate."

And he'd risked capture to come after me. "Is there anyone you know who can help me?" After hours tramping through the woods, I was pleading for more help from them. It was hard to believe, though I'd do so much more to save Karl. The question was, could I trust them?

"I think sleep's what we need," Louis said, gesturing to Tobias. But he meant me.

"I'm sorry. I don't know what to say," tears were trying to get out. I fought and won.

"You have reason to be tired, anyone would be exhausted," the doctor said. "We'll talk in the morning."

I lifted Tobias to my shoulder, he was heavy but he smiled in his sleep. Full and warm for the first time in weeks, no wonder he was smiling.

The stairs were steep, the creaks deafening. I went slow but still tripped twice.

"Here," he pointed to the room at the top of the stairs. What did he think of the doctor helping me, putting him and any others here in danger?

"Thank you," gripping Tobias with both hands I couldn't shake hands but he didn't step towards me anyway. And the half kiss I'd come to expect here in France, he made no move to extend.

He opened the door and went in, closing the door behind us. Light from the window streamed in, his eyes were deep with worry.

"What is it?"

"Later. I'll come when I can," then he hurried away.

I stood in the room, fancy by any standards, but there was a bed, which was all I cared about right now. I threw back the lace cover and laid Tobias down. Then I grabbed a blanket from a chair and threw it over him.

It was rougher material, out of place in this room.

I looked at it closer.

Why was it familiar?

A gentle knock and Louis was back. "He's a collaborator, he's going to turn you in tomorrow."

I sat down on the bed. "Why are you telling me this?"

"I can get you out," he clasped his hands behind his back. "But it's your choice."

He could be lying. Why should I trust him?

"The decision is yours. I have no proof to give that I'm not the one who's lying."

I looked at Tobias. His future depended on my choice. Which was right? I had no time to think, I had to decide. "I'll go with you."

He nodded.

"What do you want me to do?"

"Sleep. I'll come back in an hour or two, when the doctor's asleep."

"Thank you," I wanted to say more, to say something that mattered but I had nothing. "Thank you."

He nodded and was gone.

Who should I trust? Louis or the doctor. Both seemed to know too much about me, but I couldn't stand any longer. Last night I hardly slept after sneaking out to see Karl. It seemed like it had been so much longer than one night. I clenched my teeth, I needed sleep. Whatever happened, being tired would make it that much harder.

I pushed Tobias to the middle of the bed and curled around him.

TWENTY-SIX

*D*arkness was bliss for a few seconds, or was it hours? Something woke me, I lay frozen and searched the room with my eyes. The noise came again, from behind me. I took a breath and looked over my shoulder.

Nothing.

I slipped to the carpet, then reached up to the bed and pulled the blanket tight around Tobias.

He moaned and reached out his hands but I tucked them in. After a moment I crawled to the wall by the window and stood. Holding my breath I peeked out the window.

A man crouched on the ledge, but it wasn't Louis. That much was clear. He nodded to the window.

I took a deep breath and pulled on the latch. But it was stuck. I pushed hard but the whole frame was stuck.

He tried from the outside, pulled so hard the veins on his neck stood out, but it didn't budge.

And this wasn't an accident. The doctor told Louis to put me in this room for a reason.

The man outside used his knife, working at a corner he kept

scraping something away but I couldn't see much. Then he looked straight at me. "It's nailed shut and there's no time."

"What do I do?" A rabbit in a hutch, sealed in. Quite a price to pay for a little sleep. Was I trusting the right people now?

Time after time I'd made the wrong choice. I told them about Karl. A sickening lurch made me want to throw up all the food I'd taken from him, but my body needed it too much. No wonder he had so much food.

A creak came from the floor boards outside the door. I braced myself against the wall for a second before I darted to Tobias.

The door opened. A man.

I tried to see which man it was through the darkness. I'd seen too many the last few days. He closed the door to the crack and turned and held up his hands before him.

"I was outside," he took a step closer. "If Louis disappears the doctor will suspect him, so I'm here to get you safely away."

"Who are you?" I whispered, then turned to look at the window. "How'd you get in?"

"The window in the next room," he came a step closer. "We don't have much time. If you're going with me it's now."

I looked at him, trying to decide. I guessed wrong last night. What was to make this right? Or had I guessed right last night and Louis was the liar? How was I to know?

I swallowed. "I'll go with you," I turned to Tobias.

"Let me," he bent and pulled him into his arms in one fluid motion, keeping the blanket wrapped tight around him.

Would Karl be good with Tobias like that? *Stop*, I yelled at myself. We have to get out of here.

"Careful around the doorway," he whispered. "The boards are too loud for it to be an accident."

I tried to step where he did but his legs were longer and I almost screamed three times when a board creaked under me.

We went down the hall to the next room and this one was so

empty even the sound of our breathing echoed. The shiver that shook me was not from the cold.

The window was open, he threw one leg over the window sill and then the other, Tobias asleep his arms. He ducked his head through and was out, as calm as if he carried children in their sleep every day.

I took hold of the window frame then remembered, my bag was downstairs. There wasn't anything in it of value, but it was the only thing I had left. Just a bag, but there was no way I was going back for it. I stuck my head out the window and the cold wind hit my face. Where was the man with Tobias?

The roof sloped down, it was a tall two story house.

I closed the window behind me and took a deep breath.

"Hurry," a voice said right beside me. It was the same man, but without Tobias.

"Where is he?" I stood up. "Where did you go?"

"He's fine," he whispered. "But we have to hurry."

I followed him around the corner of the chimney.

He grabbed my arm. "Careful of the edge."

I bit my lip hard, but my heart was racing. The panic inside was crawling up my throat. "Let me go."

He pulled his hand off. "Sorry."

The edge of the roof ended only centimeters in front of our feet but a shed stood a few steps away, beyond a sickening black gap. One man stood opposite us, another disappeared over the other side with Tobias over his shoulder.

He was disappearing with a stranger, I couldn't lose him again. But to jump across?

"He'll grab you if you start to fall," the man whispered. "Don't scream, alright?"

I nodded and tried to imagine jumping across the distance before me. I'd jumped this distance on the ground. I could do it.

"Can you do it?" Now he sounded worried.

There was no time to think about whether I could or

couldn't. Tobias was over there. I had to get to him and away from that man who'd put me in a room with nailed down windows. I jumped and the earth pulled me down, I wasn't going to make it. The rushing wind, the ground coming to hit me, then my legs hit the side of the building while two hands almost crushed my arms. Then I was yanked up and set on the cold roof.

"Open your eyes."

I obeyed.

The roof was empty, but a light came on in a downstairs window.

"Are you ok?"

I nodded. Strong hands pulled me up and I almost collapsed from blood rushing from my head. I bit my tongue, focused on the pain, and followed the man down the ladder as fast as I dared.

Three men stood in the alley, one held Tobias.

He was awake and watching me, but he seemed alright. Curious more than frightened.

I let out a breath.

"He didn't wake up till we passed across the roof," someone said.

My heart jumped, thank goodness I didn't see that.

"Where are we going?" I whispered.

The man walking beside me shook his head. This was the man who'd caught me on the roof and seemed in charge.

I straightened my shoulders and followed the silent men through the streets. Every other minute I looked at Tobias, but he didn't seem to mind the midnight walk.

The fear that made me jump off the roof was seeping away.

My heart had quit trying to jump out of my chest and now there wasn't enough blood to keep me moving.

"It's not long now," someone said.

I looked up. I'd been following the man in front of me and missed the change from the streets to the woods. There wasn't a bit of path but the man in front didn't hesitate.

"Why are you helping me?" I asked. "Who are you?"

He grabbed me and pulled me behind a tree.

I opened my mouth, his hand was over it. I couldn't breathe. I jerked away but his hands were tight, my back against the tree, my arms pinned to my sides. All the blood in my veins was boiling, I'd chosen wrong again. But why would they go to all this trouble to kidnap us? Where was Tobias?

A flickering light shone ahead and a few voices came through the woods.

His mouth was by my ear. "Forgive me. There wasn't time."

I focused on breathing and not thinking and stopped digging my nails into his arm. Tobias was with one of the men. I wouldn't scream. Was he indeed trying to help?

He had grabbed me and covered my mouth to keep me from being caught. He took his hand off my face. "Sorry." His hand on my arm tightened.

I froze, but my eyes searched the woods. Where was Tobias?

There was light from the moon but there was no one in sight. Even the lights ahead had gone out now.

"The others are close, up a tree with the boy," he whispered.

Searching the tree I found a few shapes that could be people.

He released me, keeping a light hold on my arm. "There wasn't time for anything else."

"I'm sorry I clawed your arm."

He coughed then let out a low whistle. A few thuds sounded around us and the next moment I was standing in the center of them once again.

"Poppy," a little voice said from the dark.

I turned around. "Toby," then he was in my arms. "Were you in the tree?" I hugged him close.

"He was a good boy," someone said. Was it the man I'd seen in the house? "So quiet."

Tobias snuggled against me. "I watched that man cover your mouth."

I held him closer, so glad of the darkness to cover my face. "He was keeping me safe, like the man kept you safe in the tree."

The men whispered in hurried voices. What they were planning, I couldn't imagine.

"You were so good to be quiet, Toby, and not to fuss when you found someone carrying you."

"He said we were keeping you safe. He said you wanted me to be quiet," he leaned back and stared into my face. "Did you?"

I forced on a smile. "Yes. That's what I wanted. You did so good."

"It's dark," he said looking around. He shivered the same time I did.

I looked at the others. I longed to tell them I'd take Tobias and go, but I couldn't. I needed their help. Whoever they were, they weren't the law. So they were my best chance to get Karl out.

"We have to get you away from town," one of the men said, suddenly close.

I flinched but opened my mouth to protest.

"And tomorrow we'll talk about Karl. You're no help to him if you're picked up yourself."

I couldn't argue with that. But how did they know about Karl? How did the doctor know about him?

"He'll take you on, the rest of us must be seen in town," he said. "Till tomorrow."

"Thank you," how many times would I be saying that to people I could never repay?

"He'll carry the boy, you'll wear yourself out," he said. "And he's a good man, you can trust him."

Tobias looked at me and I nodded.

One of the men stepped closer and reached for Tobias. "We should go."

I could've seen his face if he'd looked towards me.

The others were gone now and the last man carried Tobias and led the me the other way. He didn't hesitate but he didn't make me hurry.

I didn't even know this strangers name but I wouldn't have been able to carry Tobias. Not after walking this far and in the dark and after so many days without sleep. I had no choice but to trust this unknown, unnamed man walking so quiet beside me. "What's your name?"

"Call me Jean."

"It was high," Tobias said.

I walked faster. So it was this man that had him up the tree.

"And we were quiet," Tobias said.

"Yes. You were a quiet boy," the man said.

He was the one who came in the house and carried Tobias out the window. The one who said he knew Karl. But there was something different about him, what was it?

We trudged through the forest one slogging step after another. The stars were gone now, the sky had become the color of ash. How long had we been walking? Hours for sure.

The path grew wider and with Tobias asleep over his shoulder, he slowed, walking beside me.

"They would've brought you but they have to avoid suspicion." Any words would have been surprising after the hours of silence. "In the eyes of the law, I too have no right to exist. That's why I'm free to bring you here."

But his accent. "You're not German, are you?"

"No. Though it's no point asking where I'm from. I'm a sinti."

Sinti, gypsy. They'd been outcasts longer than we had. No

wonder he was so comfortable in the woods and hiding in a tree.

"Karl is a good man. He's worth fighting for."

I shuddered at what that could mean. "How do you know him?"

"We worked together for a time. When you were at the bakery, I'd check on you for him."

I looked up, the sky was gray now, almost a pale light. "I've never seen you before, or any of the others."

He shifted his arms under Tobias and picked up the pace. "We have to hurry. It wouldn't do to be seen."

What did he say? "You checked on me?"

A barn loomed large straight ahead.

We'd passed several but this time he didn't skirt around it. He looked around the clearing for a long minute then lowered Tobias into my arms. "Wait here." Then he walked across the clearing toward the barn.

I held my breath and pulled Tobias closer.

Still fast asleep, his eyes were sweaty and there were smudges of dirt on his cheeks.

Something tightened in my chest. He was so beautiful. And I had him back in my arms. I hugged him tighter.

My legs were getting numb. Tobias was getting so big.

At last the man came back out of the barn and back towards us.

I backed up, almost tripping. He didn't look worried, but trusting what I thought people were thinking had never worked in the past.

"It's alright," standing before me in the almost light of the morning I could see him at last.

No wonder he could carry Tobias up a tree. Shorter than Karl, he looked stronger somehow. He probably could have carried me. I bit my lip. Why must I compare him to Karl? He reached for Tobias, but looked at me.

I nodded, letting him take Tobias. My arms were tired. I was close to falling already.

The clearing before the barn seemed to stretch farther and farther. It was pale in the sky, almost light. A small door stood open and I followed him inside.

"All the way to the end. Can you get the door?"

I moved in front. "This one?"

He nodded.

I opened into a room, a simple room with a bed and a chest and a chair. I grabbed the back of a chair and held on. I'd been holding my breath for too long.

"You ok?"

I nodded, keeping my eyes closed.

"You should sleep now."

I forced my eyes open.

Tobias was on the bed, asleep. The man stood a few steps away, watching me.

I looked straight at him. "Who are you?"

He didn't flinch. "They call me Jean."

I almost fell when my knees gave way. I clenched the wood and made myself stand. "Why did you check on me?" I had to have at least one answer.

He came towards me. With slow measured movements he took hold of my arms.

The same strong grip that caught me on the roof.

I forced my lungs to keep breathing, to ignore his tight hands on my arms. He was trying to help. I let go of the chair and walked to the bed and sat down.

"Karl is an important man," he said, raking his hand through his hair. "He's intelligent and brave and what he knew helped us a great deal." Why did this sound like an excuse for something bad?

"Us?"

"And he was brilliant, his plans always worked. Always. And

he never lost his nerve or focus no matter how stressful the operation, except when he was worried about you. Any time he'd be gone more than a few hours, especially at night, one of us was assigned to protect you." He waited, unblinking.

I pulled the blanket around Tobias, then looked back at him. "Why are you telling me this?" This confusing jumble of information, what operations was he talking about?

"It's why I know you. Karl was silent about his family, his past, the reason why he helped, but we all knew the most dangerous task of any mission was for whoever was watching you. If you tripped and hurt yourself, or burned yourself on that blasted oven, he was tense for days. He didn't say much but we all knew how he felt," he shook his head and looked down. "When he heard about your son..."

I sank to the bed, burrowing my head against Tobias. "He must've been furious."

"He was torn up for days," he whispered. "And more careful of you than ever. He demanded I be your guard and no one dared cross him."

I opened my eyes. Light streamed in and there were no shadows to hide in. I could see every line on his face.

He believed what he was saying.

"I don't understand."

He sat in the chair an arms length away. "He refused anyone else after he learned about Tobias. You mattered more than any information we needed to get or installation we needed to get into. Anything that would bring officials closer to you was shot down, anything that would take him too far away, impossible."

I held my arms against my stomach and gasped for a breath.

Karl knew about Tobias. He knew before I left him. Why didn't he tell me?

He stood up. "Please get some sleep. It's safe here, even for us." A scar over his brow was enough to remind me that we were never safe.

TWENTY-SEVEN

*D*emetri.

The name swirled in my head. In a real bed, curled around Tobias. *No.* My arms were empty, Tobias wasn't next to me.

I sat up, and looked around.

A chair stood against the whitewashed walls, but no Tobias. Where was he? I stood and my feet cramped inside my shoes. They were still on. The blanket was smeared with dried mud. But it was hard to care because he was gone.

Tobias was nowhere to be seen.

I opened the door, the hallway was empty.

Of course it was empty. My shoelaces dragged as I tiptoed down the hall, stopping at each door to listen till I got to the end and pushed through the heavy door to the outside.

A breeze chilled my face and the light was wrong. Afternoon?

Ringing blows came from nearby. Loud thuds followed every ringing blow

"Yay!" Came a voice. It was Tobias.

I ran around the corner and something hit me in the side. A log.

"Poppy."

All I could see was a huge pile of wood rising higher as I slid to the ground.

"I'm sorry. I'm so sorry," that was Jean.

I blinked, leaning back against the barn.

Tobias's little hands patted my arm. "You woke up."

I felt him all over, he was fine. That's what mattered.

Then I saw him, Jean, crouched a few feet to my side. Strong and dark. Familiar.

"Are you alright? I didn't see you," he ground his teeth.

"Demetri?" I asked. "Don't worry. I'm not hurt much."

He started and took a step back. "What?" he whispered looking around and then he came closer.

I pulled Toby closer. "Isn't that your name?"

"Where did you hear it?"

"Didn't you tell me?" I tried to think. "You must have. It's yours right?"

"Let's go inside," he looked around and held out his hand. Then paused and backed up. "I'm sorry. I wasn't thinking."

"Can we eat?" Tobias said. "I'm hungry."

"Would you like help?" That was Demetri, or Jean. What was his name?

I swallowed and fought down too many emotions. It was an offer of help. That's all. I closed my eyes and shook my head. "I'm alright."

"Can you walk?" he asked.

I gripped the side of the barn and stood. My side only hurt a little where the log had hit me.

Leaves crumbled under every step. Tobias held my hand while we walked and I held my side with the other.

Demetri walked nearby. It was different to be with someone else. He was safe, I was convinced of that, but I hadn't realized how much more it was with Karl. So much more than just safe.

Tobias held onto my skirt. "We ate when I woke up. But now I'm hungry."

I forced my mouth into a smile. He was happy with that. Somehow we made it to the kitchen.

Demetri almost pushed me into a chair. "Sit." A pitcher in his hand, he came to the table. Tobias climbed onto my lap.

"I like milk," Toby said.

I had to do something and soon. I needed help to save Karl.

"I'm sorry that block hit you."

I looked up to find Demetri's intense dark eyes boring into mine.

"We can talk about it, everything, later on if you'd like," he glanced at Tobias then back at me.

I nodded, my head still be spinning. "Later would be good."

He set a glass of milk before me, and smiled. "Perhaps a bath tonight, Toby?"

I waited to see what he'd say. He'd hated baths since he was old enough to know that boys usually did.

"Do I have to?" He asked, his eyes innocent as he tried to worm his way out of it.

I sucked in a breath. How I missed him trying to get away with something. "Yes, you have to."

He went back to his milk. Not surprised or even unhappy.

Demetri pushed my cup closer till it was almost in my hand.

All at once the smell of the kitchen, the odor of meat or sour milk or something made my stomach heave. I ran outside and lost my dinner, burning like acid as it came up my throat. I pressed my forehead into the barn, gripping the wood, trying to stop shaking.

"She's ok. Why don't you get your car from where you slept?" Demetri said, no doubt to Tobias. Then his feet were standing beside me.

"I'm ok," I said. "But not to eat."

"You don't have to," he said. "But Tobias will worry if you stay out here. And it's better not to be seen."

I held onto the rough board wall. Why was I so weak now?

"How about some water?"

"Yes," I still flinched when he put his arm behind me.

The hall sounded hollow, the kitchen still smelled off. But Demetri got me water and gave Tobias some spoons and a roll and put him in a cupboard. The door was open and Tobias was happy.

But I looked up at Demetri.

"Growing up we played in cupboards," he spoke only loud enough for me to hear. "Saves time if we needed to be hid. They'd just close the doors."

I shivered at that. Growing up always afraid.

"I didn't know that's why till I was older, of course."

I nodded. "Of course."

He sat down opposite me. "What are you planning to do?"

"I don't know," it was all I could think about but it seemed impossible. I glanced at Tobias. "But I have to get Karl out."

"Good. I agree."

"Why? Why are you helping us? Why did you come in the first place?"

Demetri put his hand on the table in front of me. "Karl's important to the underground," he lowered his voice. "And he's my friend."

I took a sip of water and then another.

"The trouble is thinking of a plan. And convincing the others."

Tobias was happy, eating and playing with his car.

"You got inside?" He whispered.

I nodded.

"How?"

"I pretended to be with the Swiss aid unit," I whispered. "It took days, doing the work so I didn't arouse suspicion. That last day I felt I was close and lost track of time."

"What vehicles go in and out?" He asked. "Are there any civilians? Are the guards all French or are some German?"

I closed my eyes. "I was only there one night."

"You were there overnight?"

"It was an accident," I took another drink of water. "I didn't get to the truck in time, so I hid."

"Try and think. Is there any way I could get in?"

"I saw the guards changing duty," that guard. "One of the guards was kind to Tobias and the man who took care of him. All I saw were French."

"A man was taking care of him?"

"Yes. He helped me get away. And he helped me talk to Karl once too."

Demetri's face darkened, his jaw tight.

"Tell me I'm not the stupidest person ever," I leaned forward. "Tell me I didn't get Karl in more danger."

"What was his name?"

"Toby called him Uncle Fritz," I swallowed. "I meant to ask him his name a few times but I always forgot."

"Describe him."

The cup in my hands was warm now, the edge digging into my hand.

"Taller than you. His hair was graying and he was going bald, but only on the top of his head." I waited for him to talk, to say something. "Is he someone you know?"

He shook his head. "No. But coincidences are rare. He found the boy and took care of him and made friends with the guard and helped you talk to Karl and then escape."

"How can we save Karl?" I asked. "I'll do whatever it takes."

"Think," his voice was hoarse. "Who goes in and out of those gates besides guards and the relief workers? Is there anyone at all?"

Think I did.

Demetri sat up. "You have it?"

"I don't know if it's helpful or not," it was disgusting. "I don't know how often, but they haul troughs of waste out of the camp. I don't think soldiers did the work."

He clapped his hands together. "Now we have something to work with."

I shook my head. "What am I to do?" I leaned closer. "And why are you so good with kids?"

"I had a lot of cousins." It wasn't a good answer, but it was all I was going to get. "Ready to try some food?"

After I swallowed a little soup and Tobias had eaten two bowls, a slice of bread and another cup of milk, he got a bath.

Demetri filled the tub and left.

I stripped Tobias and put him in. Scrubbing him off with a washcloth I felt the lines along his ribs, only a few weeks in there and he'd lost his baby chubbiness. But it was quiet and peaceful here. I was giving him a bath and he was safe and warm.

I poured water over Tobias's hair, combing my fingers through it. There was the thick scar above his ear, where he fell on the furnace last year. Thank goodness it wasn't lit.

"Why did you go?"

The question hit me. His beautiful dark eyes serious, staring up into mine. He needed to know.

"I didn't want to leave you," I held his arms and sat down, at eye level. "They didn't give me a choice. They took me, Toby."

"But you pushed me into Nana's arms and said be good," he leaned closer to me. "Why did you say that?"

"I was trying to keep you safe," I poured water over his back. "I didn't want to leave, but I thought it was safer. I wanted you to be safe."

"You weren't there when I woke up. You couldn't cry with me when I got sad."

260

"Baby, I cried more when I was alone."

"Are you leaving me again?" He whispered. His whole body was tense.

"I have to help my friend. He's still inside there, all alone." I traced his baby chin. "He saved me, Toby, I can't leave him."

"Don't leave me," he grabbed my neck and pulled me tight. "Mama, don't leave me."

Never before had he said those words to me. "Poppy, my name is Poppy."

"You take care of me," his little eyes were serious. "And you love me."

My throat was tight, my heart hurt so much I could hardly breathe. "I do love you. And I will always care for you. But Poppy is a good name too, don't you think?"

He cocked his head to the side, the little wheels turning. "No one else says Poppy."

"Lucky, aren't you?" said Demetri.

I jumped, my heart pounding in an instant.

"A special name all your own," he stood a few feet inside the door.

Tobias looked at him and then finally turned back to me. "Is my bath done?"

"Yes."

"Is this our home?" Tobias asked.

"No, we're visiting," I wrapped him in the towel and carried him to the bench by the stove, glad he couldn't see my face.

Demetri picked up the tub and carried it out.

A minute later Tobias was dressed and dried and I took him to the bedroom. I tucked him under the blankets, rubbing his back to warm him and remind him I was near. To feel again that he was here. "Goodnight, beautiful."

He smiled at me and rolled over, exhausted but not ready to give up.

I rubbed his back and waited for the heavy breathing, for his hands to relax and sleep to take him.

Before I always struggled to stay awake. But tonight I was wide awake and he fell asleep too fast, I wasn't ready to leave him. I wasn't ready to face Demetri and decisions.

Karl.

The thought pulled me off the bed. I bent down and kissed Tobias once more on his little chin, his forehead, his soft little hand.

I swallowed hard. It shouldn't be possible for two different loves to both be so all-consuming. The pain in my chest wasn't from cold or hunger. It was a terrifying pain that was so much worse.

I went out and closed the door behind me.

Demetri was waiting in the hall. "He's asleep?"

I nodded. "Thank you for taking care of him today." I went back to the kitchen, still steamy from the bath and the extra warm fire.

He closed the door behind us.

I flinched. But closing the door would keep in the warmth. It made sense.

"You said you aren't going to leave him," Demetri sat at the table.

How long was he listening outside the door? "And?"

"Nothing. The others will be here soon."

"From last night?"

"Yes," He cleared his throat. "I asked them to come. So we can make a plan."

I nodded. "Thank you. So much."

He cleared his throat. "I do have something I need to ask," he stood staring at me, so serious.

"Did you hear something?" Karl. Something happened. "What is it? What's wrong?"

"No. Nothing like that," he sat down. "But how did you know my name? Did Karl tell you? Everyone here calls me Jean."

"He never mentioned you."

He stared at me. "But you know my name. How did you know my name is Demetri?"

"I don't know, I'm sorry. I thought it was your name."

He rubbed his hands together and looked away. "Would you call me Jean? The others don't know my name and I'd like to keep it that way."

"Of course," I swallowed. How did I know? Did Karl say it in his sleep? "I'm sorry."

"That's alright. I'll give you a few minutes," he stood and left the room.

A few minutes for what? Then I saw a basin and pitcher, steam rising from it. Life was simpler when no one noticed me but it was very kind of him. I soaked a cloth in the hot water and held it to my face. When did washing my face become a luxury? I soaked the cloth again, the warmth impossible to resist.

"They'll be here soon," Demetri said. "Sorry if I startled you."

"It's alright," if there was anything to be done to save Karl, this is when it would be decided. "But why are you here?"

"Karl," he threw another log on the fire. "I owe him."

I pressed the dry towel to my face. It sounded like so much more. "That's why you're helping me?"

"Yes."

The bluntness was reassuring. I dropped the towel to the table. "Thank you."

"I haven't done much and don't know if they'll agree to help us." The lines were being drawn.

"But they are coming," the gnawing inside was growing. "They're coming to make a plan?"

"I don't know if they'll want to risk it," he pressed his lips together, the lines along his jaws suddenly sharp.

"Why me and not him?" I whispered, clenching my hands inside the towel. I had to stay calm.

"I'm not saying they won't help, but there's no guarantee. I thought you should know."

The walls of the room closed in. The waiting was old and it'd just started.

"Last night you had questions."

I looked up. "What?"

"Any more?"

"Last night's a little blurry," I could feel the blood rush to my face. "I don't remember much."

"You had questions about Karl."

My pulse picked up. That one day Karl was late getting back, I knew something was off, I should have asked what was going on. He might have told me. We might have gotten honest.

"Karl knew about Tobias," if Demetri started shouting, it couldn't hit me harder than when he told me last night. "What else did you find out?"

"Is there something else?"

Footsteps in the hall. Someone was out there.

I bit my tongue. Who found us this far out, in an old barn?

The door opened and a man stepped into the light, the man who'd come in the house for me. "You're here," he said, letting out a breath.

Another followed and they closed the door behind them. Both were panting.

Demetri brought glasses of water to the table.

"Were else would I be?" I asked. "Did you think I'd run off?"

"You've done it before," the leader laughed. He whispered in French and the other guy joined him. "I'm Marcel."

Demetri tried to hide his smile.

I was small in this group of men. Both in stature and in

status. They risked so much to help others in the underground. And this man before me, sitting across from me was the leader. Yet I didn't feel threatened.

"The town's quite torn up, the commandant's furious you got away with the boy."

"I don't understand."

"We did a lot of the searching," he said. "You're important for some reason and they spared no pains to find you."

"But I'm not important," I looked from face to face. "Why does he want me so much? And Tobias? This doesn't make sense. I'm nobody."

Demetri slid closer. "Karl isn't."

My stomach knotted.

Marcel leaned in. "We need to get Von Liedersdorf out."

Demetri's hands were under the table but the veins in his neck were taut.

"Do you have any ideas?" Louis asked.

I swallowed, looking from face to face. Should I trust them? I looked at Demetri, he knew Karl, a little.

"We want to get him out," he said, "But are you sure it's Karl?"

"I spoke with him. I'm sure."

Louis whispered something and Marcel looked back at me. "What sort of building was he in? How well was he guarded?"

I closed my eyes. "It was one of the few buildings by the front gate. There were bars on the window but the guard was in the other room. He came in to check twice in ten minutes."

"Was that at night or during the day?"

"Night."

"But Fritz spoke with him during the day," Demetri said, looking at me. "The one who was friends with the guard."

"Friends with a guard?" Marcel looked from Demetri to me. "What did he look like? How did you come in contact with him?"

My spine crawled. "I found Tobias with him. He helped me hide overnight and helped me get out."

"What's his name?" Marcel gripped the table, all the veins in his arms stood out. "What does he look like?"

"Tobias called him Uncle Fritz. He never said anything else," I was shaking inside and out. "He was thin and tall, taller than you. Thinning gray hair, balding on top."

"He was fluent in German?"

I nodded. "Who is he?"

"We believe they planted someone inside. That explains how they know you were there, and that you escaped with the boy."

My head sank to the table, too heavy to hold up. I'd brought Karl more trouble than ever. "Why did he help me get out?"

"Doubtless you were meant to be caught, but something went wrong and you got away. But we want to get Karl out."

My head bobbed up. "You're still going to?"

"We have to get in though."

"Lena has an idea for that." Demetri said. "Civilians do go inside."

I cringed at the thought. When they turned to me, I cringed even more. "It's the waste troughs. I saw the wagons go in and out a few times. I wasn't paying much attention but it wasn't guards doing it."

Marcel sat forward. "Did they use prisoners?"

"I don't think so."

Louis said something.

Demetri cut him off. They were speaking fast, low. It was hard to make much out. Marcel straightened, "Impossible," Louis said something and Demetri slammed his hand on the table.

Marcel turned to me. "We have an idea."

"No," Demetri stood and shook me along with the table.

"And what do you suggest?" Marcel stood opposite him. "It's worth a try."

I swallowed hard. "What's your plan?"

"The Abwehr is sending an officer to pick up Liedersdorf. We're going to send someone else early in his place," Marcel glanced at Demetri then looked back at me. "An officer and his wife."

Demetri clenched his teeth. His tension almost palpable.

"Wife?" The rest of the plan was explained, but I couldn't focus.

It got quiet and I looked up.

"What do you think?" Marcel asked.

I looked at Demetri.

He was staring at the table, tense. Still.

I swallowed hard. "If it will save Karl…"

Demetri met my eyes and sighed. Did he think I wouldn't do it or that I couldn't?

"I'll do it," I said. "But I'm not good at pretending."

Demetri shifted on the bench. Then he said something, leaning forward he whispered in a furious rush.

"We'll risk it," Marcel said, nodding.

"What?" I asked pushing back in the chair. "Talking in front of me isn't nice."

Marcel shook his head. "It's nothing of importance."

"Tell me what you said," I stood and faced Demetri. "Tell me now."

He sighed, "I told them something Karl said once."

I felt my face heat up, and the chair back in front of me now was clasped in my hands. "I don't know what would have been so funny."

"He told me you acted once, he thought you were convincing."

My hands were numb from squeezing the chair so tight. "He said, what?"

"He wouldn't give details," Marcel leaned over the table, his voice was low. "You could share those now if you'd like."

"We were together for months," I turned away. "It could have been any number of times."

"It's of little consequence. Will you do it? There aren't many girls in the area who speak enough German and are willing to go in. We'll set it for tomorrow afternoon. Sooner the better if someone's on their way."

"I don't have anything to wear," I saw the problems now we'd decided to do it.

Louis said something fast to Marcel.

He turned to me. "His sister will bring clothes tomorrow. And she'll stay with Tobias while you're gone."

They stood now, all of them, and Marcel turned to Demetri. "I'll send the uniform over first thing, and the car."

Uniform? "I missed a few details." A little or a lot.

"It's late. He can fill you in," Marcel said, nodding to Demetri, then he and Louis were gone. The door clicked behind them in the silent hall.

Demetri and I were alone.

"If there was another way I wouldn't have agreed," Demetri said. "But I couldn't think of any." He opened the stove and threw in a log. A speck of coal flew out and hit his hand, before I could say a thing he'd smacked it, a smudge of soot the only thing left.

"It'll work," I said sitting down. I could sleep after he told me the plan.

But he didn't' seem to remember that. He sat and stared at the fire through the slits above the door, his mouth tight and tense. He was always tense.

"Could you tell me what I'm doing? I think I missed some of it," all would be more accurate, but I didn't need to say that.

He didn't look at me. "I'm your beastly husband sent here on official orders, and we're to make a scene. I was sent here to investigate Karl's story and take him back with me."

I waited. There had to be a reason for me to go along.

"You came along and we have to make a scene. A big commotion is what we're after, with yelling. Something that gets them on edge, to distract the commandant."

I flinched. "I can do that."

He looked up. "I know, but they didn't. That's why I was rude. I had to prove that you could get angry. I apologize for playing you, but I don't know how much time he has left."

"I behaved perfectly then," I traced the line on the table. "But it won't be like that tomorrow. It'll be for real and it'll matter. What if I mess up?"

"By this time tomorrow you'll be with Karl. Remember that and you'll be fine."

"Are you willing to bet your life on it? What makes you risk so much for him?"

"Without Karl you don't have much chance of getting anywhere. Getting him out is the best way to save you. I promised him," he swallowed and looked away. "And I don't have anything to lose."

"Why is it you going in?" I asked. "Is it so dangerous you're the only one who would?"

"It's because I won't be recognized, the others are local. But Marcel is smart, if there wasn't a good chance of success, we wouldn't do it."

"I suppose."

"You should get some sleep."

I nodded but my eyes wouldn't listen, the table was so soft.

The table sank beneath me, the world swayed and I pulled away from the arms gripping me.

"Stop screaming," the voice was close but it was wrong. It wasn't Karl. "Stop screaming Lena."

The whole room swam, but then my hands were on the table again. I was standing again. I sucked in a breath but couldn't. Then a hand left from my mouth.

"I'm sorry."

I opened my eyes.

Demetri stood few steps away. His hands in the air.

"What happened?" I asked looking around the room, coming back to Demetri.

"I couldn't wake you, I swear I tried. But you need to get some sleep so I thought I could…I'm sorry."

I nodded, though now with my heart racing it was hard to believe I'd get to sleep at all. "Sorry I screamed." At least I didn't claw him. I looked at his arms, no marks, I forced myself to look at his face.

"What is it?" He backed up. "I won't touch you." He said, holding up his hands.

"Did I hurt you?" He looked at me.

I shook my head. "Did I scratch you or hit you? Did I hurt you at all?"

He sat down and worked at his boot laces. "Just screamed."

At least I didn't hurt him. I went to the door.

"So much for exaggerating."

I sucked in a breath and turned back. "What?"

He looked up. "Nothing."

I waited. Karl wouldn't have given into this, but maybe Demetri would.

He sighed. "When Karl had me watch you, he was specific that I never startle you, especially not to wake you."

"He told you not to wake me."

He dropped the boot. "Not that I was to be seen, ever. But just in case, he made that clear."

"He told you I startle easily?" If he told everyone that, he may have told them more.

"He demanded I always guard you and then gave me specific instructions. You didn't do well with, contact. I thought he was exaggerating."

"You guarded me?"

"I told you last night. When Karl was away for more than a

few hours someone was close," he stood up and took a few steps closer. "He said you needed watching."

I backed to the door.

He stopped. "He was right."

I flung open the door and hurried to Tobias's room, went in and closed it behind me, holding the knob with both hands. My heart was so loud it was hard to hear Tobias.

The clouds covered the moon, keeping even a little light from the room.

I needed sleep. Tomorrow I had to be calm and controlled and then make a scene, but I couldn't do that if I was tired. I found the bed and froze. Then felt further on it.

The bed was empty.

The silence of the room gripped my chest, no one else was in the room. I searched the bed again, then the floor. Tobias didn't fall out of bed but the bed was empty, it wasn't even warm. We'd been talking yes, but not that long. Not an hour. Someone had come and taken him. I'd lost him again.

I ran from the room.

Demetri was inches from the door, his hand reaching for the handle. He saw me and backed up.

"Tobias is gone. He's not in bed," I looked up and down the hall, as if he would appear and disprove me. I wouldn't have minded being proved wrong.

"It'd be hard to find him," Demetri pointing at the door behind me. "If you looked in that room."

"What?"

"That's where I sleep. Tobias is in that room," he nodded to the next door over.

"I'm sorry," I moved towards the door he'd pointed out.

"Now you know where to find me," he seemed to be joking, but with so little light it was hard to be sure.

"Thank you," I said and disappeared into the right room. Tobias's breathing greeted me and I sank down beside him.

What if something went wrong? What if I said goodbye tomorrow and never saw him again?

It was too horrible to consider. I pulled him close and wrapped the blankets around us both.

He sighed and curled into my neck.

I bit my lip. I had to do this. I had to save Karl. But how could I leave Tobias?

My heart was tired from pounding so often, my eyes ached from holding in the tears. All of me was tired but my mind wouldn't stop spinning.

Tobias nestled into me. I had him back. I had him, but my heart was breaking.

TWENTY-EIGHT

$\mathcal{I}$ didn't move. I didn't want to and I didn't have to and there was nothing that could make me.

Little footsteps clattered up to the door.

Tobias. The door opened and he ran up to the bed. "Poppy, are you awake?" His eyes were so bright, but wide.

I pulled him onto the bed.

"I'm sticky with jam," he pulled back.

But I pulled him closer, kissing his nose and his cheeks and his mouth. "I like jam," I brushed the hair from his forehead. He was still my little boy. "And I like you."

He wrapped his arms around my neck. "I like jam too."

The door creaked.

"I'm sorry to intrude," it was Demetri, but he wasn't alone.

A girl stood there, beautiful and clean and close enough to my age. Then I remembered I was in bed, with the wear of weeks on me. And Demetri was here, though it was hard to say if that made this better or worse. He turned and left.

Tobias licked a smear of jam off his finger. "We got your bath ready. I helped."

I watched the girl. "I'm taking a bath?"

Tobias kissed me, his little hands patting my hair. "I get to help outside," he wriggled off the bed.

I smiled at her and pulled my knees up, exposed without him beside me.

She smiled back and nodded towards the kitchen, then left the room. She must be Louis's sister, she looked like him.

I followed her and Tobias trailed along, his little hand snuck into mine. "What've you been doing?"

"Eating," he said swinging his arm and mine with it.

"Eating? And then what?" Bits of bark and woods shavings trailed after us. So much for his bath last night.

"Looking at stuff."

I stopped and swung him up into my arms and pressed my nose into his face.

"I love you," I whispered and he giggled. Then I tickled his side and he laughed out loud.

"Celine's here to help you get ready."

I spun.

Demetri stood in the doorway of the kitchen. "Need anything before I take Tobias outside?"

Celine looked uncomfortable now.

"No. But Tobias can stay here."

"You need to hurry. Marcel will be here in a few hours," he stepped closer, reaching for Tobias. "Tobias likes playing outside," his eyes were on me. "There isn't much time."

"Very well," I smiled down at Tobias. "Be a good helper."

He smiled and slid to the ground.

"Thank you," I looked up at Demetri.

He nodded and they were gone.

The kitchen was silent.

Celine stood looking at me. Then she started pouring water from the stove into a tub.

I took one of the other buckets and poured it in. "Thank you for helping us."

She nodded. "I'm happy to help. I'll leave you to soak then I'll come back." She left the room.

I struggled out of all my clothes but my drawers and stepped into the water. It was warm and the tub just big enough. Then all I could think about was how perfect and warm the water was. Warmth covered me and I sank into it.

A few minutes later someone knocked on the door. Then knocked again. Celine came in, keeping her eyes away.

"It's ok," I said. "But I can't do a thing with my hair."

She exhaled, perhaps relieved I left something on. "I can help with that," she must know what sort of character I was acting. I wanted to ask what she knew about us and why she was helping, but I kept my mouth shut.

The minutes ticked by, each tick eating into my nerves till I was sick. Today was dangerous, someone could get hurt. I could make things worse.

But the water felt so good. I kept scrubbing my arms and my legs and my neck while she worked with my tangled hair.

"I'll leave you to dress," she pointed to the pile of clothes on a chair, stood and went out.

Stripping quickly I wrapped the towel around me and stepped out of the water.

A pile of white sat on top, new underthings.

All my slips were past repairing but these were so fine, so lacy and expensive I couldn't wear them. I looked around, there wasn't anything else. I was playing someone rich. A jolt went up my back.

The strings tangled the instant I slipped into them. Breathing heavy I slowed down and worked through it, laces up the front, ties on the sides. Where they'd gotten these, I didn't want to know.

Then Celine was beside me again. "Shall I?" She raised her eyebrows, reaching forward.

"Thank you," I was likely to rip something if she didn't help.

She twisted the bodice halfway around, then pulled it down and tied it up the back. Pulling the towel off my hair she sighed.

She'd left me for one minute and I found a way to mess something up.

"What's wrong?"

"Your hair is lovely," hers was short and bobbed, but clean and smooth and shiny.

"So is yours."

She shook her head and laughed. Then she gasped and pulled back.

"Celine?"

But she turned away and took up the dress, her lips pressed together when she turned back holding it up for me.

I slipped it on, numb. What did I do wrong?

She turned for something else on the table.

I grabbed her arm. "What is it? What's wrong?"

"I'm sorry. I shouldn't have done that," she nodded to the chair then stood behind and toweled my hair. Sitting by the fire it dried fast, and soon she was brushing it out.

She was helping because she believed I could help Karl, but I might be the worst person to trust. I'd never been good under pressure before.

Knotting my hands in a sock I stared at the wall over the stove, at the table, but all I could think about was what I'd say to Tobias when I left him.

Only for a few hours, lord willing, but there was no guarantee. He was out of the camp and the underground would find a safe place for him if it...if that was necessary. But I had to try and help Karl. I owed it to him even if it was only to say goodbye.

I refused to think if, there was no if.

Karl's arms through the bars holding me up. His command to take Tobias and leave him. I couldn't leave Karl after he'd come back to help me, and I couldn't leave him without trying to help.

Celine braided my hair, her hands gentle. Her fingers stilled when they came to the ridge along my forehead.

It was healed now but I shivered, remembering the night I got it. He'd rescued me then too. I was right to try.

Celine rested her hand on my shoulder.

I twisted my head back to her. "It's ok," I said touching her hand and forcing a smile.

We couldn't be late. A knock at the door made me jump.

"Come in," Celine called.

The door opened and Demetri came in, Tobias in his arms. Demetri stared at me for a long minute.

Tobias stared too, then lunged forward. "Poppy."

I jumped to catch him and fell into the tub.

Demetri had Tobias, he was fine, but my sleeve was soaked. I already messed up.

Celine was at my sleeve with the towel.

"I'm sorry."

Demetri said something under his breath, but I kept my eyes on Celine.

She looked up and said something to him, in French. She looked angry.

"Demetri, what is it?" Oh no, why did I have to forget and use that name? Now they were both angry. "I'm sorry. I didn't mean to. I'm sorry."

Demetri leaned down to me, Tobias in his arms. "I'm not mad at you and neither is Celine. She's mad for you."

They both believed I could help Karl.

Demetri went to the cupboard with Tobias. "We came in for a bite to eat," he poured a glass of milk.

My stomach cramped. I should eat. But to take more from them, whoever it was, it seemed wrong. They had already provided so much.

Celine threw down the towel and picked up the comb again.

Demetri came over with another glass and held it out.

"I'm alright," I said.

He held it out further. "Karl will give me hell if you don't eat something."

I had to smile, it did sound like Karl. Blaming Demetri if I hadn't eaten. I brought the milk to my lips and closed my eyes. I didn't deserve to be here with my little boy and people trying to help.

Little hands touched my face.

I took a breath and forced my eyes open. Tobias was on Demetri's knee, crouched beside me.

"The milk is good," Tobias said.

I smiled but my eyes were blurry. "I know. You drink yours and I'll drink mine."

Demetri stood up. "Now I have to get dressed," they left, Tobias still holding the cup in his hands.

Celine worked on my hair, twisting it and pinning it up.

I looked down at the milk. A few bubbles were on the edge when I raised it. I listened for Tobias. For footsteps, for something or anything to go wrong. I took a drink.

Celine stopped with my hair and stepped away. She pulled at the bodice, saying something under her breath. Then she came around, her eyes stopping on my arm.

I grimaced. How could I have been so clumsy? "I'm sorry."

"It's nothing," she took a clean towel and rubbed at it. Then she had me stand, taking the cup from my hand.

"Thank you so much," if only I could make her understand how grateful I was.

"I'm happy to help."

Shiny buttons caught my eye and I froze.

A soldier stood in the doorway. How did they discover us? How?

I turned to face them and let out a breath.

It was only Demetri, dressed as a Wehrmacht officer. As Karl used to dress. "Tobias is tired. And Marcel will be here soon."

I lowered my eyes to Tobias.

He looked from person to person ending on me.

I came forward and crouched, watching where my skirts touched the floor before settling on Tobias's little face. "Toby," I said reaching out a hand. "I have to go help a friend."

He let go of Demetri and clenched my hand with both of his.

"I'm going to help a friend, and then I'm coming back to you."

He leaned forward. "Why are you leaving me?"

"I have to help him. He saved me and he needs my help. Celine is going to stay with you. She's so nice. Look how she fixed my hair," I held his hands in mine and let him press his forehead into mine. "I'll come back."

Celine wrapped a sheet around Tobias then nodded to me. "Go ahead."

Tears filled my eyes, I pulled Tobias into my arms, crushing him to me. "I love you. I love you so much."

He hugged me and I hugged him back. Standing up I held him close. I didn't want to know what the others were thinking. Was I too emotional to play my part? Why did I already have a three-year-old child? "Can you be good for Celine?"

He shook his head. "No. I want to go with you."

"Please, Toby. I have to go, I have to. But I'll come back." A car drove up outside.

Tobias raised his eyes to mine. "Don't go."

Celine stepped towards me, her hands held out.

I choked down a sob and pressed my face into his. "I love you."

"We'll be back tonight," Demetri said. "Don't worry, Toby. I'm going to keep Poppy safe."

I jumped when I felt him so close. I hadn't noticed him come up.

"And Celine knows you like jam on your bread," he added.

Tobias was still staring when I looked down at him again. Begging me.

Marcel appeared at the door of the kitchen. "It's time. Are you ready?"

I handed Tobias to Celine.

She held him and whispered to him.

But he didn't see her, he was just staring at me.

The walls spun in a circle and my stomach lurched but there wasn't enough to lose.

"Poppy!" Toby screamed.

Two hands caught me, I clenched my nails into my hands and didn't scream. I took a deep breath and opened my eyes to see Demetri. His arm was tense around my back.

The quiet was worse than the screaming a minute before.

"I'm okay," I held onto his arm. "Toby, I'm better now. I got dizzy, that's all." I moved towards him and Demetri came too. I leaned down to kiss Tobias and the tight circle of Celine holding Tobias, and Demetri holding me was enough to make anyone nauseous.

"I'm sorry," Marcel said. "But we have to go."

"I'll come back," I touched Toby's face then turned and walked from the kitchen.

Demetri had one hand on my back.

I clenched his other arm. "I'll be fine in a minute."

The hallway was long and dim, but when we stepped outside I took a deep breath of the chill air.

"You look perfect," Marcel said, opening the back door of a shiny black car. It looked familiar, my heart jumped to my throat.

Demetri's arm tightened. "What is it?"

"Nothing," I said pushing away the memory of the last black car I rode in and stepped inside.

Demetri slipped in beside me and shut the door. "Are you sure you can do this?"

"I have to," I whispered back.

"I mean, are you sure you want to?" He lowered his voice. "Leave Tobias?"

My pulse picked up. I couldn't answer but I nodded and looked away to hide my tears. Toby's eyes were stricken when I handed him to Celine. How could I hand him over to a stranger when he was begging me not to? No matter how nice she seemed, I left him.

The front door of the car slammed shut.

"The plan is unchanged from last night," Marcel said and started the engine. Then he twisted in the seat and looked back at us. "Any questions?"

Demetri shifted closer to me, though his whole arm tensed up.

"Who are we?" I asked. "And what are we supposedly doing here?"

Demetri's arm couldn't get any tenser.

Karl. I was doing this for Karl.

"Newly, but not happily married, and you," he pointed to Demetri, "were sent to investigate what Karl was doing here."

Married. I drew in a breath.

He looked at me, taking in my attire. "Your job is to be distracting, get them on edge. Get into an argument and if that isn't enough, slap him. It has to look real. We're not comfortable with displays of emotion, especially from Germans. The idea is to make them want you to leave and not pay attention to what doesn't make sense."

My stomach turned at the thought of slapping Demetri. Why did they always seem to think of that?

"Let's go," Demetri said then he turned to me. "You're free to slap all you want. Let's just hope Karl doesn't see."

The car was loud and we were moving now.

"He'll be furious," Demetri was laughing now, but he wasn't joking.

"He'll be grateful you came. But I'm…" scared to death didn't cover half of it. What if I couldn't get him out? What if I got caught and left Tobias again? And what if he did get out, what would happen next?

"You haven't done anything wrong," he said. "Though he'll be mad I'm letting you go back in."

The drive was silent for a while.

"But there's something we have to discuss," he swallowed, loud beside me. "Something I need to ask."

I held my breath.

"We have to make this believable."

"I know."

He shook his head. "This won't work if I can't even touch your arm."

"I'm expecting that."

"So, if I put my arm around you, will that be alright?"

I nodded.

"We can do this. Focus on why we're going in, on getting Karl out."

I looked at him. "What happened?"

"Nothing. We wouldn't go in if we didn't think we could save him. Try to breathe."

The car swerved off the road.

"We're meeting your driver. I can't go in," Marcel said before I could open my mouth. "One more thing, the commandant is known for disliking women in general and childish ones in particular."

"Is that what I'm supposed to be?"

Marcel shrugged. "I'm telling you what we know. Use it as

you will."

"You're an officer?" I asked Demetri.

"For the day," he shrugged. "For today, I come from a long line of military heroes."

Marcel wrenched the car to a stop and ran for the trees a few yards away.

What if it was a trap and Demetri got arrested along with Karl and Tobias, all because of me?

A private ran out of the woods, a German private or someone in that uniform. He slid into the seat and slammed the door. Jamming the stick forward he drove in a circle and we were back on the road a second later.

I raised my eyebrows at Demetri and he did the same back.

He addressed him in French. No response. "What's going on?" He asked, in German this time.

The young man looked back for a fraction of a second before focusing on the road again. "We're driving to the camp as you instructed. Has there been a change since we left the inn, sir?" His German was perfect, his tone and behavior almost had me convinced.

"No. That will be all," Demetri said and he put his arm around my shoulder.

I shivered.

He moved it and stared at the window, shaking his head.

This was not going to be easy.

The gates ahead were small, but I could still see them in my head even when I closed my eyes.

"For Karl," he whispered, too close.

I bit my lip and stayed still.

"Lena."

I opened my eyes.

"You need to be distracting," he rolled his head to the side. "You know what I mean?"

"I understand. What's the rest of the plan?" I asked. "The part that matters?"

"It's better if you don't know, that way you can simply respond."

I pushed down the lump in my throat.

"This won't take long" he leaned even closer now. "If you feel faint or it's getting too hard..."

The blood pounded in my head, the need to get away filled me. "Yes?"

"Dig your nails into my arm or hand or something. Let me know, I'll keep you up."

"It seems I'm more trouble than help."

"No. We need you," Demetri didn't hesitate. "You'll see."

"You needed a girl who spoke German. Not me. I'm—"

"Perfect for the part."

We were at the gate now, and out of time to argue. The guard at the gate came forward.

I ignored all the talk and focused on looking bored.

"I'll speak to your superior," Demetri said after a few minutes, his impatience not lost on the guard. "And hurry. I don't appreciate my time being wasted." Then he turned his back on the guard and put his arm on the seat behind me.

Out of the corner of my eye I watched the man go back to the gate.

"What's he doing?" Demetri asked.

"Talking to the other guard," I whispered.

It was hard to pay attention to them with Demetri here, paying so much attention to me.

Real or fake, he was sitting very close.

I thought I was more controlled but I'd been fooling myself. All those times with Karl, when I didn't freak out, it was because it was him, not that I'd gotten better. "He's coming back, and he brought someone with him."

"That's good," he said, but his arm became hard as iron.

Leaning into Demetri I kept one hand inside my coat, clenching it tight while I sighed like a child. "How long will we be here?" I raised my voice when they were a few steps away.

"Not long, I'm sure," Demetri said and stepped out of the car.

I rolled the window down and rested my arms on the door. A distraction was what we were going for. Was this the right sort of distraction? If this was what they wanted, someone beautiful would have been a better choice.

The new man saluted and bowed.

"Are we going inside now?" I interrupted.

The man looked at me, his eyes already tight. He wasn't happy with me.

I sighed, trying to be dramatic. "I'm so tired of traveling in this car."

Demetri looked back at me. "A moment, I'm finding out who's responsible for blocking my orders."

"How are we to finish if we don't go in?" We had to get inside. I willed the men to let us in. "And I need to use a washroom."

"Be still for once," he spoke angry and low but loud enough for everyone to hear. Then he straightened and turned towards the men again and held out his papers. "My orders were specific. We don't want to risk him escaping."

I sank back after Demetri's correction, then smiled at one of the guards. My stomach clenched but I looked at Demetri's back and then back at the guard again. It was worth it, if we could get Karl out. This was what I was supposed to do, wasn't it? Be distracting?

My heart sank.

If getting him out depended on how well I could pretend, we were doomed.

TWENTY-NINE

"*G*ive me a moment," the man went back inside the guard house.

I heard the rumbling of a truck before I saw it. Turning in the seat, I could see it behind us,

We had to get inside. Excitement welled inside and though it didn't make sense I went with it.

Peeking out the window, I winked at a guard. Then I opened the door and got out. I smiled again when Demetri wasn't looking. "I'm so tired," I said leaning against the car.

The soldier in charge came back out. "You may come in the gates, but stay in your car until I get confirmation."

Demetri held the door open and waited for me. "Quickly now."

Once the rumble of the engine had started up, Demetri leaned close, he put his arm around my shoulders. "Focus on the main guard especially, then the commandant. Is this too much?"

I shook my head and leaned back against the seat. "One of those guards is the one who looked away when I sneaked Tobias into the truck."

He smiled at me. "Which one?"

"The taller one, who didn't talk."

Demetri's hand was on my shoulder.

"You're doing great," he smiled, but his eyes were worried.

It took a minute but I got my heart still enough to answer. "You're fine," but it was awful to think how Karl would feel if he saw. "Karl isn't going to see though, is he?"

"Breathe," the car was slowing in front of the buildings, he had one second before the man standing on the porch would hear us. He leaned in and whispered. "You can do this."

Short and to the point. My stomach dropped.

"Smile," he said and stepped out of the car, straightened his jacket, then reached in and held out his hand to me.

It was wrong, every part of me screamed in protest but I had to do it. I put my hand in his.

A commotion started behind us, a man on the porch saluted as we came up the steps. "I'll be right with you," he said and stepped around us.

"When are we supposed to be distracting?" I whispered to Demetri. "What are we trying to keep him from noticing?"

"Them," he nodded to the two men who'd climbed from the truck that followed us in the gate.

"I'm starving, Gustav," I said, loud. "When are we going to eat?" Demetri held my arm.

The commandant looked back at us from the men he was talking to. "I have other things to deal with," his steps came pounding back up the steps.

I groaned and swayed.

Demetri caught me, his arm was hard, he was so close.

I froze at his touch and clenched my teeth. It had to look real, I'd known what we'd be doing. I found Demetri's arm and squeezed.

He squeezed back. "If she can rest on your sofa while we talk, she'll be fine. She's exhausted from the drive."

Footsteps came closer.

287

"Of course," a man said, and we started up the steps.

The swaying made my head spin, now I wasn't acting at all. I dug my nails into my hands, I couldn't even feel it. I kept my eyes shut. I wanted away from Demetri's arms and his watchful eyes, seeing everything I was thinking.

I'd messed up. I'd let Karl down.

His arms tightened.

I breathed and opened my eyes, I had to keep everyone's attention. "You know I get carsick and yet you made me come," it was the first thing that popped into my head.

"You need to eat something, that's all," Demetri said then looked away from me. "I apologize for this."

"Not at all. I have a wife myself," his sigh wasn't an act.

Demetri let me down on the seat and turned to the man. "I'm sure we can finish our business quickly if we leave her to rest here."

"Don't leave me," I grabbed Demetri's coat. "I'm scared to death with all these criminals here. Can't you talk in here? I won't be any trouble." The commandant sighed and looked at Demetri.

"My business won't take long. As you know I'm here to investigate the soldier you discovered," Demetri glanced at me. "If everything's in order, my instructions are to bring him back for questioning. Quietly. I assume you've made the arrangements?"

"I wasn't informed you'd be taking him."

I needed to say something. To get him focused on me instead of what Demetri was saying. "I'm starving, can't you have someone prepare a sandwich or at least some tea?"

"Yes," the commandant nodded to the man standing at the door. "See to it."

"And I need to use your washroom," I smiled up at him. "I won't be gone a minute."

"Are you certain you can walk?" The commandant could scarce keep his manners.

"I was carsick. It happens you know," I said standing. "I won't be long." I clenched Demetri's hand briefly and went the way the man pointed.

Once outside the door I took deep breath. Why did I leave? Instead of helping distract that French Commandant I'd left Demetri alone with him.

I went back in.

"I changed my mind, washing my face isn't worth it. Anyone might be hiding around the corner in a place like this," I settled on the couch beside Demetri. "Are you through with your business?"

"We haven't started," Demetri said. "Sit quiet and wait for your tea while we talk. I don't want to hear another word."

The commandant's lips twitched. He liked Demetri putting me in my place.

"I couldn't bother you if you'd left me home instead of dragging me endless kilometers through this wilderness," I stood up. "Or at least left me at the inn."

"Sofia," he stood and pulled me against him, turning us both a little from the commandant. "don't do this right now." But his whisper was too loud to be real and his hold on my arm was gentle. His back to the commandant he leaned in till his mouth was only a breath from my ear. "Keep going."

"Let go of me," I pulled away. "Take me to the inn and come back tomorrow. I'm tired and—"

"That's enough," he took my arm again. "I've had all I'll take."

The commandant stood and watched.

Demetri mouthed. "Slap me."

I shook my head. "No, let go."

"Stop behaving like a child," he said stepping closer. "And do as I ask."

"Stop being a bully and grow up yourself," I pulled away. My foot caught on the carpet and I fell into a table. A lamp crashed to the floor with me.

Demetri stood still in shock, this wasn't part of the plan. His mouth hung open.

I was sprawled on my back, the lamp in shattered bits around me. I sank back and closed my eyes.

"Sofia."

I sat up and looked at my hands. Blood oozed from the bits of glass sticking out of a dozen gashes. Every time I moved a fraction something twisted in the pit of my stomach.

"I didn't mean to push you," Demetri crouched down, but the lines of worry weren't pretend. "Are you alright?"

"Look what you did," I held out my arms. "Do I look alright to you? I'm covered in blood."

He took me by the elbows and pulled me to the couch. "It was an accident," he turned to the commandant. "I do apologize and I'll pay for the damage, of course."

"Of course, blame it on me." The room spun and the smell of blood made my stomach clench. I closed my eyes and focused on breathing. Now I had to give him a few minutes to work this out.

Their voices were hushed and hurried. "The evidence is clear," Demetri said at last. "I'll take him with me."

"This is unexpected. I have nothing prepared. No guards I can send with you even to Oloron."

"Have him bound and gagged, that will last the drive to town where I left my squad," Demetri wasn't asking. "We'll leave at once."

"I had no orders to release him. Only to assist in your investigation."

"This is a matter of military intelligence. It's of great importance that I get him back without delay."

Be a distraction. "How long does it take to bleed to death?" I tried to sound scared but even to me it sounded forced.

The commandant looked at me then back at Demetri. "He's your soldier, as you say," the hesitation in his voice made me want to scream. "I'll have him brought out. If you'll excuse me."

"Thank you," Demetri said.

The commandant bowed and left the room.

Demetri came to me now. "So much blood, I wouldn't be surprised if you fainted for real this time."

"I'm fine," I said, but I dug my fingers into his arms, letting him pull me to my feet.

He held me steady for a moment, then nodded and put his arm around me. "You okay?" He whispered. "Really?"

I nodded. "Did it work?"

He held me up, one hand on my elbow. "We'll see." And led me out to the porch.

The commandant came up the steps and nodded to Demetri. "I've done as you requested."

Did I do it right? Was I distracting enough? I let out all the worry and looked up at Demetri. "I'm sorry I ruined your trip. I'm sorry." I choked on my sobs. And then I felt someone else's eyes on me. I looked around and lost my breath.

Karl stood beside the car, staring at me and Demetri. At the blood on my hands, and Demetri's arm around me.

I shook my head.

His face was murderous in an instant. And the next he was running towards us.

Then everything spun and I was on the ground.

The voices faded for a moment, then I was dragged back out of the blissful darkness.

"Bound and gagged, I said," that was Demetri and he laughed as he held me tight. What was going on? He'd been working with them all along, he just wanted to show Karl he had me too.

"No. She's fine," he sighed. "She faints at the sight of a mouse, I expected as much."

It was too bright now. I couldn't get my eyes open and I

didn't want too. I'd ruined everything and lost both Tobias and only made things worse for Karl.

Then there was more shouting, Karl's voice rang out. And then there was thud on the ground.

"Use chains if you must, but tie him up and throw him in the back." Demetri shouted. "I don't have time for this."

Then the talking was fast and blurred. Demetri picked me up and put me in the car.

My head swam, but it was nothing to what I felt inside. I held myself frozen. Was this his plan to get Karl out?

"Gagged, I said. I don't want to hear his cussing all the way to town."

The door was closed and I was alone. Nothing moved, nothing made a sound. I opened my eyes and looked at the driver. He was staring ahead, unmoved by the events around him.

Then the door opened again and a rush of cold air made me shiver.

Demetri's hands were gentle, he wrapped handkerchiefs around my arms. He was gentle with me, but having Karl gagged? Why was he having Karl gagged if he was trying to help him?

"Don't struggle, the glass is still in your arms," then he shut the door.

Was he helping me and trying to rescue Karl, or did I take a risk and lose everything in one horrendous mistake?

"Lena," someone whispered. "Lena."

Someone's arms were around me. Holding me, not tight, but holding me close.

"She's okay."

"What do you mean she's ok? She's covered in blood." The voice was deep, angry and familiar. It was ...no, it wasn't.

I drew in a breath and struggled to sit up but my hands were dead and my arms were on fire.

"Lena."

I had to face reality, whatever it was. I opened my eyes.

It was Karl holding me close.

I tried to sit up.

"It's ok," he said, but he didn't let me up.

"What's wrong?" I was still in the back seat, but Karl was here now too. "Why won't you let me up?"

"I will, but slow. You lost a lot of blood," he cupped my face with his hand. "You didn't need to be that convincing." His voice was so gentle.

Like he was about to tell me something.

"He was helping get you out," did he know his name was Demetri? "He got us away from the doctor and was trying to help. I think he was." The car swerved and I fisted my hands. Every bit of glass in my veins bit deeper, sending a jolt of pain singeing down my spine.

"I'm still here," that was Demetri, in the front seat. I hadn't even noticed. "Karl isn't mad I had him tied up."

I looked at Karls hands wrapped around me, thick red marks streaked his skin.

"And gagged," Karl said pushing a strand of hair off my face. "I never saw you with your hair up before."

My stomach flipped. I'd tried to forget how I felt around him.

"You should've seen her before she cut her arms open," Demetri said. "A better distraction we couldn't have had."

A distraction. That's what we'd needed. "So I didn't ruin everything?" I looked at Demetri and slowly leaned back against Karl.

Karl's arms pulled me closer, turning me to face him. "You were perfect," he said, then his teeth gritted. "Though it about killed me, listening to that. I heard you get hurt and I couldn't do a thing."

"It wasn't the plan, I fell on accident," a bump in the road and we were all jolted sideways, my stomach dropped with a sickening lurch.

"You need to be more careful," he whispered in my ear.

I shivered at the warmth and smiled. "Maybe I just need someone to catch me." I didn't open my eyes.

The bumpy road was getting bumpier.

"You knew they were going to tie you up?"

"It's alright," Karl fingers worked at my clenched fist. "He had to make it look real. I guess all the blood wasn't enough. You always were thorough." He was talking towards the front now, towards Demetri.

"I couldn't take any chances. We wouldn't get another shot."

Karl's arms tightened around me and his heart thudded faster, but he didn't say a word.

I opened my eyes. "What was going to happen?"

He shrugged his shoulders.

"Tell me."

"I don't know for sure."

I reached my hand up and traced a red line around his neck.

"How did you get this?"

He straightened his neck a little. A muscle in his neck jerked. "I wasn't prepared to see you covered in blood, in another man's arms. Even if it was Demetri," the lines on his face edged deeper. "I guess you've gotten over some of that."

"No, Karl," Demetri said. "She hasn't."

I was too tired, I closed my eyes and let go, resting on Karl's chest. His steady breathing easy to follow.

"I saw, Demetri. You don't have to say anything."

"You saw but you don't know. I always thought you were exaggerating."

"Your arms were on her, you picked her up," Karl said his voice harder now.

"I kept my hands on her wrists to keep the blood inside her and keep her from falling when she passed out."

"She used to—"

"This morning I caught her when she tripped, one hand on her arm...you said she's sensitive. What the hell happened to her?"

The darkness was nice. Karl's arms were right around me again, I was safe.

"It was for you, Karl. She put on this smile and acted the part, but she had her hands clenched so tight I thought she'd break through her skin. She's not over anything."

"And Tobias? Is he safe?"

The pain in my arms grew. I held my breath but it didn't help. "It hurts," I whispered then relaxed into the darkness.

THIRTY

*T*he silence woke me.

It was dark now and there were trees all around. Too many trees. We should have been back to the barn by now, the camp wasn't hours away.

I sat up and opened my mouth, it was covered before I could get any air.

"Shh," it was Karl. He watched my face while he moved his hand.

There wasn't much moonlight but I could see his face, I could see it was him. "What's going on?"

He put his finger to his lips. "We're avoiding some unpleasant people."

Demetri sat behind the steering wheel.

"Where's the driver?"

"We let him off awhile back. After you," he paused and looked out the window. "Fell asleep."

What did Karl say about Tobias before? What did he know about him?

I shivered and pulled my arms around me.

"Don't," Karl whispered in my ear, his voice breaking. "Don't pull away. Tell me what's wrong, what is it?"

I shook my head and kept my eyes closed.

Worry was hiding how furious he was. And once we were away, when he knew I was somewhere safe and he'd fulfilled his responsibility, then he'd leave and I'd never see him again.

"I can't," my heart was pounding too hard, too fast. I couldn't say what had to be said.

Demetri cleared his throat. "I'll go make sure they're gone." The door opened slow and careful and then it was quiet.

Hot breath on my forehead made me let go and I opened my eyes.

"What is it?" Karl asked, swallowing hard.

I swallowed when he did and made myself meet his gaze. "You don't want me, Karl," I said before I could think about what would follow. But I held onto his shirt, I couldn't let go. "Tobias is mine. I know what men think about girls like me."

"Listen to me," he said. "Lena. Look at me."

I stared at the lines of his shirt. How could I have started this conversation?

His hand cupped my chin and made me look. "I wouldn't change a thing about you. You're perfect."

No matter how hard I bit my tongue I couldn't keep the tears from streaming down my cheeks.

"I want you, Lena. And your son."

I let go of his shirt.

He wiped the tears off my face.

"You're not mad?" I gasped out. "For leaving? For lying?"

"You didn't lie about leaving, you told me," he said. "And I knew why you were going."

Demetri opened the door and sat down, rocking the car. "I'm sorry. It's clear and we should get going." He started the car and a second later we raced along the pitted road.

"How? How did you know about," I hesitated. "About Tobias?"

The moonlight shone into the car right in his face.

"When did you find out?"

Karl sighed and sat up, keeping me in his arms the whole time.

Blood rushed to my head but I ignored it. I had to know.

"What did you think I was doing all those hours I was gone? Never at the same time. At night more often than not," he pushed a strand of hair out of my eyes. "Never telling you a single thing about it." He watched my face. No doubt he could see plenty.

"You were working with the underground," I wasn't asking because it wasn't a question. I already knew from Demetri. "But no one knew about Tobias but my Uncle and Aunt. And my father." Pressure in my head made it hard to focus on talking. "And he wouldn't have admitted to having a daughter, let alone one with a child."

"There's ways to find information."

"No one else knew," I touched his face, smears of dirt hiding the scar by his ear. "Tell me how you knew."

"I'm sorry, Lena," he said. "You're not as good at lying as you think."

My heart started thumping. "What does that mean?"

"Your uncle knew all along."

"You spoke with my uncle?"

"Not directly," a bump in the road pulled me towards the seat, but Karl held me close. "And he knows you're safe."

"Safe?"

"Well you were safe at the bakery, before you left. We were finding a way to bring Tobias to us, your uncle and I. But then they got Tobias..." his mouth tightened and he looked out the window.

"What happened? You have to tell me," I grabbed his shirt. "Is it my uncle?"

"I'm sorry," he said pulling me close.

The tears didn't come, I waited but they didn't.

"Are you ready to leave now?" Karl asked after a few minutes.

"What?" Leave what? The car?

"The barn won't be safe for quite some time," he nodded. "A daring rescue like this will heighten everyone's awareness."

I hadn't had time to think about this. About Karl and Tobias. "I'm not leaving Tobias."

"Of course not," Karl stopped me before I could finish. "I'd never dream of that. Never."

"Alright," Demetri said. "We'll be at the barn in five minutes. We don't have much time."

"Thank you," Karl said. "And I won't forget this."

"I still owe you," Demetri said. "I don't forget either."

What Karl saved him from, I didn't want to know. "And I owe both of you."

Demetri coughed. "Helping you was the best way to help Karl," he didn't turn around. "So, you don't owe me."

Karl sat watching me, waiting.

"It would seem that I only owe you," I pushed my fingers through his hair. Last time I did was a miserable moment, knowing I'd have to leave him.

He'd known all along I was going to leave.

"How can I ever repay you?" I asked tracing his collar bone with my free hand.

His breath sped under my fingers. "Well," he began, then he looked to the front and back at me.

Knowing our thoughts were in the same exact place made my stomach clench.

"Here we are," Demetri said. He parked at the edge of the clearing and cut the engine. The barn looked empty, dark.

"Why are we waiting?" I started to pull out of Karl's arms, but he held me tight.

Both the men were staring, straining to see round the clearing.

"It's been three minutes," Demetri said.

"Not enough," Karl said. "I'll go."

"No," Demetri got out and went to the barn, disappearing inside.

The minutes dragged by. Karl's hand on my back grew tenser, his hold on me tighter and his breath came faster.

Then Demetri appeared at the doorway and he nodded towards us.

Karl got out and held out his hand to me.

I took it and we walked towards the barn, my heart so loud there was no way he didn't hear it.

Demetri held the door open. "Celine's in the kitchen."

I stopped. "And Tobias?" It was so late.

"Celine says he didn't want to sleep," Demetri said leading the way to the kitchen. "He's waiting."

Karl put his arm around my waist but waited.

"Poppy."

That was all I needed to hear. I rushed around the corner and saw him. Standing next to Celine he was staring at Demetri.

"Toby!" I cried, dropping to my knees and hugging him to me. After a minute I realized he was crying too.

"What is it?" I asked letting a small space come between us so I could see his face. "Why the tears, beautiful?"

"You came back," he said. "I thought someone got you and you weren't coming back."

"I said I'd come back, remember?" I said pushing his hair out of his eyes. "I said I'd come back."

"She got me supper. Two times," he pointed at Celine. He leaned closer, cupping his hand. "I like her." His whisper was loud enough for everyone to hear.

I smiled; he was a little boy again. Then I felt a hand on my shoulder, Karl's hand, reminding me we had to go. "Tell her thank you, Toby. And goodbye. We have to go now."

"At night?" He asked walking towards her, but staring at me the whole time. "Where are we going?"

"Say thank you," I said standing up. "And I don't know where."

"Thank you," he said to Celine.

She smiled and hugged him. "He was a very good boy."

"But I didn't eat the fish."

She laughed.

"Don't worry. Not everyone likes fish," Demetri stooped down to Tobias. "And I'll see you again sometime, I'm sure of it."

Tobias turned back to me. "He's not coming?" Then he looked at Karl standing behind me, seeing him for the first time. "Is he your friend? He's bigger than you. Why did he need help?"

I held out my hand and Tobias came and took it. "Sometimes big people need help. And when you have a good friend who needs help, you help them." I lifted him up and hugged him, my wrists tingling but I ignored it.

His little face studied Karl.

"I did help him, but he saved me first, Toby," I whispered rubbing his back.

Karl leaned closer and pulled me against him. His arms came around me and held Tobias up.

"Hey, Toby," he said. "Ready for a car ride?"

Toby looked at him hard, then leaned down to my ear. "Is he coming with us?" So close to Karl, but he was loud enough Demetri and Celine could hear half the room away.

I had to smile. "Yes. He's coming too."

"We have to be gone, and soon," Demetri said. "There isn't time."

"Are you sure we should take the car?" Karl asked, letting go of me. "I don't want suspicion thrown on anyone because of me."

"It's all arranged," Demetri said. "And you have the contact once you're over the border."

I wasn't going to argue. I wasn't ready to run for the speed we'd need to get far enough away, and Tobias couldn't handle that.

Tobias sighed and dropped his head to my shoulder. Rocking a little, I looked around the room and found Celine watching me.

Watching us.

"Thank you," I said nodding at Tobias. She'd been such a calm person when I needed that, and the assurance that Tobias was safe had helped. Holding Tobias with one hand was a strain, he'd gotten big so fast, but I moved him and held out my hand.

She took it and touched the handkerchief. "What happened?"

"It was an accident."

The guys stopped talking and Karl came back. "I forgot."

Celine didn't let go of my wrist. "I should take care of it. Before you go."

"Here Toby," Demetri held out his hands.

He was almost asleep, but I couldn't hand him off now. "He'll sit quiet," I said, sitting down and letting him rest on me, then I held out my arms. "Please?"

Celine was already in the corner, digging through her bag.

"I have to go," Demetri said, looking from Karl to me. "But good luck."

"Thank you," I whispered.

He took my hand.

I held my breath. After everything today, couldn't I keep it together for a moment?

He let go and laughed, looking back at Karl. "I guess you don't have to wonder."

My face heated, couldn't I shake his hand? Fresh blood seeped through the handkerchiefs on both wrists.

Karl muttered something under his breath and went out the door with Demetri.

Celine untied the handkerchiefs and her quick intake made me sit up.

I looked from my wrists to her face, but it was just the slashes from the glass.

Sitting beside me she pulled out a piece of glass.

I winced and closed my eyes.

Tobias was asleep on me, and breathing heavy. Oblivious. Thank goodness he was exhausted or he'd have to see this.

Another jab from my wrist pulled a noise from my throat. My stomach heaved but I pushed it down.

Her hands on my wrists stilled. "I'm sorry, I'm trying to be careful."

"It's okay," I said nodding, keeping my arms before me, on Tobias's back. "Thank you."

She took my wrist again and pulled out another shard.

Something twisted inside me and my head swam. The blood dripped down my hand. I closed my eyes. Then a deeper jab made me clench my fists. Pain licked up my arms, making it worse. Tobias slept on, but I was about to throw up. The room sank in towards me and everything spun.

Celine said something, but I was too tired to listen.

"Lena."

I should answer. I needed to answer.

"Open your eyes," it was Karl, and that was a command. "Now, Lena."

A weight was lifted off my chest, I could breathe better then. "No," I forced my eyes open. "Tobias." The room swirled into focus.

Demetri held Tobias a few steps away and Karl's arms were around me. "Breathe."

Pressure on my wrists, I sucked in a breath trying to push past the sickening in my stomach. I pressed my head into his neck, waiting for the world to stop spinning.

"Talk to me," he said.

"Why'd you take Tobias?"

"You fainted," he said, the tension in his hands loosening at last.

I looked at my wrists. They were wrapped now.

"I'm sorry. We have to go now," Karl said, looking at the others also. "We all do."

Demetri nodded.

Demetri was still here? "I thought you left."

"Celine called, when you passed out."

I wanted to hide, I was always getting too much attention.

"Passing out isn't something I can ignore," he looked from Tobias to Karl. "I'll take him to the car."

"Where are your things?" Karl asked.

I swallowed looking around the room. Did I have anything?

Celine held out a bag. "His car is in there too."

I took the thin small bag. "Thank you."

Karl lifted me in his arms and held me tight.

I needed to be strong and responsible, to stop being so much trouble.

"Don't be upset," Karl whispered, walking down the hall.

I shivered when we hit the cold. "I suppose I should be glad I pass out from blood or pain," or fear. But I couldn't bring myself to add that out loud.

Karl set me on the back seat.

Demetri laid Tobias next to me, wrapped in a blanket.

I grabbed Demetri's hand before he could straighten and leave. "Thank you for everything."

He nodded and closed the door.

I sat in the car and watched Karl and Demetri. They walked a few steps away and talked but I couldn't hear a thing. So I lay down and stroked Tobias's hair. "I love you, baby."

He stirred, snuggling closer to me, deeper into the blanket.

What time was it? How long had I been out before I woke up in Karl arms? In his arms. How much I wanted to be there now.

Had we actually made it? Were we out and free? It didn't seem possible.

Karl walked towards the car. Demetri was halfway to the barn.

The door swung open and Karl slid into the front seat. "Ready?" He asked, looking over the seat. He was smiling, that was good. At the very least Demetri's talk hadn't made him mad.

"Yes," I answered. I'd always wanted to say yes to him. I knew that now.

"Is he warm enough?" He asked, looking down at him. Then he reached down and rubbed his back.

I lost my breath.

Our eyes met. He reached his hand out and covered half my face with warmth. A moment ticked by, his hand against my cheek grew hot, then he pulled away. "You must be tired. Why don't you get some sleep too?"

I didn't want to sleep.

He handed me another blanket.

"Thank you."

The engine roared to life. I waited for Tobias to wake, but he slept on.

I curled around him, half slipping off the seat. Sleep didn't come, but every curve of the road, every touch of the brakes almost threw me to the floor. I pulled myself away from the sleeping Tobias, dropped to the floor and sank into a miserable half sleep.

THIRTY-ONE

$\mathcal{I}$t was the sudden silence that made me start up.

The car's engine was off. And it was light, almost light outside, the shadowy gray before morning.

I turned and caught my breath.

Karl was looking at me over the seat. "Did you sleep at all?"

"I don't know," I moved to sit and something dug into my back.

"Care to join me up here?" He whispered.

I looked into his eyes but couldn't speak.

He leaned over the bench, his arms so close.

Then Tobias stirred in his sleep.

Karl froze, his gaze moved from me to him.

"He's okay," I said, ready to be off the floor.

He gave me his hand and I took it. I climbed the bench and found myself in his lap.

The fog outside was heavy, I couldn't see a thing. "Where are we?"

"Close to the border," he said, his arm pulling me closer.

I sucked in some air, breathing past the tension in my back.

He froze.

"I'm sore from yesterday and sleeping on the floor," I pulled his arm closer. "I'm not scared of you anymore."

"You were scared before?" He asked.

He knew I'd been terrified. "Sometimes you're funny," I said, glad he could only see part of my face.

"It's not funny," he said turning me around so we faced each other. He traced something over my eyebrow. Then he brought his lips to my forehead and kissed me. "I didn't think it possible."

I shivered at his lips on my skin, his hands on my back. But what was he thinking now? "What?"

"I love you more every minute."

I sighed, leaning forward, resting my head on his chest. "Aren't you tired of saving me?"

"Never," he said, his mouth by my ear now. "I will never be tired of saving you."

"But Tobias, you didn't plan on him," I closed my eyes. "And you've never asked me."

"I didn't plan on anything. On seeing you and falling in love with you. You can't plan destiny," he kissed my closed eyes. "You don't have to tell me anything. And I won't try to find out."

My head was hot and spinning, I clenched his shirt. "Please, tell me you don't know."

Then both Karl's hands were on my face. "Breathe," he said, "Lena, I'll tell you everything I know but first breathe."

I kept my eyes closed but took a deep breath.

Karl swallowed twice then took his hands off my face. "I know your uncle and aunt posed as his parents to protect him."

Maybe he didn't know. "How did you find that out?"

"I worked with the underground."

Of course, that's why he went to the camp. "What else do you know?"

He laid his hand on my back. "I know he's not your brother."

My heart hammered.

"You don't need to tell me anything, I swear. I love you. I don't need to know."

"Is he still asleep?" I pressed my face in the corner of his neck, gripping him tight. "Check."

He twisted under me, shifting us both for a moment before he sank back down. "He's asleep."

"I have to tell you," I said. "You have to know."

Karl put his finger on my lips. "Only if you want to."

He had to know the truth. "I don't want to keep hiding things from you. All along I've had secrets."

He wasn't talking now, but his chest was rising fast and falling faster.

I pulled closer to him. Would he still hold me after? "I left school at thirteen because I was unwelcome. After a few months I might have tried to go back, but I couldn't, they wouldn't allow it. So every day I'd escape to the woods to read and study. I liked to learn, but it was more to escape...Father didn't make home a pleasant place." my heart was pounding hard now. I took a breath. "I did that for almost a year."

"You're safe now," Karl whispered into my hair, his hands on my back.

"That someone noticed I went out, I swear, I never knew," I couldn't stop the trembling that shook me from inside. "I never saw him coming." My throat closed. I bit my lip and focused on the pressure of Karl's hands on my back.

He didn't make a sound.

"Father said I'd been asking for it."

"Your father saw?" Karl asked.

"No. But he didn't believe me when I told him what happened, why my arm was broken. He said I'd made it up and that no German soldier would—" I stopped.

Karl's hands dug into me, but it didn't hurt as much as it would when he pushed me away. That would come soon.

"Father said I made it up and wouldn't do anything. Didn't

mention it again until—" I choked. This was harder than I'd thought. "Till I couldn't hide it anymore, that's when he sent me away."

His grip was so tight I couldn't breathe. I pushed against him, he let go. His eyes were closed.

"Maybe I shouldn't have told you," I said taking his hand and holding it between mine. "But I wanted you to know the truth about me," I swallowed, choosing my words with care. "And to know that I've never loved anyone else." Reaching up to his face I traced the raised welt along his chin. "That I've never wanted anyone else."

He opened his eyes. "You're not just shy of people or scared of men. It's soldiers," he fell back against the door. He was backing away.

"I'm not scared of you now. I trust you."

"All those times I carried you, pulled you next to me," he covered his face with his hands. "That night in the woods."

"You kept me alive and you didn't know. You couldn't have known," I reached out and laid my hand on his arm.

He tensed at my touch.

Did this change his feelings for me? It wasn't a surprise. "I should have told you sooner. I'm sorry."

"No."

I dropped back on the seat, out of his arms. "You had to know the truth."

He groaned and leaned forward, closer to me now but his eyes were still closed.

I shrank against the door but there was no way I could get far enough away. He was in pain and I'd caused it. "I'm sorry." How he must hate that I kissed him. That he'd given up so much for a girl like me.

His eyes shot open. "You're sorry?"

"That I misled you."

"How did you mislead me?" His voice rose. Then he looked

at Tobias and took a breath. "I'm not mad at you." But his hands fisted.

I pulled my legs to my chest, tight against my heart that was tearing apart. I fell in love, the one thing I swore I'd never do and now he regretted me. My throat wouldn't let me talk. I fought to keep the tears inside.

"I'm not mad at you," his voice was gentle again.

I closed my eyes. The pain worse, so much worse than I'd imagined. "I shouldn't have—"

"What? Saved me?"

I gripped my head in my hands. "Stayed with you. I knew how you'd feel once you found out the truth."

"How I feel?" He leaned close, his breath warm on my hair. "You have no idea how much I love the sweet and strong and perfect girl I see before me. The more I learn, the more I want to have you in my life forever. I'm in love with you. Can't you see that?"

"I can see that you're mad."

"Of course I'm mad. I just found out," he paused. "That you needed someone to save you a long time ago, and suffered great pain because no one did. I'm furious at a level that frightens me," Karl's big hands circled my shoulders. "But I'm not mad at you."

I shivered, the chill of the car creeping up all at once.

"You said you're not afraid of me," he said.

I nodded.

"How not afraid of me are you?"

My chest was tight but I peeked up. "What are you asking?"

His face was a foot away, his eyes dark but he pulled back. "A few minutes ago, you didn't seem to mind where things were going. Be honest, do you want me to back off? That last day at the bakery, I still don't know why things happened the way they did. But I think about it all the time."

A touch away, all I had to do was reach out. "Karl."

He stopped, his throat working.

I moved to my knees so we were face to face. I wanted to smooth out the lines on his face. To touch him again. "Does this mean," I swallowed. "You still want me?"

His eyes widened. "You thought this would change that? That's what you're worried about?"

My lungs were tight. I couldn't get a word out.

He took my face between his hands, his mouth hovered above mine.

"I want you, Lena. Forever and always."

I choked. "Why?"

He stared into my eyes, the seconds excruciating. "There are no words for why. You defy explanation. But that isn't what matters most," his eyes were worried.

What was it now? What could matter more? "What matters most?"

"Do you want me?"

I grabbed his shirt and pulled his face to mine, melting into him and tasting his breath and knowing I was crying and not caring.

His hand on my back pulled me closer, the other in my hair, every finger sent a spark of energy through me.

The guilt of the last kiss nowhere to be found, he knew my secrets and wanted me. I broke away for a breath and he kissed my neck, pulling me in without a word.

His heart was pounding so hard under my hand.

I swallowed and sucked in a breath.

"Lena," he groaned.

And my stomach clenched. I froze, then opened my eyes. Karl's were wide and so alive. A new Karl I wanted to know, the one who loved me.

"Poppy."

Tobias. What did he see? Karl was lying on the front seat, I was on top. I looked over the seat.

311

Tobias was sitting up. "What are you doing to your friend?"

I swallowed. "Come here, Toby. I want you to meet him."

He crawled out of the blanket and shivered. "It's cold."

"Not up here," Karl sat up, shifting me off him and reached back, picking him up with the blanket and setting him between us.

I pulled the blanket around him. "Toby, I was all alone and this man came and rescued me. When I came to find you, he followed me and tried to help me again and that's why he got caught."

"Behind the bars."

I nodded. "That's right."

"He's driving us somewhere safe?"

I looked at Karl. "I don't know where we're going," I pulled Toby close against my chest. "Because I trust him."

Karl held out his hand to Toby. "My name is Karl. I'm very glad to meet you."

Toby looked at it and wriggled his arm free from the cocoon of blanket. "I like you, too," he placed his little hand in Karl's big one.

"I like your..." he looked at me. "Your?"

"Poppy," I said. "My name has always been Poppy."

Karl nodded. "Well, Tobias, I like Poppy and I like you and I want to stay. What do you think about that?"

Tobias looked up at me. "Stay where?"

I kissed his face. "With us, baby," I let my hair hide my face. It was hard to wrap my head around it, Karl wanted to be with me and my little boy.

Karl pulled a bag from under the seat, rummaged in it, pulling out a packet. "Are you hungry?"

Tobias nodded, peeking out from my hair to see Karl. "Yes."

Karl handed him the package. "I'll trade you, this gingerbread for a hug."

I loosened my grip but kept my mouth shut.

Tobias looked at Karl and then back at the package of gingerbread in his fist. He reached out to Karl. "Yes."

Karl pulled him from my lap and hugged him tight. Toby's little head rested against his neck for a second.

I blinked and looked away. It was too much.

"Now, Tobias. Do you want to eat your gingerbread?"

"Yes."

"And I think Poppy wants a hug."

"You hugged her. I saw."

I swallowed and peeked through my hair. How was Karl going to answer that?

"We did. But sometimes people need more than one hug. Do you want another hug?" Karl didn't look at me once, which was a good thing considering how hot my face was.

"I want to eat."

Karl was still holding Tobias. "Right. So you want to eat. How about I fix you up in your blanket to keep you warm so you can eat. Then Poppy and I can hug before we start driving. Does that sound good?"

Tobias kept looking at Karl. "Yes. I like gingerbread."

Karl had Tobias wrapped in blankets and on the back seat in two seconds, the gingerbread in one hand and an apple in the other. "Are you warm now?"

"Yes," Tobias said. "Are you warm?"

"I will be."

I choked on my laugh.

Then Karl looked at me. He closed the space between us.

I leaned back against the door.

Karl's arms were on the seat on either side of me, he leaned in and whispered by my ear. "I have permission."

My heart was beating, burning, exploding. I pressed my hands against his chest then moved up to his ear. "He'll see," I whispered back.

Karl looked back over the seat. "Is that good?" A muffled something came back.

"Stay warm in the blanket little man, can you do that? Me and Poppy need a few minutes to talk."

"Okay."

Karl looked back down at me. "We'll have to make the most of our moments," his hand was on my back then, the next moment he pulled me under him. "And get creative to keep a little person busy."

I stared up at him, his face rough from days of not shaving, his eyes focused on me. I reached up and traced the line along his jaw.

He kissed my fingers. "You're so beautiful."

I caught my breath.

He froze above me. "What?"

I shook my head, turning away from his searching eyes. "Nothing."

"Lena," he leaned down and pressed his lips to my neck in one gentle, careful kiss. "What did I do?"

I wrapped my arms around his neck. "Having you close makes it easier to be honest."

"Tell me what I did."

I closed my eyes though he couldn't see me either way. "You said I'm beautiful."

His breath against my neck was distracting. "Is that a problem?"

I swallowed. "No one's ever called me that before. I never thought of myself that way."

He pulled back. "You are so beautiful I don't know what I'm going to do. Everyone will think I kidnapped you."

"I'm serious."

He backed up more. "So am I. You're so gorgeous I'm scared you'll wake up and realize you can do so much better than me," he stared down at me, his arms were by my head holding him up.

I turned my face away from his gaze, it was too much to believe. My stomach stirred and I pressed my lips to his arm and waited.

He came close again. "You don't know what you're doing," he whispered.

I looked straight into his eyes. "Are you sure?"

He groaned.

"You promised me a hug," I wrapped my arms around his neck and pulled his head to mine.

He gave in, pressing me into the seat of the car. His lips weren't so careful now, his hands hot and strong.

I dug my hands in his hair pulling him closer, wanting this perfect moment to never end.

Then he pulled away. "It's a good thing we have Tobias with us."

"He's not done yet. And neither am I," I pulled him down, pressing my lips to his for one short, gentle kiss. Then I broke away. "And why is that?" I whispered.

Karl shook his head and pulled way, panting. "We'd never get anywhere."

I sighed and sat up.

Tobias was eating his apple, his little face peeking out of the burrow of blankets.

"Are you warm?"

He looked at me and swallowed his bite. "You like to hug a lot."

I laughed. "Yes."

Tobias nodded. "Now you have two persons to hug."

Karl cleared his throat. "So, you think hugging's a good idea?"

Tobias nodded. "I'm good for bedtime, but when I'm busy you can do it."

Karl wrapped his arms around me and pressed his face into my neck.

"All children have to sleep sometime," he whispered in my ear.

I sucked in a breath.

"And there's bound to be a preacher sooner or later."

I shivered. "Karl."

He pulled away and looked into my eyes. "I love you, Lena. Will you let me love you forever?"

I reached up and wrapped my hands around his neck. "Yes. Because I love you."

The End

EPILOGUE

*D*ying for another glimpse of Lena and Karl together? Go to https://BookHip.com/XPFVJV and read it now!!!

Enjoy this book? You can make a big difference!

Reviews are the most powerful tools when it comes to getting notice for my books. And I don't have the financial muscle of a New York publisher, or my own marketing team behind me.

Not yet anyway...

But I do have something far more powerful and effective that the big publishers would give anything for.

A committed and loyal bunch of fans.

Honest reviews help bring my books to the attention of other readers.

If you enjoyed Unguarded, I'd be so grateful if you'd go to Amazon and spend just five minutes leaving a review (as short as you like!).

Thank you very much.

*I*n a perfect world our favorite books would never ever end. How I'd love that.

But we don't, and Unguarded couldn't last forever. . . however I can give you the next best thing, another story in that world.

And so I present to you . . .

UNSPOKEN
The Ties of Blood #2

When Gabriella finally finds the man of her dreams, she never imagined she'd soon be doubting every choice she's every made and a dream soon becomes a nightmare. . .
But when a way out of the nightmare is offered. . .can she accept it?

ACKNOWLEDGMENTS

So many people helped in such enormous ways and I have to try to thank you- but don't hate me. This is ridiculously hard!

To the Lake House Writers, you kept me going when I wanted to give up, reminded me why I started and encouraged me in so many ways. I'm blessed to have found you. Thanks for putting up with me.

To my first critique partners, Cindy and Ruth, you helped me at the beginning when I was beyond lost in this writing journey. And thanks for the editing Ruth.

Anabelle, you're the first to read one of my books. I shudder when I recall that version, but you made me believe you liked it. Whether you lied or told the truth, thank you. I really needed that.

To Amanda, three-years-old is pretty young to find a best friend. So blessed to have found you. Thanks for never giving up on me.

Most of all I want to thank my family. It goes without saying, but I'd be lost without every single one of you. Thanks for stretching and loving me. For showing me what matters in life and exactly what I'm made of.

You guys are everything to me.

ABOUT THE AUTHOR

ABOUT THE AUTHOR

MaryAnna Rose is the author of The Ties of Blood historical romance series.

Connect with her at www.maryannarose.com

Printed in Great Britain
by Amazon

85840427R00192